T0247887

Ranger McIntyre:
The Stones of Peril

RANGER MCINTYRE: THE STONES OF PERIL

JAMES C. WORK

FIVE STAR
A part of Gale, a Cengage Company

LIBRARY OF CONGRESS CATALOGING-IN-PUBLICATION DATA

Names: Work, James C, author.
Title: The stones of peril / James C Work.
Other titles: At head of title: Ranger McIntyre
Description: First edition. | Waterville, Maine : Five Star, a part of Gale, a Cengage Company, [2021] | Series: Ranger McIntyre
Identifiers: LCCN 2020008558 | ISBN 9781432876456 (hardcover)
Subjects: GSAFD: Western stories. | Mystery fiction.
Classification: LCC PS3573.O6925 S76 2020 | DDC 813/.54—dc23
LC record available at https://lccn.loc.gov/2020008558

First Edition. First Printing: May 2021
Find us on Facebook—https://www.facebook.com/FiveStarCengage
Visit our website—http://www.gale.cengage.com/fivestar
Contact Five Star Publishing at FiveStar@cengage.com

Printed in Mexico
Print Number: 01   Print Year: 2021

To Nancy M., who made this a far better book
and
To Jan M., who gave it authenticity

AUTHOR'S NOTES

ONE

By the early 1920s, when this story takes place, the United States government had assumed responsibility over dozens of natural and historical places in the American West. Some sites were famous, such as Yellowstone (1872) or Yosemite (1890), while others were virtually unknown. There were two different agencies charged with the management of America's lands, history, and resources. One was the National Park Service, a branch of the Department of the Interior, formed to preserve designated parks and monuments for future generations. The other, under the Department of Agriculture, was the Forest Service, which supervised the wise utilization of natural resources including logging, mining, grazing, and recreation.

The two assignments seemed clear and straightforward: protect unique areas from human exploitation and manage natural resources for the benefit of all. Soon, however, both agencies found themselves facing a maze of complications, among which were the archaeological dilemmas. The big question was, what should they do about prehistoric human sites? Should these be "stabilized" to protect sightseers, as was the case with Mesa Verde (1906)? Should they be "restored" to their original appearance? Scientifically explored? Or allowed to decay?

Confusion included the basic question of who would make the decisions. Laws were handed down, policies were written and rewritten, guidelines were issued, but the final judgment call often had to be made, and enforced, by just one person: the district ranger.

Two

Black Elk, the Lakota mystic, spoke of "vision places" and "the sacred hoop." A Cheyenne elder named Dreams of Horses told me about vision circles, beginning places, sacred hoops, and medicine circles. The medicine circle in the following story sits on a level tundra meadow in the northern Rockies. Resembling an antique wagon wheel, it is seventy feet from side to side. It is comprised of stones weighing anywhere from ten pounds to more than thirty. The central circle, the hub, is seven feet in diameter. Connecting the hub to the rim are twenty-four lines of stones radiating like spokes. It is obviously prehistoric, but who built it, and why?

Some non-native investigators, including anthropologists who should have known better, formulated an astronomical explanation. According to this notion, Paleo-Indians built the "strange" wheel of stones in order to track the seasonal movement of the sun. The fallacies in this theory are obvious. Nowhere in the legends and folklore of the Northern Plains Indians will you find any reference to a circle of rocks being used for astronomy. Nor would the nomadic Indians have any use for a calendar in such a remote location.

Instead, according to Dreams of Horses, the circle is a Place of Becoming. Its location is one of those spots on the physical earth where the spirit of place seems especially strong, making it a revered or sacred site suitable for coming-of-age rituals. It is remote, solitary, and difficult to reach. Being above tree line at nearly 12,000 feet elevation, it gives the initiate full exposure to the four sacred elements of sun, earth, air, and rain. The location was also chosen because of its unobstructed 360-degree view of the world.

How is it used? A young man seeking recognition as an adult, or "warrior" in the parlance of the Anglo-European, undertakes a long trek to the Circle where he will fast and pray for his vision, sitting in the center of the Circle for hours each day. If he is successful, he will begin to feel completely united with earth, air, and sun. His people would say that the Spirit takes possession over his mind. As this possession takes place he will find his physical eyes returning time and time again to a certain point on the horizon. When that happens, he is then to gather stones, stones that he will arrange in a straight line leading from the Beginning Place and pointing toward the distant Place of Being. One stone for each day and night of vision-fasting. Vision-seekers who came before him may have been drawn toward the same faraway spot, in which case there may already be a line of stones. He adds his own stones to the existing line.

There is no expectation that he will travel to his horizon point. It is only symbolic, a confirmation of his spiritual medicine-direction. Dreams of Horses likened it to a Christian gazing at a cross: the Christian cannot travel to the original cross, but the cross shows the direction in which the Christian's thoughts and actions should go. And what, you may ask, is a medicine-direction? In many of the Northern Tribes each of the four directions represents what we might call an "attitude" or "habit of thought." Thus, the North represents seeking deep wisdom, the East leads to enlightenment, the West is the place of introspection, or "looking within," and being drawn toward the South means approaching one's problems from an attitude that is innocent, curious, and nonjudgmental.

Fasting and vision-seeking reveals an initiate's general "medicine direction" or "beginning place." The medicine circle then gives sharper focus to that intuition or feeling. It might be compared with a modern aptitude test: after showing your inclination toward public service, your answers to the aptitude questions might go on to suggest a specific career in government, welfare, or teaching.

Let me try to clarify. First of all, the person who came to look for guidance at the Medicine Circle would already know the significance of "sacred" directions. That knowledge would be part of his life from early childhood. Meditation and contemplation show him his own personal way of being, symbolized by his line of stones. Let us say that his line does not point directly south, nor does it point directly west, but somewhere in between. This tells him that the gifts of both directions will be his best guides whenever he faces a life decision or a complicated problem. Or perhaps when he simply seeks some inner peace. He will know to look at a decision as someone who is naïve and innocent—the south direction—but tempered with a degree of introspection, the direction of the west.

The different lines on the circle also tell him he is not alone: many others have traveled the same life road. Over the centuries, countless young men placed their stones in the circle, each stone representing a kind of epiphany, an emerging awareness of the nature of his selfhood. Looking around him at all the lines and how they fill the hoop, the circle of life, he is aware of his place in the greater world.

Curious people ask many questions about the ritual. There are only two I can answer. First, did the Seeker go alone? No. The Seeker was accompanied by one or two trusted friends who camped in the forest farther down the mountain. They brought him water and saw him safely home after his fasting. Was there really an alpine herb that, when properly prepared, enhanced the vision experience? Yes.

DISCLAIMER

The following story, with its settings, happenings, and characters, is fiction. It is about what happens when humans try to exploit—or protect—sacred places that they do not understand. While there is no intention to represent actual places, people, or events, the Rocky Mountain National Park [RMNP] "Eve" incident is a matter of historical record from the 1920s. History also records how Japanese contract crews were brought to Colorado early in the 1900s to labor on the Grand Ditch irrigation project. The ditch, approximately fourteen miles northwest from Flattop Mountain, can still be seen as you drive across Trail Ridge Road.

CHAPTER ONE
DANGEROUS RESCUE

The prairie falcon saw it happen. The hunting had been good. Her hunger was satisfied and her wings craved flight, yearned to be drawn skyward by the lifting breeze coming up the mountainside. Therefore she rose from the rock into a lazy spiral above the alpine tundra, soaring and turning with an almost insolent ease, her sharp eyes indifferent to the sight of pika spreading grass on the rocks to dry or voles dashing from rock to hummock. She briefly considered stooping for the small bird picking berries from the kinnikinnick bushes, but it would be too easy a kill and besides, her stomach was already full.

The man who slept in a bag near the circle of stones was a curiosity to the prairie falcon but nothing more. He had worked with his ropes throughout the morning and now he rested. Maybe he took note of the heavy clouds coming up from behind the mountain and knew they brought chilling wind with them and sought refuge in his bag. He left the two ropes at the edge of the cliff. Later on he might go back to them and climb down to the ledge fifty or sixty feet below and back up again.

She saw him wriggle out of the bag. He stood up to look at the gray skies. She saw two smaller men come up over the slope to the north: from head to foot they were covered in brown cloth. The small men became excited to see the rope man. One of them held back; the larger one, however, the one with the stone-tipped spear, walked toward the rope man and he was shouting at him. The rope man backed away. The spear man

13

followed, threatening. The falcon saw the rope man run to the edge of the cliff where a coil of rope lay on the ground, one end tied to a metal stake driven into the rock. He dropped the rope over the edge, looped it over his shoulder and under his thigh, and threw himself off the cliff.

The falcon's sweeping spiral took her out and past the lip of the rocks in time to see him hanging halfway to the ledge, struggling with the ropes, caught as if in a snare. Something was still holding the rope: the larger man cloaked all in brown used his spear to chop and pry until the spear's stone point broke.

He screamed like an angry eagle and he raged at the broken spear point. His companion came to him. For a few minutes they stood looking over the cliff at the man hanging in the ropes, and then they went to the circle of stones where both of them scrabbled at the dirt with the broken spear.

The falcon wheeled around and came gliding back over the mountain, but the two small men had vanished down into the trees. The hanging man, unable to free his body from the snarled ropes, had ceased struggling. A new stone, glaring white, had been added to the ancient circle where the two brown figures had been digging.

The telephone at Fall River Ranger Station jangled mercilessly. Ranger Tim McIntyre grumbled and put his head out of the blankets. The cabin was dark. The windows were dark. He sat up, put his feet to the ice-cold floor, shook the remains of a pleasant dream out of his head, and groped for the bedside lamp. The phone kept up its harsh, insistent noise. The ranger crossed to the desk and lifted the earpiece.

"Fall River Station," he said. "Ranger McIntyre."

"Tim? This is Ken. At Bear Lake Lodge. Sorry if I woke you up."

"It's okay," McIntyre said. "I had to get up to answer the

phone anyway. What's the problem? President Harding planning
to stay at your lodge while he makes a surprise inspection of the
national park?"

"No, no. President Harding's visit turned out to be a rumor.
Tim, I think we've got a stranded climber. One of our guest
couples were coming down the Flattop trail. They'd been hiking
all day. It got late, started to cloud over. A mist began falling.
But they're sure they saw a man hanging in ropes from the cliff
on Flattop. They got in a panic, I guess, and came running back
to the lodge. Couple of my men rode up there. They think the
climber's dead. But they couldn't tell and they couldn't reach
him. They thought about hauling him up with his rope, but they
were afraid he might be alive and might fall out of the tangle he
was caught in if they tried to move him."

"Right," Ranger McIntyre said. "I'm on my way. Why don't
you ring up the ranger barracks and tell Jamie Ogg to meet me
at the lodge. Tell him the situation, have him bring the climbing
gear and extra rope. We'll need a couple of your horses. Can
you loan us a canteen, maybe provide some sandwiches if we
have to be there a while?"

"Sure thing," Ken replied. "But hurry, okay?"

"Be there as soon as I can," McIntyre assured him. He turned
on the desk lamp and squinted at the alarm clock. "We ought to
be able to make it to the foot of the Flattop cliff by first light."

"On belay!" McIntyre called up to Jamie.

"On belay!" Jamie repeated from the top of the cliff. "You're
secure!"

"Descending!" McIntyre called. "Give slack!"

"Slack!"

The ranger rappelled as delicately and as slowly as possible,
following the victim's rope while being careful not to jostle it.
When he came alongside, he saw how the man's rope had

become twisted over his shoulder and around his waist. *Like he's wrapped up in a giant square knot,* McIntyre thought. *How in hell am I going to get him out of that mess?*

The man moaned. He was still alive.

"Who . . . who there?" he muttered.

"A ranger."

"Oh."

"We're going to help you out of here," McIntyre said. "I guess you've been here all night, huh? What happened, anyway?"

"Dwarf," the man muttered. At least it sounded as if he said "dwarf." His next words were equally indistinct. McIntyre heard them, but they didn't make sense.

"Stones?" the hanging man moaned. "Spear. A spear. Short. Hit my head."

McIntyre cautiously turned the man in order to see the back of his skull. Blood from a serious scalp wound had caked in his hair.

"Looks like you slammed into the rock when you came down. Well, let's see what to do here. No way in hell we're going to lift you back up to the top. Must be fifty feet or more and you're dead weight. Jamie! Jamie!"

"I'm here!" Jamie called down.

"We'll need a single belay. Tie off this guy's extra rope and toss the end down to me. We'll see if it's long enough."

In a couple of minutes the rope dropped next to McIntyre. Suspended in his own belay rope, McIntyre made bowline loops in the second rope's bights, two for the legs with a half hitch around the chest. He called to Jamie to take up the slack.

"Can you rig his belay so you can lower his weight by yourself?"

"You bet! I've got him! Hey, Tim! I can see some guys riding up the trail. Looks like we're gonna have help."

"Can't wait for them," McIntyre shouted. "Watch our belays

while I fix a couple of pitons."

McIntyre, hanging in his rope, groped in his belt pouch for a six-inch flat piece of steel and a small hammer. The whanging sound as he drove the steel into a crack was reassuring; it meant the rock was solid and the steel was good. As a precaution he hammered a second piton into a different crack and connected them with a loop of cord from the pouch, making sure his belay rope was inside the loop.

The next step was to untangle the giant square knot.

"Victim on belay!" he shouted once the victim's original rope was no longer fastened. Jamie was now holding the man's life in his hands. Literally.

"Belayed!" Jamie called out.

"Hang on!" McIntyre shouted up to Jamie. "I'm going to drag his first rope down to me."

Like McIntyre's rope, the victim's had been doubled through a piton loop. Two equal lengths hung down about sixty feet. The arrangement allowed the climber to pull on one end and bring the rope down where he could secure it again and continue his descent down the granite wall. McIntyre threaded the rope through the new piton he had pounded into the cliff, looping it over his shoulder and under his thigh, and then he was ready to say a prayer, go off his remaining belay, and get this poor guy down to the ledge below.

"Going off belay!" he shouted. "Jamie! Lower away but make it easylike! I'll be rappelling beside him!"

The slow progress of the descent was agonizing. McIntyre did his best to keep the victim from scraping against the cliff as inch by inch they both dropped to the ledge. When they were safely down, McIntyre undid the ropes, made the victim as comfortable as possible, and gently explored legs and arms for broken bones. There was nothing else he could do. He sat himself down to wait for the trembling in his muscles to stop.

"Hey!" Jamie shouted down to him. "Look there!"

McIntyre looked. Three men from the rescue group had dismounted and were headed for the talus slope below the cliff. McIntyre understood what they were doing: they intended to scramble up the unstable rock and make a fairly short and relatively safe free climb up the remaining few yards of cliff face. They carried long coils of rope over their shoulders.

"Colorado Mountain Club boys," McIntyre said. "Thank God."

CHAPTER TWO
SUMMONED TO APPEAR

"RMNPSO" stood for "Rocky Mountain National Park Supervisor's Office." Dottie, the S.O. secretary, stood for no nonsense. Therefore when she telephoned Ranger McIntyre on the evening of the rescue and ordered him to be at the Pioneer Inn hotel in the village at seven o'clock sharp the following morning, he was out of bed, shaven, dressed in his uniform, and fifteen minutes early. He found Assistant Ranger Jamie Ogg already in the dining room at McIntyre's favorite table by a window overlooking the village, with a spectacular view of the Front Range of the Rocky Mountains beyond.

Neither of them saw Supervisor "Nick" Nicholson coming. His official car did not come up the side street beneath the window. He did not come along the sidewalk in his businesslike stride. The man had been a hunter and fisherman all his life and, as several inattentive RMNP workers had discovered, he had an unnerving way of appearing out of nowhere. On this occasion Jamie and McIntyre were watching out the window for their boss to arrive. Hearing someone clear his throat, they both turned and found him sitting in the third chair.

"Good morning," he said cheerfully. "What are you boys having for breakfast?"

No surprises there. Jamie Ogg, energetic, quick, and efficient, ordered his usual large bowl of oatmeal—with extra raisins, please—accompanied by slices of Charlene's homemade bread and jam. Milk or tea was his usual drink, but this morning he ordered hot cocoa instead. McIntyre, taking advantage of the supervisor's invitation, asked Mari to bring the gut-stretcher special. Which came on two plates.

"I've never been able to figure it out," Supervisor Nicholson said, looking at McIntyre's breakfast.

"What?" McIntyre asked.

"Your breakfasts. I can't figure out if the pancakes are the main course and the sausage, eggs, and bacon are on the side, or if it's the other way around."

"If you ask me," Jamie Ogg volunteered, "I'd say his main course was syrup and salt."

"Nice jab, Ogg," Nicholson said. "But let me tell you why we met here, other than to watch McIntyre deplete the larder. I need to hear your reports on the rescue—I guess you heard the victim didn't make it. Exposure, the doc says. You two did your best."

"Jamie deserves credit," McIntyre said. "If he hadn't done the rope class last year and learned all about rock climbing, and if he hadn't figured out where to buy the right equipment, we couldn't have done anything to help the guy. Would have had to wait for the Mountain Club men to get there."

"The other reason we're here instead of at my office is because a reporter phoned from the *Denver Record* newspaper. He's coming for a story this morning. But before he arrives, I need to make sure we all agree this was a straightforward rescue and a very unfortunate accident. No drama, no mystery, nothing to write a sensational story about. After the incident with the Lady Eve, the superintendent has been extra touchy, very sensitive about sensational publicity."

Jamie and McIntyre did their best not to smirk. Or laugh. Two seasons ago the "Lady Eve" had shown up accompanied by a flock of photographers and reporters. She was dressed in a sort of cave girl, stone-age leopard-skin costume with sandals.

She announced how she intended to spend a week in the park alone, living *au naturel* off the land. While flashbulbs popped and reporters scribbled, she posed with the regional superintendent and several local politicians before she went prancing off into the forest. The superintendent pronounced it "a perfect use for the new national park, a demonstration of what it means to return to nature," etc. Park attendance soared as weekenders came hoping for a glimpse of "Eve" and letters of support arrived at the S.O. every day, some containing offers of marriage. The truth came out several weeks later. She had actually spent the week at Hillside Lodge—in a tourist disguise and perfect comfort. Her demonstration of being at one with Mother Nature was nothing but a publicity stunt to sell newspapers.

"Well . . ." McIntyre began, biting into a strip of bacon, "the rescue had one interesting thing about it."

"Do not tell me," Nicholson said. "McIntyre, Ogg, don't you two dare tell me it was anything but a routine rescue. Don't you dare. There's a Washington senator talking about putting a national park in Death Valley and they'll need rangers."

"Sorry," McIntyre said, "but there was something strange."

"Go on," Nicholson sighed.

"The boys from the Colorado Mountain Club didn't have much trouble reaching the ledge. They knew the victim. They said he had been teaching himself how to rappel and how to do something . . . what did they call it, Jamie?"

"Called it 'chimneying.' You get into a wide crack, see, like the one on the face of Flattop. Get your back against one side, brace your feet on the other, and work your way up."

"Go ahead, Tim. What next?"

"Like I said, they took charge of the victim and did first aid on him. They lowered him off the ledge. People from Bear Lake Lodge were down below with a litter to take him to the trailhead. Nothing more for us to do, so I went down to the trail. I left the ropes and stuff there while I hiked up to where Jamie was. We'd need to load up the guy's gear and pack it out."

"Except there wasn't any," Jamie said.

"Any what?"

"Gear," Jamie said. "No gear up there. There was signs of a campfire near the stone circle. Plus, you could see where a tent had mashed down the tundra. Me and Tim looked all around but there was nothing except his two pitons hammered into the edge of the cliff. We kept on lookin' around and Tim, he spotted the guy's stuff 'way down in the trees at the far side of the cliff face. Somebody'd pulled up his tent and thrown it over the edge, see?"

"I'm telling you two right now, I do not like the direction this is heading," Nicholson said.

"We found one other thing," McIntyre said. "It's back at my cabin. Half of a stone spear point. A wide spear point, large as a man's hand. You can tell it was broken recently, from the sharp shiny edge. Made recently, too. Oh, and one of the victim's pitons was scratched up and bent, but not from him hammering it into the rock. I think somebody tried to use the spear point to pry the piton loose. Maybe the victim did it. Except we never found the other half of the point. We lay down on our stomachs and tried like heck to pull his pitons out of the cliff but they wouldn't budge. But that one piton had definitely been messed with. And it was the one securing his rappel rope."

Nicholson's long, deep groan could be heard all the way across the dining room. He signaled Mari to bring the coffee pot.

"I see what you're leading up to," the supervisor said grimly. Nicholson would really love it if Ranger McIntyre could someday investigate a normal accident and not find it tied to some sort of crime or conspiracy.

"You think somebody interfered with the man's belongings

and maybe tried to make him fall down the cliff," he said.

"I do. And there's one more thing, or two, maybe," McIntyre said. He impaled the last bite of fried egg together with the last piece of pancake and wiped up a spot of syrup.

Supervisor Nicholson took a slug of coffee. It was scalding but he didn't care. He was picturing himself trying to keep the newspaper reporters from turning an accident into a front-page sensation. At times such as this he wondered if he could resign from the administration business. There might be openings at the proposed Death Valley park, mostly ranger jobs. It would mean a demotion, but once in a while it looked very tempting.

"What?" he asked.

"While I was taking care of him, the guy mumbled something. At first it didn't make sense. I think he said 'stone spear' and something about a small man or little men. No, wait. I remember. He said 'dwarf' and 'short' before he passed out."

"And that's all?" Nicholson asked. "Maybe he'd been drinking? Prohibition is big news these days. Could we maybe come up with an explanation involving illegal booze? Alcohol and high altitude? Please tell me that this rescue—recovery—isn't going to get weird."

"Plus . . ." McIntyre continued, "I think somebody added new rocks to the Indian circle. White ones. I've got no idea where white rocks would come from. Quartz, maybe, but they don't look like quartz. Exactly. More like limestone, except you don't find limestone at that altitude."

Nicholson sighed again and hauled out his wallet to pay for breakfast.

The three men in green stood up and put on their flat-brim ranger hats and waited for Mari to bring Nicholson his change. The supervisor reached out and straightened the name tag on Jamie Ogg's tunic.

" 'Assistant Ranger Ogg,' " he said, reading the name on the tag. "Ranger Don Post. Ranger-Naturalist Eleanor Pedersen. Rangers Gray, Williams, Torkein. Ranger Russ Frame. I've got over a dozen ranger names on the national park payroll. Why is it, do you think, whenever a routine task turns into a damn jigsaw puzzle, or whenever there's a ranger who's gone fishing while tourist vehicles stack up at the entrance station waiting to pay their fee, why is it that the name 'McIntyre' is always involved?"

"Dumb luck, I suppose," McIntyre said with a grin. "Or maybe I'm naturally more active than the other rangers."

"Sure. I should have thought of it myself," Nicholson said. "You're more active. When you're not taking a nap or fishing. Jamie Ogg, you come back to the office with me and sign your report as soon as Dottie has typed it. Then you can go about your duties. McIntyre, same thing. Only after you sign your report I want you to drive your tail back to Fall River Station and stay there. Talk to visitors, hand out brochures, pose for photographs or whatever. But stay there. And for God's sake watch what you say to reporters."

It was noon and Ranger McIntyre was about to hand over the entrance post duty. The summer temp could stay there to collect entrance fees and give away free maps. The day was full of sunshine and somewhere under all those endless blue skies there were trout waiting to be caught. A man deserved a lunch hour, and if it happened to stretch into, say, two hours beside the stream, would there be any harm?

He nearly made it to his cabin door when the voice behind him made him stop and turn.

"Ranger McIntyre?"

It was more of a wheeze than a voice. It was the sound of someone from down in the city who didn't know enough to take it easy when he came to the mountains. The park entrance was nearly two thousand feet higher than Denver.

McIntyre turned. The young man's city suit looked strangely tight and uncomfortably warm, and he wore it buttoned all the way up and with the jacket belt cinched tight. No wonder he was breathing hard.

"Ranger McIntyre," he repeated.

"Yes?"

"Hi! Hi, I'm Norman Duggin. From the *Denver Record?* Supervisor Nicholson sent me. He said if you weren't busy tomorrow you might take me to this sacred Indian circle place where the climbing fatality took place. You know, for photos? We'd like a story with local color. Sort of tell the newspaper readers what you ranger guys do all day."

"I see," McIntyre said. "I guess if it's what Supervisor Nicholson wants."

"Is this your ranger cabin?" Duggin asked. "Geez, it's like what you see in one of those *National Geographic* articles! I've never seen a national park. Is everything built out of logs around here? What do you do all winter? You suppose we'll see any elk tomorrow? I've seen deer but I'd love to see an elk. By the way, I need to bring a photographer along. If it's all right?"

"More the merrier," McIntyre growled. "New to Colorado, are you?"

"Sioux City! I was on the *Star-Herald* newspaper out of college, three years, but I got lucky and this *Denver Record* job opened up. Say, look at the pickup truck! I always wanted a pickup truck. The newspaper gave me a Ford coupe to drive. I guess it's okay. Why does your pickup say 'Small Delights' on the door, anyway?"

"I got it from a tourist resort when they went out of business," McIntyre explained. " 'Small Delights' was the name of the place. Haven't gotten around to painting the doors yet."

"Gosh. Say, can I have a look inside your cabin? How many

guns do you have? Did you ever have to shoot anybody? I guess I don't really know what a ranger does."

Ranger McIntyre showed the young man the inside of his "ranger cabin" and took him on a tour to see the stable and the woodshed, the outhouse, and the corral where Brownie stood eyeing him with as much curiosity as a mare will allow herself.

"Do you ride?" McIntyre asked.

"Oh, heck, yes. Back in Sioux City there's a young lady. We sort of stepped out together and she loved to go to the park—city park, I mean—and rent horses to ride. We rode in the city park all the time. Tell me, do you live alone? Any girlfriend? How would it work, with you being up here in the woods and all?"

"The job keeps me busy," McIntyre said, leaving out the part about two-hour breakfasts and frequent fishing trips, which he didn't want to appear in a newspaper story. "But as a matter of fact I do have a lady friend. She works in Denver. A sort of secretary, you might say. We like to . . . what was your phrase? Step out together?"

"Wow," Duggin exclaimed, "all the way down in Denver. Holy cow. Well, listen, thanks for the tour! Really good to meet a real ranger! Now, about tomorrow. I meet you here, all right?"

"No," McIntyre said. "Let's save time and meet at Bear Lake. You and your photographer can hire horses at the lodge. Make sure the wrangler provides you with slickers in case it rains. Bring along your own lunch and canteen. In fact, if you don't already have a place to stay you might consider renting a room at Bear Lake Lodge where the story begins. Mr. Outman was staying there—Charles Outman's the name of the accident victim. The people who found him are also lodge guests. Be there early. We'll need to be on the trail by first light."

"Great idea!" Duggin said. "I'll go find Bill—Bill Roget is my photog—and we'll drive up there this afternoon. Great to meet you! We're going to have a great time tomorrow!"

Great, McIntyre thought. *Nothing I'd rather do.*

Chapter Three
The News Gets Around

At timberline Ranger McIntyre reined up to wait for the reporter and photographer. Brownie twisted her head back and cast a disapproving look at the two livery horses plodding up the rocky track. *You'd think they could at least make an effort to hold their heads up,* she thought. One looked like he was walking in his sleep while the other one simply looked dejected. Pitiful.

McIntyre looked back, too, noticing how Duggin squirmed and fidgeted, a sure sign his saddle didn't fit him. The hot spots he was feeling on his butt could soon grow into saddle blisters. Time to call a halt.

A few minutes later they came to a flat place where the ground around a hitching rail had been worn down to bare dirt by many shod hooves. Other than the rough mountain trail, the hitching rail seemed to be the only man-made thing for miles around.

"Dismount," McIntyre said. "Time to have a drink and stretch our legs."

The photographer lifted his head and smiled at the word "drink" until he realized the ranger meant water. Damn prohibition, anyway.

"Great view," Roget said, easing himself to the ground and wincing as he attempted to stretch his spine back into its normal shape. "I'll shoot a few pictures."

"It is great," Duggin wheezed. "You can see for miles in every direction! Look at all the mountains you can see from here!

Ranger, what happened to the trees? Somebody cut them down?"

Brownie snorted. McIntyre checked his tongue and remembered that any national park they might build in Death Valley wouldn't have trout streams.

"Ever been above timberline before?" McIntyre asked.

"Gosh no," Duggin said.

"If you look down there, all along the whole Rocky Mountain range, you can see where the trees stop and the granite and tundra begin. See? At this latitude, timberline is somewhere between 10,000 and 10,500 feet above sea level. In other words, you're nearly two miles high right now. I don't know if it's due to the cold, or the wind, or maybe the lack of oxygen, but up here the trees don't grow. Except for those real scrubby little bush-like ones, all twisted. Like those over there. They survive in places where there's shelter from the wind. Folks call it 'krumholtz.' German word, means 'crooked timber.' "

Roget had his camera on its tripod. As most first-time hikers in the park have discovered, up here on the roof of the continent, in the pure clear air, there seem to be perfect, ideal, panoramic scenes to photograph anywhere you cared to point a camera. Someone once called it a bewildering abundance of distance.

"Where's this Flattop Mountain?" he asked.

McIntyre laid hands on Roget's shoulders and turned him until the photographer was looking at the gray wall of granite a few hundred yards away.

"You're looking at it."

"You mean . . . up there?"

"Yup. We'll be able to ride the trail along this shoulder of the mountain until it's too rough and steep for the horses. From there we go on foot, up and around the back side. We'll come out on top of that cliff you're looking at. But from here you can see where the accident happened. Take these field glasses. Focus on a long crack up the far side, the one that looks like an open chimney running all the way up the cliff. Follow it to the top. Now slowly scan to the right. See the knob of rock? Looks like a tooth? It's fairly close to where Mr. Outman started his descent. Scan straight down fifty, sixty feet and you'll see a wide ledge. Wide as a city sidewalk."

"I see it!" Roget said. "And you ended up there! Cripes!"

"We did. The Mountain Club boys were able to scramble up the slope of loose rock—you can see it over there—and they got to the ledge. The loose rock is called talus, if you want to put it in your story. If the Mountain Club hadn't come along I was planning to lower him by myself."

Ranger McIntyre let the newspapermen sit and rest while he scouted the flat summit of the mountain. The dry soil, being mostly coarse sand, showed only a few scuffs and small indentations where the climber had pitched his tent. He had also made a campfire without a sheltering circle of rocks, leaving scorched lichen and grass.

McIntyre got down on his stomach and looked over the edge of the cliff. The two pitons hammered into cracks in the cliff had held the poor guy's climbing ropes, one for rappelling and the other for a self-belay. How did they end up all tangled around his body? Maybe he tried to switch from his climbing rope to his belay rope in mid-descent and ended up with both of them twisted around his hips and shoulders. Or he tried to tie a loop in one, under his arms and over his chest, to belay himself and the knot slipped.

McIntyre confirmed what he and Jamie had told Nicholson. One of Mr. Outman's pitons was scratched and scarred as if someone had attempted to knock it loose with a rock. Why not cut the rope instead? Simple: a cut rope looks deliberate. A piton pulling out of the crack looks accidental.

He got up and walked back to the medicine wheel, where he found Norman Duggin.

"Feeling better?" he asked.

"Yeah, once my legs stopped shaking and my lungs stopped burning. My chest still hurts. Boy, this magic circle is sure a spooky place, isn't it? Makes you feel like something's about to happen. Know what I mean? Anybody know who built it? I wonder when it was built. Are there Indians around here, I mean, it had to be Indians, who else could it be? If it was merely a wide circle of rocks, I'd say it was for doing dances, you know, ceremonies. I've seen Indian ceremonies where they dance in circles. But not with all those spokes, those lines of rocks. So you say this climber fellow, he probably wasn't interested in the circle at all?"

"No, I don't think so . . ." McIntyre began.

"Yeah, probably not. Like you said, he was probably practicing. Good place for climbing, you said? Solid rock, good ledge to aim for, nice chimney to climb? Nothing to do with the circle, but we'll shoot some pictures anyway. Main story is the rescue and the risk you two rangers took. I'll do a sidebar on the hazards. You know, don't hike alone, pace yourself at this altitude, watch the weather, the handy hint kind of stuff."

McIntyre wasn't really listening. He wanted a closer look at those new rocks, the white ones. Each had been placed in a gap in one of the spokes; together with the white rocks already there they almost made a kind of pattern. He stood musing, looking at the wheel as he would look at one of his jigsaw puzzles. If a man were to put three or four white rocks connecting two of the spokes . . . it would look like the symbol on an oriental vase his mother owned.

The rocks certainly weren't small. Not the kind of stone a man might carry in his pocket. These ranged from the size of a

31

loaf of bread to the size of a cinder block or larger. They weren't like any rocks he'd ever seen anywhere near Flattop Mountain. McIntyre was no expert when it came to geology; he knew barely enough about it to answer tourist questions. But he did know white quartz when he saw it. Some people called it milky quartz. These rocks were white, but they weren't quartz. Using a granite boulder as a hammer he chipped off a sample of the stone to take back.

There was another thing. Not only had someone carried these rocks from God knows where and not only had they added them to the ancient wheel, which hadn't seen any new stones in many decades, but whoever did it had taken the trouble to dig out a place for the white stones to sit in. Each white stone had a pile of freshly dug soil in front of it.

"Any idea what it's for?" came the voice behind him. It was Roget, the photographer.

"Who knows?" McIntyre replied. "Got all the pictures you need? Those rain clouds will be coming over the mountains soon. We'll want to be off this peak before the lightning starts."

"Let me take one photo of you, if you don't mind," Roget said. "I wish we'd brought a climbing rope you could be holding. Duggin had himself a peek over the cliff and decided you're a really gutsy guy to drop down there. Said he might do another sidebar on this medicine circle thing but mostly he'd like to push the hero angle. But I'll bet he's gonna write how spooky this prehistoric stone circle is. Wow."

"I hope you'll tell him to keep in mind how Charles Outman died on the way to the ambulance. I mean, think of his family. What his family's going through is the real story. They need to know exactly how he died, and why. And without the drama."

The other man would never know it, but McIntyre knew exactly what Outman's family was about to go through. He had gone through it himself when the woman he loved had died in a

32

car at the bottom of a cliff. Why didn't someone find her sooner? What did anyone do to help her? How did she die, was it quick? Was it over before she knew it was coming?

"Old mountain men say these mountains can kill you," McIntyre said. "They're right, too. These mountains have a dozen ways to kill you. Let me ask you a favor? Before you and Duggin start writing any thrilling front-page stuff, let's remember the family. Try not to upset them with theories until we find out why it happened. See?"

Roget got his picture of the tall ranger posed near the medicine wheel, and another of McIntyre at the edge of the cliff gazing off into the distance like some kind of 1920s Daniel Boone. To the west, ominous dark clouds were filling the sky behind the mountain range.

"Lightning, you said?" Roget said, quickly folding his tripod and packing his camera.

"Yup. We'll make it to the tree line, at least. Down in the forest the rain might catch us, but there's less chance of getting electrocuted. Maybe."

They collected Duggin, who had been sitting with his legs hanging over the cliff busily scribbling in his notebook, and the three went sliding and stumbling down to where the horses were waiting.

It took until evening of the following day for McIntyre to shake the sound of Norman Duggin's persistent queries out of his head, but at least he had done his duty to the world of journalism and could put it behind him. He slept well all night and woke the next morning looking forward to a day off. He was even humming a little song while preparing his omelet and frying his hash browns. Brownie had been given feed and water and let out into the pasture, the woodbox next to the stove had been filled. His breakfast coffee tasted better than usual. A brand-new jigsaw puzzle lay jumbled on the worktable, beckoning to him to come and sort out a few pieces . . . only a few bits of border. However, with a day so calm and so clear, the trout would soon begin rising in the stream and he wanted to be there. In fact, he said to himself with a smile, he needed to be there. It was his responsibility to go fishing. Without dedicated anglers the world could be overrun by trout. But it wouldn't, not if he could help it.

As the last swallow of coffee chased the last mouthful of omelet, the telephone jangled. He got up, went to the desk, and picked up the earpiece.

"Fall River Station. McIntyre."

"Ranger McIntyre? This is Polly. Polly Sheldon? Pauline?"

Polly Sheldon. The much-animated niece of the older couple who had owned the Small Delights Lodge. The vivacious Polly who seemed to throw off energy like an electric dynamo, who rarely stood still. Everyone who met her marveled at how a young woman could be so active and eat so little and still be . . . well . . . eight or ten inches too short for her weight.

"How are you, Polly?" McIntyre asked politely. "Still living in Denver, I guess?"

"Big news for you! Front-page stuff!" Polly exclaimed. McIntyre held the phone receiver away from his ear to keep her enthusiastic voice from deafening him. "I want to hear what you've been doing, too!" she said. "On the way driving up here I was telling my friend Johnny about you and how much fun you and I had outwitting those gangsters at the Small Delights Lodge. Remember how we rigged up the fire hose together, and got the pump going? Wow. How's the pickup truck running?"

McIntyre pulled out his swivel chair and sat down. Merely listening to Polly was enough to make him tired.

"Truck's fine," he said. "Except for where the doors still say 'Small Delights.' People sometimes give me grief about it, but I kind of like it."

"I bet you would!"

"Polly, did I hear you say you drove up? You're up at the village?"

"Yes! We had a day off! Yesterday's newspaper had a great story about you. Picture and everything. Wow, you really did take a chance to rescue the climber guy! I guess you're a hero, huh? I'd love to see your ancient magical circle thing. According to the reporter it must be haunted by old Indian spirits and stuff. But from what he says you need to be an experienced climber even to get to it, but when you do it's real spooky and mysterious."

"It's only a pattern of rocks," McIntyre said, "nothing more. You can get most of the way on horseback. In fact, there's another trail, a longer one around the peak, and it brings you out a few hundred yards below the circle. But listen, Polly. The climber died, so I didn't really rescue him. I didn't save him. I don't feel like much of a hero."

"Sorry, Tim. I know how that must make you feel. Anyway, I was reading all about you in the *Denver Record* and Johnny said what did we want to do tomorrow—this was yesterday—and I said let's go up to Rocky Mountain National Park and look up my old friend Ranger McIntyre! And here we are! I'm using the public phone at the telephone exchange. Tell you what, we'll buy you lunch, okay? How about we meet at the Pioneer Inn?"

McIntyre hung the earpiece on the hook. He was all alone in his cabin and he didn't believe inanimate objects could communicate with humans, yet somehow he could sense the dirty breakfast dishes demanding to be washed, the new jigsaw puzzle complaining about being unfinished, and the fly rod on the wall glaring at the back of his neck.

He had rinsed the last dish and was drying his hands when

the telephone clattered again.

"Fall River Station. McIntyre."

"My, my! Don't we sound like a growly bear this morning! Whattsa matta, Ranger, did I drag you out of bed?"

"Hello, Vi," McIntyre said.

The caller with the silken voice was Violet "Vi" Coteau, personal executive secretary to the FBI agent in Denver, A.T. Canilly. More than once Ranger McIntyre had wished for a framed photograph of Vi to keep on his desk. In his mind she was one of the more glamorous flappers in Denver when off duty and one of the more dangerous government girls while on. In his line of work McIntyre met many women who could shoot rifles and revolvers, but she was the only one he knew who was officially qualified with a Thompson .45 submachine gun. She drove a six-cylinder Marmon convertible coupe at terrifying speeds. Her zest for life knew no bounds, and she enjoyed teasing him with two questions that always remained unanswered between them. The first question related to her three passions, three things she confessed she couldn't resist: one was egg salad sandwiches, one was chocolate nonpareils, but the third was a mystery, something that she said he might learn someday. The other mystery about Vi Coteau was her concealed pistol. On two occasions she had produced a deadly .38 snub-nosed revolver and McIntyre couldn't figure out where she had it hidden.

"It seems I know a hero!" Vi said. "Where did you learn to be a mountain climber?"

"Jamie did," McIntyre explained. "The park service sent some men to climbing school at Yosemite. Brought in an Austrian expert to teach them about ropes and pitons and stuff. Jamie took the course and came back and taught me. Turns out to be something I like to do. But you can scrub the hero stuff. The victim died."

"You'll have to show me how to rock climb. And I absolutely have to see this sacred haunted medicine circle of yours! The newspaper makes it sound dreamy! We need to fix ourselves up with some of those egg sandwiches from Tiny's store and climb up there."

"Ride," McIntyre said.

"Sorry?"

"We could ride horses. Almost all the way."

"Okay. Better yet! Mysterious white rocks, too. What else?"

"Keep it secret?"

"You know me."

"Yes, I do. That's why I'm asking. Keep it secret?"

"Oh, okay. Spoilsport. What's the secret?"

"Charles Outman. The climber. He was still semiconscious when I got to him. It sounded like—and keep this under your little cloche, okay?—sounded like he said small men in brown had forced him over the edge of the cliff and tried to kill him. He wasn't real coherent. But I think it's what he meant."

"Therefore it's a new puzzle for you!" she said. "It must be your birthday. What a treat! I really wish I could drive up this weekend and help you solve it. But I'm afraid we've got a case of our own right now. Remember Agent Canilly telling you how he suspected rumrunners were using airplanes? Flying illegal booze up from Mexico, or down from Canada, landing out there on the prairie? We got a hot tip about airplane pilots using a certain landmark in order to find the rendezvous point. This weekend we'll stake it out. I guess you're on your own."

If I was on my own, McIntyre thought glumly, *I'd go fishing.*

True to her customary nature Polly Sheldon took charge of the lunch conversation. When Johnny asked questions about Mc-Intyre's job it was Polly who answered for McIntyre. She spoke for Johnny when McIntyre asked him what he did in Denver.

McIntyre began to think that the two of them might as well leave and let her go on talking to herself.

"And after the Small Delights Lodge closed and I moved to Denver—along with Uncle John and Aunt Hattie who are both fine, by the way, and love living in the city—and I found a job in a sewing store where one day who should walk in but Johnny here, looking for some heavy fabric to patch an airplane wing and boy! Did we hit it off quick! Naturally I told him about my Jenny, like you used to fly in the war?"

"Polly told me you flew a Curtiss Jenny," Johnny said. "But I didn't know we used them in France?"

"We didn't. I trained on the JN-4 in Texas but in France we flew Nieuports."

"Wow," Johnny said. "You need to come down to Combs Field and have a gander at our new babies. We got a swell Douglas mailplane, except it only seats one man, the pilot. But . . . ready for this? A couple of Douglas M-2s! The Army National Guard uses them."

"I've read about those. Like to have a look," McIntyre said.

"Anyway," Polly interrupted, "Johnny has a job with the Geologic Survey taking aerial photos and plus he's a pilot and mechanic. He took me out to the field lots of times and it turns out I've got a natural bent for mechanical stuff."

"I knew as much," McIntyre said. "Remember the burning garbage truck? And the sabotaged safety valve on the boiler?"

"Right!" Polly said. "Well, to make it short, I am now . . . guess what! An aircraft mechanic-in-training! My Jenny has a nice home in a hangar right there, too. The flyboys all tell me I'm an absolute whiz at troubleshooting an engine. So there, and what do you think of them apples, hmmm?"

"Fantastic," McIntyre said. "Congratulations!"

When they had finished with lunch, the trio took their coffee out to the wide porch of the Pioneer Inn where they could sit and admire the Front Range panorama. Polly asked which mountain was Flattop, and the conversation returned to the thrilling newspaper story. Overly thrilling, in McIntyre's opinion.

"Jeepers, the news reporter made this magic circle seem spooky," Polly said. "Love to see it. I wonder if it's like the other one? I've only seen it from the air, not up close. But, of course, I haven't seen yours up close neither."

"Other one?" McIntyre asked. "From the air? What other one? Another medicine circle? Where is it?"

"Out on the prairie. Let's see, how to tell you how to find it? Okeydokey, here's what you do. You fly north out of Denver, follow the Platte River along . . . until you come to Route 34. Well, heck, you could keep on following the Platte, I guess. Either one brings you over Fort Morgan. There you pick up the Bijou Creek. No water in it, usually. Usually it's nothing but a wide strip of sand. Turn south and keep the Bijou Creek off your right-hand wingtip and you'll find yourself flying over a whole lot of empty prairie. Keep watching to the left and you'll spot a circle of stones like the one in the newspaper photo. Looks like a wagon wheel, maybe fifty yards wide."

"No kidding," McIntyre said. Polly could spew details like a geyser. "Is there a way to drive to it?"

"There's a dirt road," she replied, "but I don't know where it comes from or goes to. We could fly up there one of these days and trace the road from the air. It'd be terrific! Back when you and I were trying to save Small Delights from the mobsters you said you'd like to fly my Jenny."

"Sure," McIntyre said. "Write down your phone number for me. While you're at it, write down where I'll find this Combs Field place."

The ranger had another thought.

"Johnny," he said. "Polly says you work with the U.S. Geological Survey?"

"Right. Aerial photos, mostly."

"If I gave you a rock sample, would you know somebody who could tell me what it is?"

"Sure, several guys. Geologists. What is it, gold ore from a lost mine?"

"I wish. No, it's a chunk of white rock. Maybe you could swing by my cabin before you two leave?"

"Speaking of which," Polly said, "we need to roll the Firestones on down the macadam. I want to drive Johnny out to see the Small Delights Lodge and the lake and everything. I know it doesn't look the same as when you and I had our adventure there but I told him all about it and he sure would like to see it. Besides, what could be nicer than driving around in the mountains on a gorgeous day like this?"

"Flying, maybe?" McIntyre said with a laugh. "Or fishing."

"There you go!" Johnny agreed.

"By the way, Johnny," McIntyre said. "These Douglas M-2s you've got at your airfield. Is there any way the park service could maybe rent one or lease one? If we ever needed a plane, of course. What's the service ceiling on it, anyway?"

"Ceiling? They claim it can go to 16,000 feet. I'll look into the rental idea for you and let you know."

"Great, thanks," McIntyre said. "Boy, 16,000 feet. You could fly over Longs Peak! It's about 15,000."

"Depends on the air temperature, humidity, fuel load, whether you flew solo or had an observer in the other cockpit. Might not make it. Mountain air currents can be tricky, too."

"But listen here, Mister McIntyre," Polly said. "You're not taking my Jenny flying over any mountains and I'll let you know it right now and for free. Nosir, my girl stays where the ground is flat and where she can make emergency landings if she needs to."

★ ★ ★ ★ ★

When they drove away from his cabin, Polly waving merrily out the side window, McIntyre was sorry to see them go. He realized how much he missed the aerodrome chats among pilots and mechanics. Back during the Great War, airplanes were often the only topic of conversation at the squadron mess and in the barracks. Men were always going on about what kinds of planes they had flown, airplanes they had seen, airplanes the Germans were flying, which machine gun was best to have in a dogfight, how to do a safe dead-stick landing, on and on and on.

He had enjoyed seeing Polly again with her perpetual cheeriness and unflagging enthusiasm. He promised himself he would try to arrange a day when he could drive to Denver and take a ride in her Jenny, although his summers were busy and his schedule unpredictable. A Jenny wouldn't go as high nor as fast as the newer models, but it was solid, stable, and a pleasure to fly. Kind of like his Small Delights pickup. A fast, heavy roadster like Vi Coteau's Marmon Six was exciting, but for a pleasant day's drive he'd prefer his pickup.

Ranger McIntyre stood on his porch, hands in pockets, squinting into the afternoon sun. Four hours of daylight left, or more. The trout would be feeding. Upriver, not far from Fall River Lodge, there were deep pools in the shade where lunkers would be coming to the surface for bugs. A couple of nice rainbows or browns would be good for dinner. Maybe with those small potatoes. And he could open a can of peas.

He was in the cabin with his fishing rod in one hand and lifting his creel from its peg with the other when the telephone went off. Again.

"Fall River Station," he said warily. "McIntyre."

"Good afternoon, Grumpy. Have you seen the newspapers?"

It was Dottie, Supervisor Nicholson's secretary. Three phone calls from three women in one day, McIntyre was thinking.

"Hello, Dottie. Haven't seen the Denver paper, but I heard about it."

"Supervisor Nicholson would like to invite you to meet with him at his office in the morning, at eight o'clock sharp. In uniform."

"Do I have to wear a gun, too?"

"I can't see where it would do you any good."

McIntyre groaned. A meeting at the S.O. first thing in the morning was never a nice way to start the day.

"Okay, see you then."

"Right-o, ranger. Bye!"

CHAPTER FOUR
FIRST ENCOUNTER

McIntyre hoisted his camp pack into the bed of the pickup and jiggled the trailer to make sure the hitch was secure. Inside the trailer, Brownie pricked up her ears and snorted.

"Brownie seems eager to go," Jamie Ogg said. "You got any idea how long 'til you're back?"

"No idea at all," McIntyre said. "I don't even know what it is I'm supposed to do. Once I find Nature Girl, I mean."

"Okay," Jamie said. "I'll keep the station hummin' along. Any special chores you want done?"

"No, I guess not. You know the daily patrol routes. If you happen to think of it, you might change the oil in the government pickup."

"Can do. This crazy female you're after. Eve's really her name?"

"Nicholson doesn't think it is. A couple of years ago when she pulled that embarrassing stunt on the U.S. National Park Service—not to mention the village politicians—she gave her name as Agatha. The 'Eve' stuff was all for the newspapers. The whole stunt was for the papers. This time she claims she wants to avoid all publicity. Wants to be alone with Mother Nature. Wants to 'commune' with plants and animals and use her 'extra sensory perception' to visit the spirits of the dead Indians. Among other things, the spirits are supposed to tell her what the medicine circle was used for."

"When you say 'commune' . . ." Jamie said. "I mean, that

word, it conjures up a kind of image in my head. You know? You're not saying she's a nudist? I saw pictures of a commune in a magazine, once. Didn't buy it. I only looked at it."

"Bull's-eye," McIntyre said. "According to what she told Nicholson and Dottie, she's only going to carry a blanket, a chunk of bread, and some tea. At the medicine circle she means to disrobe and lie down in it until the spirits speak to her. Apparently that's how she thinks the Indians did it in the old days."

"What about sunburn? And altitude sickness?" Jamie said. "Not to mention insect bites, hypothermia, all that kind of stuff. Anyways, what are you supposed to do when you find her, carry her down the peak? Throw her across your saddle and haul her back to civilization?"

"I'll hire a horse for her from the Bear Lake Lodge livery. I'll arrest her if I have to. But between you and me, I think we ought to leave her there, if it wasn't for our dead climber telling me he'd seen somebody there, saying he'd been threatened with a spear. It keeps nagging at my mind."

"Yeah," Jamie said. "Almost like somebody took it in their mind to keep people off the place, huh?"

"And I'd like to find out who's been fooling around with the circle's rocks, too. If I wasn't so curious about the medicine circle I'd be tempted to go camp at Lulu Lake instead. I'd spend a couple of days fishing and report to our beloved supervisor I couldn't find the nature girl. Except the way my luck's been going, the damn reporter from the *Record* would show up at Lulu with his photographer."

"Maybe you'll catch whoever's messing with the rocks," Jamie suggested.

"Which reminds me," McIntyre said. "Polly's friend Johnny said he'd show the rock sample to a geologist. One of them might be phoning the station."

"What do you want me to do, ride up and find you and tell you what they said?"

"No, no. But if it turns out to be anything weird or seems important, don't talk to anybody about it."

"Mum's the word, chum!" Jamie said with a grin.

" 'Chum'? No more days off in Denver for you," McIntyre said. "You're starting to talk like one of those city sheiks."

"Hey!" Jamie said. "Speaking of sheiks and flappers, what if your glamorous city lady friend shows up? Or phones the station? What do I tell her? Vi Coteau?"

McIntyre clanged his door shut and pressed his foot to the starter button. The Small Delights pickup coughed into life. Inside the trailer, Brownie stamped one hoof and whinnied. Truck, horse, and ranger were ready to go.

"Tell her I'm looking for nude ladies at timberline. And tell her I don't need help."

One good thing came out of the Great War, in McIntyre's way of thinking. He was once again reminded of it as he set up his camp among the wind-twisted trees below timberline, a hundred yards off the Flattop trail. Trench warfare had been muddy, grotesque, and inhuman but it forced the Army to come up with lightweight waterproof tarps, excellent rubber ponchos, and efficient short shovels. McIntyre also appreciated his lightweight mess kit and canteen.

"Hadn't been for the war," he said to Brownie as he rigged a tarp to shelter her from rain and the intense alpine sun, "you wouldn't have this nice protection. And you and the livery horse would be loaded down with iron pots and a long shovel."

Brownie looked around at the short alpine grass, the exposed rocks, the scorching sunlight. *Open ground. Cold nights. Not to mention it being bear country. And mountain lion country. Plus having to be nursemaid to a timid, overfed livery gelding. You stay close, buster. Those afternoon rains are ice-cold and bring lightning and thunder with them and if you start acting up all dancy-nasty, you'll end up with my hoofprints on your butt.*

McIntyre staked his tarp with the open side facing his fire circle and went out into the trees and krumholtz in search of firewood. He walked in a zigzag pattern across the slope of the mountain, carefully noting the location of each usable piece of dead wood. It was an old mountaineer trick: you don't pick up wood as you go, because if you do you'll end up far from camp with a heavy armload. The trick is to spot the pieces and pick them up as you walk back toward your camp.

On his second fuel-gathering walk, McIntyre was startled by a glimpse of brown movement among the rocks. Good thing he had his service revolver. No, bad thing: the gun was in his pack, which was back in camp. He crouched down and froze. After a minute, through the tangle of twisted pine trees and branches, he saw it again. Something dark brown or black, something moving slowly. Without taking his eyes off of it, McIntyre felt around until his hand closed on a rock the size of a tennis ball. He lobbed it as far as he could into the krumholtz beyond. It had the effect he expected.

"Whuff!!"

The black bear stood up on its hind legs to look toward the sound. It was not a grizzly. It wasn't even a very large black. Probably a female too young to mate, or maybe a male whose mother had recently pushed him out of the den. McIntyre stood up. The bear turned and saw him.

"Whuff?"

"What's for supper?" McIntyre asked. "Having berries, are you? Grubs, maybe?"

The young black bear whuffed once more and headed downhill in that funny, awkward, butt-swaying way of the bear. The ranger watched it go, remembering the previous summer when a couple of campers ran up to him to breathlessly report a bear near their tent. McIntyre had been checking campsites but hadn't seen hide nor hair of a bruin.

"Where, exactly, did you see the bear?" he had asked.

"Over there, over there!" the woman had said. "By the big rock in the meadow!"

He had been able to see it. But the car-size boulder in the meadow was hardly "near" their tent. It was so far out, in fact, that McIntyre had not been inclined to walk all the way to it.

"What was this bear doing?" he had asked. "Did it threaten you?"

"Well, no. I think it was . . . well, it seemed to be sunning itself on the rock."

"Large, was it? About the size of a big dog, for instance?"

"Like a Saint Bernard? Uh . . . not that big. Not especially large. More of a cocker spaniel size. What are you going to do about it?"

"Nothing," the ranger had said. "I promise it won't attack your tent. It won't even bother your food, because it won't be prowling around at night. I promise."

"How can you be so sure?" the woman's companion had asked.

"Because marmots don't move around after dark. Marmots like to sun themselves. They don't go near humans. And they don't forage at night. Especially older males like the one you saw."

McIntyre smiled at the memory. After all, a mature marmot spread out on a rock would look much like a small bear. Plus, the light in the mountains tended to make people see better, farther than in the city. The transparent air and eye-dazzling sun can make the mountaintops look closer than they actually are. Sharply outlined shadows look like animals, animals can look like bushes or rocks. Alpine lakes can look shallow enough to walk across and yet are ten feet deep.

With his firewood stacked under the tarp, McIntyre resumed putting on his tunic, flat hat, and gun belt, and once again looked every inch a forest ranger.

"I guess I ought to hike up to the medicine circle and see if the crazy lady's been there," he said to Brownie. "I've tied the livery horse to the long picket rope, but you might keep an eye on him anyway. If he broke loose we'd have to spend the rest of the day following horse tracks."

Speaking of which . . . all the way up the Flattop trail there had been no tracks. Not since the last time it rained. There were long stretches between the rocks and roots where the dirt was as fine as flour and showed tracks of birds and small animals, but no horse tracks and no footprints of bare feet, moccasins, or boots. He was all alone on the mountain. There were no newspapermen looking for a story, no nude woman looking for publicity (or God knows what), no little brown men carrying white rocks and spears. There would be nothing to find at the medicine circle.

The argument Ranger McIntyre had with himself went something like this:

In a wilderness situation the first four things you need are shelter, water, dry fuel, and food. I got the tarps rigged, collected firewood, and the canteen is still full. Plenty of rations in the packs, but catching trout for dinner would help stretch the food supply. There's a creek about a ten-minute walk down over the brow of the mountain. I ought to go up to the scene of the climbing accident. But if I run out of food, will my mind be sharp enough to make a good investigation? Morning light shows small objects better anyway. I could wait until morning. Afternoon is better fishing. And who knows, a tourist might ask if there are brook trout in this creek and it's part of my job to know. And besides, fishing awhile would help me think through the situation. Help me remember exactly what the dead climber said and how he looked. Maybe he had the altitude sickness. It can make people hallucinate. Like the guy on Tombstone Ridge last summer. He had altitude sickness and thought the forest was on fire because of the heat. Told the people who found him it was over a hundred degrees and the sun was burning everything.

No, I think I need to check this creek and see if there are brook trout in it and what condition they're in. Tomorrow morning is soon enough to hike up to the circle. I'll give the place a real going-over tomorrow.

When he told Brownie about his change of plans the horse did not seem surprised. The ranger couldn't resist a trout stream any more than she could resist a crisp apple. Except there wouldn't be any apples. She went back to grazing the thin grass.

McIntyre found the creek narrow enough for a man to jump across. The ice-cold water was as utterly clear, transparent as bootleg gin. It came pouring down the mountain slope, bubbling and chuckling over granite boulders. Here it dropped into a deep slit in the tundra, then reappeared as a wide, flat sheet-like glass just before it went pouring over a granite ledge. McIntyre knew there wouldn't be any trout in the stream where it flowed through tundra because the alpine sunlight was too intense, the water too clear. No, they would be downhill, down where the creek meandered among scrubby, tough little willow thickets and in and out among the grotesquely twisted trunks of juniper and pine. He followed it to where it entered the krumholtz. There the current slowed and spread out, creating calm, deep pockets of water in the shadows. The scrub gave it shade from the glare of sunlight and there, hidden in the depths from bears and eagles, was the safest place for trout to feed.

He opened his fly wallet and selected a tiny black dry fly called a midge. This particular midge, and the one next to it in the wallet, was without a barb to the hook: he expected to snag undersize brookies and didn't want any trouble removing the hook to let them go. This expectation was confirmed when the first half-dozen trout turned out to be six or seven inches long. He looked around for a better spot, one with fish of a more decent size.

There it was.

An undercut bank on the other side of the creek, protected by overhanging willow. A great place to snag his line in the twisted branches, but a perfect shady place for the bigger trout to feed in safety where a predator couldn't reach them.

The ranger stepped back away from the water and bent over to sneak around through the brush to come out at a spot well upstream of the promising pool. He would gently drift the midge down with the current.

The first three drifts were successful. These were wild brook trout, unused to human anglers and unlikely to spook when one of their number was abruptly hauled up out of the water. Each time he caught one, another trout took over the vacated feeding station and went on watching for drifting bugs. In less than an hour McIntyre had his supper, three firm brook trout.

One more, he thought. *The biggest one ought to be a bit farther on. At the edge of the shade, where he can feed while keeping his eye on the smaller ones. I'll flick a short roll cast and . . . oh, damn! Snagged!*

He was indeed snagged. A root or underwater willow branch. Now the decision was whether to break off the midge and lose it or fool around for ten minutes trying to flip the line loose—and maybe lose the dry fly anyway—or go over there and feel around underwater until his fingers found the hook and he could pull it out of the twig. Since he already had caught enough for supper it wouldn't matter if he spooked the pool. He opted to retrieve the fly.

However, the snag was more than a twig. What McIntyre lifted from the little stream, his dry fly still embedded in it, was a cone made of willow sticks. At first he thought a wicker wastepaper basket had been thrown into the creek. It was the same size, but shaped like a pointed ice cream cone. He realized what it was. A fish trap. In fact, there were three fair-size brookies caught in it. The willow had been freshly peeled and strips of bark had been used to lash the sticks together. On the banks of the creek he spotted the stumps where the willows had been cut. Whoever had made this fish trap, they had made it on the spot. And knew what they were doing, except that the peeled sticks would be white and shiny and perhaps make larger fish suspicious. Better to leave the bark on.

Now there's a new wrinkle, as the man said when his dog slept on his shirt. A piece for the jigsaw puzzle. A little piece of picture, but a really interesting one. Someone was here. He—or she— not only had the knowledge and time to build a fish trap but was going to stick around and eat these fish.

The ranger jerked one of the willow sticks loose to free the brookies. He made the sabotage look natural, as if the bark lashing had slipped. He replaced the trap where he had found it. *I'll bet there's a camp someplace nearby. Not against park rules to camp here, although the fish trap is illegal. Certain people like to camp far away from the main trails. Heck, I'm one of them.*

He dismantled his fly rod in order to search the area. He had designed and built the rod as a five-piece that he could hide in a backpack in case he got an urge to go fishing and didn't want anyone to see a ranger carrying a fishing pole.

At first there was nothing to find except for a few smudges in the dry alpine sand. One of them could have been a footprint of a flat sole shoe or moccasin. He noticed a couple of broken twigs on the ground as he moved slowly through the brush. Another indistinct footprint, a couple more snapped twigs, some crushed grass, and he came out into a small clearing in the krumholtz, a flat sandy spot large enough for one or two sleeping bags, sheltered by the wind-stunted juniper. There seemed to be more open ground beyond the tangled brush. McIntyre pushed on through the branches and came to an empty alpine meadow sloping down toward the heavy timber. No people, no tracks, nothing but grass and flowers.

He returned to the secret little clearing in the krumholtz and studied the place as if he were planning to camp there. He figured it was the best place to put a sleeping bag where it could be out of the wind and have the first sunlight in the morning. The campfire should be out of the wind, too, McIntyre thought, and near the sleeping bag for the warmth . . . the fire would be exactly where that one flat rock lies.

The flat stone seemed out of place. And when he turned it over McIntyre found exactly what he expected. Scorching. And soot. Whoever the campers were, they had built a small cooking fire on the flat stone. After cooking the fish, maybe boiling a mug of tea, they let the fire die to ash, probably threw the ashes to the winds and turned the rock upside down to hide the evidence of the fire.

Cute. Not even a footprint. Not a broken branch. When they wanted firewood they probably scoured the krumholtz for dry twigs. Didn't use any from the brush around this clearing. Call me cynical, but I don't think the Nature Lady camped here. From what I heard about her, I'd say she wasn't this much of an outdoor person. If I didn't know better, I'd say an Indian made camp here. Hardly a trace left to tell. Maybe it was one of "Eve's" Indian ghosts.

He wouldn't have paid much more attention to the place had it not been for the pains the camper had taken to make it look unused. Who camps all alone up in the mountains and tries to hide where they camped? Were they doing something illegal, or were they just very conscientious? It intrigued him, much like pieces of a jigsaw puzzle scattered across a table would do. He went prowling through the juniper and scrub spruce until he spotted tiny flecks of ash on a twisted branch. Returning to the clearing, he knelt beside the cooking rock as the mystery camper must have done. The location of the ashes meant the breeze had been from the southwest. The camper must have squatted on this side of the tiny fire to shield it and to keep smoke out of his eyes.

There were no burnt matches to be seen. No scratches on any of the stones from striking a match. Flint and steel?

Kneeling there he reached his arms out, pretending he was the camper reaching for the cooking pot and food bag. The great art to cooking in the open is to have everything arranged within arm's reach before you sit down next to the fire. And to have a small smokeless fire. Be ready to cook your whole meal without getting up, using only one tin cup, one small frying pan, and perhaps one small kettle or pot for heating water. So, here was the fire. Here was the camper. The food bag, probably right there . . . aha!

They were almost lost in the fine sand among the miniature alpine mosses and grass. Three grayish grains of rice. McIntyre put one between his teeth and bit down on it. Cooked rice. Dried out, but it had been cooked. And it looked like natural stuff, not the kind you buy in a bag at the store.

Not many men carry cooked rice on a hike. He didn't cook it here, either. At this altitude it would take hours to boil rice. And he must have dropped it recently or else a vole or some other mousy critter would have discovered it and eaten it. Somewhere he cooked it, dried it so it wouldn't go bad. Then he could soak it in warm water to eat it.

He continued poking around on all fours and found a few fish bones and a couple of dried fins. Any other food remnants had probably been burned in the campfire or buried under a rock.

So now the ranger knew . . . what? That a camper who was

very skilled at not being seen had slept there recently and had
eaten fish from the creek. And rice. Finding nothing more to
learn from the site, McIntyre returned to his own camp to clean
his trout for supper. He considered trying to hide and wait for
the mystery camper to return and check the fish trap. However,
it might not be for several days. Besides which, chances were
they had no connection to the climbing accident. No, Mc-
Intyre's best course of action would be to go about his business.
In the morning, he would search the medicine circle. It was also
his duty, he told himself, to see if he could find Nature Lady.
Maybe he should call her Agatha. Or Crazy Eve.

The following day dawned clear and cloudless and without a
whisper of a breeze. The air was warm even before the sun
struck the high granite tips of the Front Range. The mountaintops, the crystalline air, and the incense of conifer were beckoning to hikers like a cheap tart in a doorway saying "come on,
come on."

Ranger McIntyre wasn't to be taken in so easily. He knew
what the unmoving air meant. He knew what it meant to see
long, long innocent-looking cloud banks lying nearly hidden
behind the western range of mountains. The day would start
out warm enough to make a man want to strip off jacket and
shirt and walk the tundra bare-chested. By noon it would be so
hot he'd be looking for shade, except up here on the rooftop of
the continent there was no shade and even the marmots and
pika who usually sunned themselves among the rocks would be
underground in their cool tunnels. Before two o'clock those
clouds would begin to move—with unnatural speed—and
underneath their gloom a cold, cold wind would begin pouring
over the Divide and down the eastern slope. And the thunder
would walk the tundra and the lightning would come to earth.

He had a plan of, kind of. As he hiked up the slope toward

the medicine wheel he was thinking he might search around—again—and sketch the wheel into his notebook for the second time as a way of making sure he had seen every detail. He wanted to have another look down over the other side of the mountain's flat top, down into the stunted trees. There might be additional evidence to find down there.

The sun, climbing the cloudless sky and stroking its way down the flanks of the surrounding peaks, arrived at the medicine wheel several minutes before McIntyre. When the ranger came up over the rim of the peak, planning to look everywhere and even crawl around searching on hands and knees if necessary, the first thing he saw was a brown shape lying in the bare spot at the center of the wheel.

He thought it must be a small deer lying there. Resting. Or dead. Maybe someone had killed a yearling and had placed it in the middle of the stone circle. But it moved and stretched out two bare arms. It was a human being, a person wearing deerskin. A woman. She lay down spread-eagle in the hub of the stone wheel, her figure covered with a badly made deerskin poncho. It looked like two rectangles of hide had been stitched into an envelope with holes for arms and head. On her feet she wore sloppy-looking boxes that were probably supposed to be moccasins.

He came to the middle of the circle and stood over her. She did not seem surprised to see him.

"Hello," she said, looking up. "Isn't it wonderful?"

"Pardon?"

"Wonderful! Do you know the lore of the Cheyenne, Ranger?"

"Some of it, yes."

"It's wonderful. If you lie here with your head to the east you can feel inner illumination flooding your entire mind and body! When your head is to the north it brings you dark thoughts, but not bad ones. More like introspection. I don't know the

Cheyenne word for it. Like a bear in his winter den, sleeping and dreaming ineffable thoughts. Head lying to the south, of course, is the way to see your innocence. You should try. All ideas of guilt, or ambition, or shame, or need, all go away as if you were an infant seeing only the present moment's joy. Sky, air, earth."

"Are you all right?"

"Certainly. Why do you ask me that?"

"Because it's my job. You're in my ranger district. I try to keep tabs on things, including hikers and other visitors. Your name is Agatha, maybe?"

She laughed as though he sounded very foolish. She sat up and crossed her legs like one of those oriental statues of the fat guy who is always smiling.

"You think I am the nature woman who came to the park three years ago! I am not that woman. She was naïve. She believed if she wandered the forest *au naturel* she would find her true bond with Mother Nature. Foolish woman. No, I am not the woman you think. As you can see, I have clothed myself in the garment of the Indian and I seek to know Mother Earth as the Indian does. Here, in this wonderful ancient circle, I have found the source of Indian wisdom. I know it will take much time to absorb it, but what joy to have found it!"

"Okay," McIntyre said. "Can you give me a name, though? For my report? Like I said, we like to keep tabs on who is in the park. Mostly for their own safety. You know, in case relatives need to get in touch." *Or we need to contact your next of kin. Or your psychiatrist.*

"*Washichu* name," she replied.

"What?"

"It means white people. I have not yet been given my true and natural name. It has not been revealed to me. You may, however, write down my *washichu* name as Fannie Painter."

"You're pulling my leg."

"Fannie Painter," she repeated. "Or Francine, if you need to be formal. I once thought I was Agatha. Are you going to go away now? I need to lie with my head facing west."

McIntyre had a dozen questions buzzing around in his brain, like where she camped and what she ate and what she was going to do next, but an unexplainable instinct told him to proceed very cautiously with interrogation.

"I do have one question, if you don't mind," he said.

"I would certainly not mind at all! In the magical circle my serenity is unflappable."

"I see. Well, the question concerns these white rocks."

"Oh!" she exclaimed. "You saw it, too! Those three white rocks, that one, that one, and that one, yesterday they were aligned perfectly with the rising sun! Perfect alignment! No doubt it was a special day. Cosmic importance. It's wonderful. Do you know what? At night they reflect the moonshine and alpenglow and can be seen at a great distance."

"Interesting," McIntyre said. "But what I'd like to know is, was it you who put these white rocks here?"

"Me?" she said, wide-eyed at the very suggestion. "Why would I? However, this morning I did notice a fresh one had been added. On the west side of the circle, making nearly a dozen."

"I've never seen white rocks like those anywhere near here," McIntyre said. "What do you really know about them? Don't you know how they got here?"

"I know of only two new ones. They appear when the clouds come over, with mist. The fog and mist come over the mountain and when they leave, the white rocks are there. They have nothing to do with me. Sometimes I believe they represent the blank empty gaps in our wisdom. After you have left, I may lie with my head toward a white rock and attempt to sense what it means."

"Fine," McIntyre said. "Let me know what you find out. I'm camped down on the eastern slope about a hundred yards off the trail."

"I know," she said.

"Good. I'll look around now. I'll try not to bother you."

"You won't," Fannie Painter said with a sweet smile.

Chapter Five
A Horrible Fright and a New Arrival

Ranger McIntyre loved a complicated jigsaw puzzle. Vague riddles and clueless quandaries, however, tended to annoy him, and both the medicine wheel and the Agatha Eve Fannie Painter woman were fast becoming the latter.

Quandaries.

Take the medicine wheel, for instance: the official mission of the National Park Service is to preserve and protect a specified area for the benefit of future generations. If a modern age person living in the 1920s defaced the natural tundra with a ring of stones, the ranger's duty would be to issue a citation and restore the site to its original condition. However, if drawings on a cliff or holes in the ground or a bunch of rocks were deemed to be "ancient" or "prehistoric" the rangers needed to protect them from removal or alteration. At Mesa Verde the rangers preserved entire buildings because they were built by prehistoric tribes. A modern tourist might be hauled into court for cementing one rock on top of another.

The Painter woman represented another dilemma. The publicity dilemma. The park depended for its existence upon tourist visitation. Publicity is what drew tourists to the park and tourist numbers seemed to be the only thing that the Washington budget wranglers were interested in. Garish posters advertising railroad excursions to national parks, newspaper releases about the latest attempt to scale the North Face or explore Grand Canyon, ranger lectures with magic lantern pictures . . . it was all for "exposure" and advertising. However, if the word got out how Rocky Mountain National Park had its own female lunatic it could bring a tidal wave of reporters and photographers eager for sensationalism. The national park might end up looking like a haven for eccentrics.

So, should McIntyre tell anyone about Fannie Painter? Or was it his responsibility to simply leave her alone? Or was it his duty to keep an eye on her and do what he could to keep her safe, even from herself? Or should he hog-tie her, throw her across a horse, and haul her the hell out of his park?

It was a meditative and morose McIntyre who squatted in front of his little cooking fire waiting for the kettle to boil. He looked up to the sky where a dark spot moving against the gray overcast caught his eye: it was a prairie falcon describing its airborne circles above Flattop Mountain. McIntyre smiled grimly. He allowed himself a fantasy in which the raptor stooped, dove earthward on mighty wings, seized Fannie in its talons, and carried her away somewhere.

Anywhere.

Ranger McIntyre figured he was ready for the rain, should the heavy overcast decide to cut loose with a late afternoon shower. He had stashed his saddles, packs, and firewood beneath the slope of the extra tarp. He had unrolled the yellow slickers and tied them over Brownie and the livery horse before picketing both horses in the shelter of overhanging krumholtz. His other tarp was rigged like a lean-to under which he had his bedroll, food bag, and campfire ring.

Where Fannie Painter would find shelter he had no idea. After their conversation at the medicine circle he had scouted the top of the mountain and had seen nothing of her camp. He hadn't seen her horse, either. Still, he told himself, both could easily be hidden in the trees down the western slope of the peak. He hoped she had a tent and blankets. The last thing he needed was a woman in wet deerskin, on the verge of hypo-thermia.

The ceiling of gray cloud flowed on across the Continental Divide, bringing cold mist but no rain. Even better, there was no lightning and no thunder. Between McIntyre's camp and the summit there was only silence. There was no moving air to whisper among the stunted trees, no birds announcing them-selves. The only thing disturbing the serenity of the wilderness was the shrill, frantic screaming of the woman who was running and stumbling down the rocky path from the top of the moun-tain.

McIntyre jumped to his feet, stomped his tiny campfire flat, grabbed his revolver, and dashed out from under the tarp. As he reached the main trail he saw Fannie Painter hurrying toward him, screaming unintelligible words. Her clumsy footwear kept tripping her. Instead of looking like a graceful forest nymph dancing along the trail she looked like an inebriate whose every lurching step threatened to send her face into the dirt.

The ranger stood his ground, pistol at the ready. *Come on girl. Keep on coming. Don't stop, come around behind me. Let's see who's chasing you. For God's sake don't try to grab at me. Come on behind me. Come on. Let me deal with it. Let me deal with it . . .*

She staggered past him and dropped into a fetal crouch behind his legs. She was no longer screaming. He could hear her gulping for air.

"What is it?" he said, his eyes scanning trail and krumholtz for signs of movement.

"Aaaghh . . ." she tried to reply. Her hands clawed at the air. She kept trying to gulp for more oxygen. She clawed the air again.

"Mountain lion?" he said. "With claws? Are you hurt? What happened, did a lion think you were a deer in your animal hide? Mountain lion? Probably gone by now. They don't like to run very far. I bet you startled it and it ran off into the bush."

"No, no," Fannie Painter gasped. "No! Bear! Big! Up there!"

She held one hand on her heaving chest and pointed at the mountaintop with the other. McIntyre helped her to her feet. She clung to his arm for support.

"Okay, okay," he said. "You're safe. What'd this bear look like?"

"Big," Fannie repeated. Her voice was hoarse. "Long claws. All I could see when he charged. Long claws, long as my fingers."

"Unusual," the ranger said. "Charging a person? Mostly they walk away from humans. Might have been a mother with cub nearby."

Fannie Painter's breathing had calmed and she let go of McIntyre's arm.

"I think it was a male. Six or seven feet tall when he stood up. Didn't you hear him roar? You should have heard him even all the way down here. Huge roar. Horrifying."

"Six feet?"

"At least. As tall as you, maybe taller. I think it was a male because he had a flat face. Not a long snout, but a flat face."

"Color?"

"Brown, brown all over. No, wait! Silvery gray markings. Rounded ears. He had a pronounced hump to his shoulders, too."

"You're describing a silvertip grizzly," McIntyre said. *And you're using words like you found them in a book,* he thought. *Sounds like you read about Ursus horribilis with its "pronounced hump."*

Fannie was shivering. The late afternoon sun was hidden by the misty fog, which had been stealthily creeping down across the tundra and into the timberline scrub.

"You're okay now," he said. "You'd better come over to my camp and I'll make us a hot cup of tea. You need a fire and shelter. Tomorrow morning I'll go up there with you and look for tracks. I'd really like to see a silvertip grizzly, if that's what it was. A few local guys say they've seen them, but grizzlies are awful rare around here."

"I don't need to go back up there tomorrow," she said. "I've had such a fright, you see. If you don't mind, I'll huddle under one of your tarps tonight. Perhaps tomorrow I'll begin to wend my way out of the wilderness. Such a fright."

Tarps, plural? How does she know I have two tarps rigged up? In fact . . . didn't she say she knew where I was camped? Who the heck uses phrases like "wend my way"? Maybe she reads too many books.

The chilly mist descended on through the krumholtz. It left dewdrops dangling off the pine needles and the kinnikinnick leaves, and as darkness approached the mist faded into shreds of cloud among the bushes and evaporated into nothingness. Much to McIntyre's relief, the sky cleared and stars began to appear. No rain. Better yet, no thunder and no lightning. He really didn't need any weather excitement tonight. He built up his fire beneath the tarp shelter, wrapped Fannie in the saddle blankets and his tunic, and poured boiling water into the pot of noodles and beef. She clutched a saddle blanket around her shoulders and sat silently staring into the flames. It took nearly an hour and two plates of food, but she finally recovered enough to thank him.

"Part of the job," he said. "You're welcome. When morning comes we'll go back up there and retrieve your camp stuff. Or I'll go alone if you can tell me where your camp is. You could stay here. Then I think we ought to get you down to civilization. As far as the lodge, at least."

"No horse?" he asked.

"No," she said. She shivered again despite the hot tea and warm blankets. "No, I am on foot. But there's no need for you to go back up there. Really. All I had was a raggedy old blanket and a tin pot, plus a sack of bread and dried meat. I would prefer to abandon it. If you should leave me alone I'd be afraid the whole time you were gone, for fear you'd run into the monster."

McIntyre smiled at the word "monster."

"How tall was this bear, did you say? Twenty feet?"

Fannie Painter actually let out a little laugh. "Oh, much taller," she said. "Thirty feet at least."

"You know," he said, "bears and trout have one thing in common. Whenever people talk about them they grow in size."

Their little exchange of humor seemed to relax her considerably. It almost seemed to change her into a normal person.

"By the way," Fannie said. "You didn't tell me what a ranger is doing camped up here on the mountain."

"Oh?" McIntyre said. "Uh . . . it's those darn white rocks. The mission of the park service is to preserve all of this area. When people start decorating it by hauling in exotic minerals we need to find out why and see if we need to put a stop to it. It's kind of in the same category as painting your initials on a cliff or maybe putting up a billboard to advertise your souvenir shop. Or you could say it's part of our duty as rangers to keep tabs on whatever is going on in the park. And by the way . . . what did you say you had for food?"

"My food? Well, when I started out I had lots of dried fruit, mainly apples and apricots, several loaves of peasant bread, or shepherd's bread, and dried beef."

"No fish?"

"Heavens, no! I cannot abide to eat dried fish. Even smoked. On my third day I did come upon a little pond among the tundra plants—what do you call it? A pond with no stream coming in or out?"

"A tarn?"

"Yes. A tarn. There were little fish swimming in a tarn. I

waded out among them with my hands in the water and spoke to them in the manner of the Indian, beseeching them to come to my hands for I was hungry."

"Did they come to your hands?"

"No. I did not have the Indian name for 'fish' you see. They did not recognize what I was saying. I did think of catching them, but I had no means. I suppose I might have used my blanket as a sort of net."

"Probably wouldn't work," McIntyre observed.

"You are right," she agreed.

"Did you bring rice with you?"

"No," she said. "Your Indians of this region, the Arapaho and Crow and Kiowa and so on, they do not know rice. Largely, I think, because of the altitude. It takes hours to boil rice or beans at this altitude. Now, your more eastern tribes such as the Ojibwa, where wild rice grows and firewood is plentiful, they do make it part of their diet. Perhaps you do not realize it, as many persons do not, but our American wild rice is not actually rice in the way we think of Asian rice. The rice in Japan is much different. I speak from experience."

As difficult as it might be to believe, the subsequent campfire conversation became even more boring. She told him what she thought were the "Indian" names of the various constellations and recited long, disjointed "Indian" legends about the moon and the peaks. Eventually she lay down next to the fire and, still talking, fell asleep. McIntyre managed to stay on watch a while, listening and sniffing the air in case a fifty-foot silvertip should come prowling, but before midnight he, too, slipped off into dreamland.

Against Fannie Painter's strong objections, McIntyre set out after breakfast to look for her camp gear. Even if it was meager, he didn't want to leave it to clutter the mountaintop. She told him to look for a prominent granite boulder several hundred yards southwest of the medicine circle; there he found the tin pot and old blanket, together with the shredded remains of her food bag.

"Varmints got the victuals," he muttered, quoting an ancient fur trapper.

The ranger found no sign of any kind of bear. However, the medicine circle looked different. Or felt different, at least. He consulted his notebook sketch. Sure enough, two more white rocks had been added recently, probably while the summit was covered in cloud and mist. One here, one over there, there was no pattern to it. Each had fresh dirt around it.

Maybe Fannie's magic silvertip grizzly did it, he thought. *Maybe the bear digs those holes to hide his meat in. Sometimes after a big grizzly bear eats its fill of a deer or elk it'll cover the carcass with dirt. Saving it for supper. But grizzlies are awful rare nowadays. Maybe Fannie's black bear is more systematic. Maybe this one separates his deer into daily portions and buries each one with a white rock over it. A very methodical bear. Anyway, while I'm thinking about "maybes" it may be I've got better things to worry about, like hauling the crazy lady down the mountain. I'll drop her off at Bear Lake Lodge and let Ken take care of her. Right now I need to figure out whether to let her ride double on Brownie, or let her ride while I walk. Or tie her on top of the packhorse.*

As things turned out, the new rocks on Flattop Mountain were not the only surprise in store for Ranger McIntyre. Another one was waiting for him when he and the nature woman arrived at Bear Lake Lodge.

"No, I'm not kidding you," Ken told him. "I don't need to find an empty room for her. She already has a room."

"Come on," McIntyre said, looking around for her. The uncombed woman in deerskins and ridiculous moccasins had vanished in the direction of the dining room. "That can't be right."

"I'm telling you it is. A woman came up to this reception desk, right where you're standing, two weeks ago. Nicely dressed. Long blond hair, snazzy hat, dark glasses. She rented a room for eight weeks, paid cash. The guy who drove the car—never seen him or the car before—he lugged a steamer trunk and a suitcase up to the room. She told me another woman, dressed Indian fashion, would be coming to stay in the room. She left and I never saw her again."

McIntyre groaned. How was he going to explain to Nicholson that the national park nature woman had a room in a lodge?

"Ken," the ranger said with a sigh, "next time there's a job opening for a busboy or bellhop, or dishwasher, let me know, would you? Being a ranger gives me the headache."

Ken laughed and handed the ranger a receipt for the hire of the livery horse.

"Couldn't afford you," Ken said. "I've seen how much breakfast you can eat. And whenever the fishing was good I'd have to go search the river for you. No thanks."

McIntyre looked at the receipt. Dottie was going to kill him. He went to the dining room to say goodbye. He would try one more ploy and if she took the bait he would be able to tell Supervisor Nicholson she'd left the park.

"I had a thought," he began, standing at her table while she waited for her meal to arrive. "A friend of mine is a lady airplane pilot. She tells me there's another possible medicine circle out on the plains, 'way out there between the Platte and the Arkansas River. Maybe you'd like to go there to continue your search for enlightenment? I think it would be a lot safer. She's only seen it from the air, but it sounds much like the one on Flattop. Very remote. No one would disturb you. Maybe I could talk my friend into flying you there. Later she could fly out and drop supplies to you. What do you think?"

"Interesting," Fannie Painter said unenthusiastically. "I will consider it."

Another twist, McIntyre mused as he walked away. *You'd think she'd show at least a little more interest. Curiosity, at least. Here I go and tell her about another vision place she could have all to herself and all she says is "interesting." And there's this thing about having a room all reserved and ready. What the heck is going on with her and Flattop Mountain, anyway? Probably turn out to be none of my business, but I'd sure like to know.*

By the time he reached the main highway McIntyre was already regretting his decision to turn down Ken's offer of a free lunch—or early supper—at Bear Lake Lodge. Now his stomach was growling at him. Truth to tell, he fled the lodge because he was anxious to put distance between himself and "Eve."

Fortunately, Tiny's store at Beaver Point sold the best darn sandwiches imaginable. He would stop there and have one, maybe catch up on any gossip. Tiny, the three-hundred-pound jovial soul who ran the little roadside grocery, was McIntyre's unofficial monitor of that side of the mountain. McIntyre's ranger station was on the other side.

"Such a coincidence you dropped in!" Tiny said with customary exuberance. "I was about to slice this beef for sandwiches! Will you have one?"

"Sure thing," McIntyre said, eyeing the joint of meat on the chopping block. "Beef? From here I'd swear it looks like venison."

Tiny chuckled.

"You mean as if a local resident hit an elk with their truck in the dark?"

"Could happen," the ranger said, pulling a stool up to the counter and helping himself to a crunchy dill pickle from the pickle jar. "What's this coincidence you mentioned? Fresh meat and a missing elk?"

Tiny's jowls and belly bounced whenever he chuckled.

"No," he said. "The coincidence is, there were two people in here—yesterday—looking for you. And here you show up! I told them you were probably fishing."

"Thanks. Who were they? Are you saying they were together?"

"Give you a hint," Tiny said, smearing homemade mayonnaise on homemade bread. "I was stocking the soup shelf when I heard the sound of a motorcar engine. It was like a cat purring? Only it was louder than any cat. I looked out and coming off the highway was a shiny new yellow Marmon convertible. Six cylinders. Wire wheels."

"Oh, God," McIntyre groaned. "Don't tell me Vi Coteau has a new car! She was dangerous enough in the old model."

"Yep," Tiny chuckled again. "I sure do like your lady friend. She was looking to show off her new coupe to you. Plus, she had a passenger. Nice lookin' gent, ten or fifteen years your senior. I took him for a scholar or professor right away, and sure enough he had been one. A professor, I mean. He's a geologist and naturalist working for a government agency. Said he had a rock sample you'd collected and he was anxious to see where it came from."

"But they left?"

McIntyre took a bite of his sandwich. Delicious as usual, but despite being sliced paper-thin, tenderized with a mallet, and camouflaged with pickle and horseradish, Tiny's roast beef tasted a whole lot like elk.

"She did. She left alone. Back to Denver. But she dropped the scientist off. He rented one of the little cabins up the hill there."

No sooner had Tiny spoken than the bell over the door jingled to signal the arrival of an individual who could best be described

as "tweedy." Knickerbockers, jacket, hat, all of tweed. Knickerbockers tucked into—what else?—argyle socks.

"Saw your truck from my cabin!" he explained. "Miss Coteau told me to watch for a pickup with 'Small Delights' let-
tered on the door. I thought it odd, but there it is. Name's
Wellington Lane and I'm glad to meet you, Ranger McIntyre.
Actually it's 'Doctor' Lane but who needs formality up here in
the mountains, eh? Call me Wellington. Or Lane. I answer to
both. Say! I am glad to see you! Or did I already say so? At any
rate, down at Geological Survey headquarters young Johnny
hands me this bit of white rock and says it comes from the
Front Range and up near the Continental Divide! Damn
interesting! I must see where it came from. Now, can we go
there this afternoon? I'm ready when you are, Ranger!"

*Maybe Ken would give me that busboy job at Bear Lake after all.
Busboys are invisible. Nobody knows a busboy's name or asks him
much of anything except maybe where to buy Kodak film or get
bootleg hooch.*

"If you're planning to have enough time for a good look
around," McIntyre said, "you'd need to stay overnight. Speaking personally, when I'm headed for timberline I like to start up
the trail before sunrise. Late afternoon rainstorms up there can
be dangerous. Anyway . . . as I was about to tell Tiny . . . a
hiker reported seeing a male silvertip grizzly near the medicine
wheel location. Probably a roamer passing through the area.
Older males have been known to travel long distances without
marking any territory for themselves. But I'm trying to discour-
age anyone from going up there for a few days."

Wellington Lane looked crestfallen and discouraged.

"What can you tell me about the rock sample?" McIntyre
asked.

"Exotic," the geologist said. "I would use the term 'exotic.'
You say you chipped it off of a larger stone. It broke off easily,

didn't it? I have it here."

He took the specimen from his jacket pocket.

"Observe the fracture. Very clean, very straight. It's because it's crystalline, you see. Now, an amateur rock hound might mistake this for Medicine Bow white quartzite, which occurs roughly fifty or sixty miles north of Rocky Mountain National Park. But if you look at it with a microscope, or drop a bit of dilute acid on it, you'll see it is actually a very pure, rather rare species of limestone. In short, Ranger, your sample is alabaster."

"Alabaster?"

"Not only is it alabaster," Wellington Lane said, "while doing my chemical analysis I found traces of diatom and sulfur residue. In short, blasting powder. Your sample came from a quarry. Or other excavation."

"I'll be darned," said McIntyre.

"Have another sandwich?" Tiny asked.

"Where could it have come from?" McIntyre asked.

"I told you. Beef. Comes from steers. Cattle."

"Not the sandwich, Tiny. The stone. Or stones. There's at least a dozen new white stones up there."

"I couldn't guess," Wellington Lane said. "I can only tell you they are not indigenous to this particular geological area. As I said, I first thought they originated in the Wyoming mountains, probably the Medicine Bow quartzite formations. There are, of course, limestone deposits to be found in the foothills east of here—north and east, to be exact—and veined alabaster has been quarried near the Cache la Poudre River. However, I suspect—deeply suspect—your medicine wheel stones did not come from those alabaster quarries. Difficult to tell from a small sample, you see. This piece has no veins nor streaks of any kind, no intrusive coloration such as is found in the Poudre alabaster. I need to go up there and see for myself. How high a place is it?"

"It sits above timberline," Tiny volunteered. "I haven't been there since the days when I was a slim, strapping youth of two hundred pounds and could hike all day, but as I recall it is probably at more than ten thousand feet elevation."

"Oh, my!" Wellington Lane exclaimed. "Even the elevation at Denver can leave me breathless. Oh, my. And you say, Ranger, there are bears?"

"One, maybe. I'm not exaggerating, Mr. Lane. It's a dangerous place to be alone."

"Oh, my."

For a minute or two the only sounds to be heard in Tiny's store were the ticking of the clock and McIntyre drinking root beer before the geologist startled them by striking the counter with his fist.

"Done, by damn!" he said. "I have a plan! Gentlemen, I have spent my time in the field, you may believe me. Haven't I camped at Niagara and among the Flint Hills, not to mention roughing it in the Arkansas forests and at the Precambrian site? I shall linger here a day or two longer in order to acclimate my lungs to the thin air. Meanwhile I'll forage among the village shops for my camping necessities. I might even purchase a firearm to take with me to this medicine wheel."

"If you get a gun," McIntyre said, "be sure you stop at a ranger station or at the S.O. in the village and ask them to put a seal on it. No unsealed weapons allowed in the park."

"Present company excepted, I presume?"

McIntyre patted the flap of his holster.

"Excess baggage, most of the time. But it's part of the uniform. If ever I was to run into a full-grown male silvertip, I sure as hell wouldn't shoot him with a pistol. You need a heavy rifle to bring down a grizzly."

"The ranger's right," Tiny said. "You shoot a grizzly with a sidearm and it's almost guaranteed to make him very annoyed with you. And you don't want to be on the mountain alone with an annoyed grizzly."

"I see you're trying to frighten me. My mind, however, is made up. I shall go."

"I can't stop you," McIntyre replied, setting his empty root beer bottle and a five-dollar bill on the counter. "But I'll ask you not to take any risks. I've already had to evacuate two people from up there. Try not to be number three, okay?"

Tiny pushed the ranger's change across the counter.

"What's on your agenda for the rest of the day, Tim?" he asked.

McIntyre consulted his watch.

"Too late in the day to start doing anything," he said. "Maybe I'll drive a long patrol loop back to Fall River Station. Might make a short detour up toward the beaver ponds in case the trout population is getting out of control. Besides, I've got two puzzle pieces to think about. A little voice inside my head keeps telling me they go together but I can't see how. Fly fishing will help me think."

"What puzzle pieces?" Tiny asked.

"Alabaster," McIntyre said. "Alabaster and three grains of rice."

CHAPTER SIX
DELAYS AND DEVELOPMENTS

McIntyre knew every pebble and twig of a certain spot on the mountain stream. He thought of it as his "meat locker," a willow-tangled pool a mile upstream of Fall River Lodge. There he could always count on catching a couple of fat German Brown trout for supper. Even as he was creeping quietly through the willows, carefully pushing the tip of his fly rod ahead of him, he was imagining a plate of trout and fried potatoes and his new jigsaw puzzle laid out on the table near the stove. If the atmospheric conditions were on his side he'd be able to tune into the Denver radio station. Maybe the Happiness Boys would be on the air. Trout, puzzle, music, in short, a relaxing evening.

The hole was ahead. Through the willows he could glimpse the reflection of late afternoon sun on the water. However . . . something about the place didn't seem right. He got down on his knees and crawled through the brush the last few yards to the stream. He saw a fishing line lying on the water and the tip of a fly rod sticking out across the pool. Putting his head out a little farther he saw the boots: someone was sitting on the bank. A whiff of tobacco told McIntyre the man was sitting there smoking a pipe. And the aroma was familiar: a half-and-half mixture of Prince Albert and Velvet tobaccos.

McIntyre rose to his feet, stepped out of the willow thicket, and stood over Nick Nicholson, RMNP supervisor and his boss.

"Kind of early to be knocking off work, isn't it, Ranger?" Nicholson asked.

74

"Research," McIntyre managed to say. "I'm, uh . . . keeping tabs on the health of the trout population."

"Better cut me off another slice of that baloney," Nicholson said. "That one's so thin I can see through it."

"Okay, you got me. I'm trying to figure out all this medicine wheel stuff. Fly fishing helps me think better."

"And a trout supper might help even more?"

"Yes."

"McIntyre, I'm glad you're predictable," Nicholson said. "I knew I'd find you here or else at your cabin with your feet up. Trouble is, there's a newspaper reporter watching your cabin. There's one haunting my office in town, too. They're after a story about the 'Eve' woman having a run-in with a gigantic silvertip grizzly bear. Which is news because grizzlies are practically extinct. According to 'Eve' she was saved by a brave ranger who carried her in his strong arms all the way to Bear Lake Lodge where the proprietor gave her a free room and meals out of the Christian kindness of his heart. Oh, and the story in the five-cent weekly says that Flattop Mountain with its strange magic circle is guarded by a gang of grizzlies. Now, who do you suppose told them that?"

"Talk about baloney," McIntyre said. "I left her at the lodge. Fannie Painter must have grabbed for the telephone before I had time to leave the parking lot."

"Why don't you go ahead and unlimber that sneaky fly rod of yours? The suspense of waiting for you to start fishing is killing me. While you're catching your supper, tell me what happened. And give me the straight dope."

The ranger dutifully flexed his fly rod, stripped off twenty feet of line, and flicked a Royal Coachman into the shady far side of the pool. In the time it took to relate the actual story of what had happened on Flattop Mountain, McIntyre had two fat trout.

"Now you know everything I know," he finished. "The longer I think about it the more I'm convinced our 'Eve' lady knows more about those white rocks than she's telling us. I'm also thinking she made up the bear story in order to keep people off of the mountain. Me, in particular. Dunno why. There's also the funny stuff with the rice, and the rocks being alabaster. The alabaster is really nagging at me. Like I think I read about it somewhere. But can't remember where."

"*National Geographic,*" Nicholson said.

A brook trout grabbed the supervisor's Black Gnat and he set the hook.

"What?" McIntyre said.

"The pile of old *National Geographic* magazines in the S.O. You know, the ones you browse through while you're waiting for me to chew you out? There was a photo article, maybe two years ago, about a place in Asia—might have been China or Japan, maybe India—where they carve bowls and urns out of alabaster. They treat it like sacred mineral. Plus they eat rice over there. So there you go."

"You might be right," McIntyre said.

"I'm park supervisor."

"In that case you are definitely right. Sir."

"I've got to start for home. The wife will be wanting to fry these fish."

"One more thing?" McIntyre said.

"What?" Nicholson asked.

"Can I come into the S.O. tomorrow and use the phone? I want to call Denver. I've got a hunch I'd like to follow up on."

"And sweet-talk the pretty woman at the FBI office," Nicholson said with a knowing grin. "Like I said, Tim, you're predictable. But go ahead and run up the long-distance charges. Do it from your cabin if you like. Whatever you do, don't give the damn press anything to write about. We need to persuade people to visit the park, not avoid it on account of bears. Once you've satisfied this hunch of yours I want you to go up Flattop again and somehow squash the story of a marauding grizzly. I don't believe it any more than you do, but we need to make certain. Go see if there's any sign of a grizzly up there. I want to tell the press we made a full investigation."

The next morning McIntyre waited impatiently for nine o'clock before he picked up the phone and asked Jane, the village operator, to put through a call to the FBI office. He was surprised to feel his pulse jump a beat when he heard the phone ringing on the other end. As he heard the receiver being lifted his throat went dry.

"FBI Denver, Vi Coteau speaking."

"I'd like you to send an agent to fingerprint a silvertip grizzly."

"Well, well! If it isn't our silly park ranger person. Haven't heard from you in a while."

"I've been busy."

"According to the newspapers you've been playing Adam and Eve with a beauty in a deerskin dress."

"Hardly a beauty. The reporter might have called it a dress, but it's more like a leather mailing envelope. When it's damp she smells like a week-old roadkill."

"Lovely," Vi said. "In other words you remained faithful to me all week."

"I stayed faithful to every living woman all week," McIntyre said. "What are you up to this morning?"

"Oh, nothing much. You know how boring my job is. Right now I'm doing my nails and drinking coffee. Later on I'll probably clean my Thompson submachine gun. We're going to raid a speakeasy tonight. I can't decide what to wear."

"Choosing wardrobe is the plus side of my job," McIntyre

said. "Because I don't have to. The park service tells me what to wear. But my supervisor also told me not to run up the long-distance charges. So I'd love to help you choose your shoot-out ensemble, but I phoned because I need a little information."

"So . . . besides silly you're going to be boring?" she said. "Okay, fire away. What's the problem?"

McIntyre reviewed the pieces of the puzzle as she listened.

"Now," he said when he had finished, "here are the bits I'm trying to put together. A climber mumbles about two small men in brown. I find a fish trap woven out of willows, and grains of rice. Yesterday I was thinking about you . . ."

"In third place? Thank you."

". . . one night in particular when you and I sat up late, swapping stories about our respective jobs . . ."

"Among other things," she said. Her voice had the hint of a purr once more.

". . . and you said part of the FBI's function is to investigate a federal crime you called 'peonage' and the Bureau tries to keep track of interstate transport of explosives. Right?"

"Right. Why?"

"I know I'm really reaching for this one, but last winter I heard guys in the coffee shop talking about the irrigation company that's digging a ditch north of the park, a ditch at timberline to bring water down from the mountains to sell to the farmers. They'd use explosives, see? There were traces of explosive on that rock sample. Maybe the Bureau has a record of the irrigation company's shipments. They'd be interstate, considering they'd need a lot of dynamite and nobody in Colorado makes the stuff. The same rumors say the men doing the work of moving rock at high altitude are Chinese. Gangs of Chinese. One of these coffee shop guys, he said that he thinks they're prisoners, or else they're slaves being forced to work off their boat passage from China. Like I said, it's a long shot."

"Why don't you simply take a stroll over to wherever this irrigation project is and ask somebody?"

"Because I'd rather talk to you," McIntyre said. "And it's a long drive. I'd need to drive down to Loveland, over to Fort Collins, then forty miles or so up the Poudre River to get to the ditch project. And some reporter would probably follow me and ask a lot of questions. Besides which, I prefer to gather my information without showing my hand. It's like fly fishing. When you want to learn if there are any catchable trout in a pool you study all the details without alerting the fish."

"All right," she said. "I'll look into it. When are you coming back to Denver?"

"Wish I knew. All this business about Eve and the grizzly bear, and the newspaper reporters, it has Supervisor Nicholson on edge. He's going to put a couple of men—Jamie Ogg and a summer temp—on my station. He wants me to go back up to Flattop and make certain there's no sign of this bear. And maybe I'll find out who's lugging white rocks to the medicine wheel. I might be camped up there quite a while."

"You know I've never done that, don't you?"

"Done what? Carried white rocks at eleven thousand feet? Neither have I."

"Silly ranger. I've never been backpack camping. When I was a teen our dad took us car camping in a tent, twice. In a campground you could drive to. Maybe you could show me how it's done in the backcountry."

After he hung up the receiver, McIntyre wandered here and there in his cabin putting dishes in the sink, stirring the embers in the stove, laying out his tunic and hat and pistol belt. His hands, however, were operating automatically without signals from the brain. His brain was showing him a moving picture film of his tent with a little campfire in front and a crystalline alpine lake in the background and he and Vi Coteau sitting shoulder to shoulder watching the sun go down over the peaks. When he came back to reality he discovered that he had washed his plate, cup, utensils, and frying pan, had dried them with a dish towel, and had then put them back into the cold and soapy dishwater.

McIntyre went on to waste most of the rest of the day. Checking his saddle, he found a torn spot in the girth strap and took time to stitch it up. He wanted his camping stove to work properly, so he spent an hour cleaning the jet and gas tube and scraping carbon off the burner. The real time-waster came, however, when he decided that he should carry his .30 caliber Winchester carbine on his trip to Flattop in case he needed it for the imaginary grizzly bear. In McIntyre's opinion carrying a carbine or a rifle was even more trouble than lugging a pistol around—and less likely to be useful—but he'd better take it anyway.

Problem: he was out of carbine ammunition. McIntyre got into the Small Delights pickup and drove over the mountain to Tiny's store at Beaver Point. Tiny had sold the last box of shells the week before and hadn't ordered more, since hunting season was still three months away; however, it was nearly lunchtime and he had tasty ham hock soup on the stove together with freshly baked sourdough bread. It was afternoon, therefore, before McIntyre parked the truck in front of the village outfitter's store and went in to buy his ammunition. Nor would it be a quick purchase: a man much given to idle chatter, the outfitter delighted in buttonholing rangers and quizzing them for information he could pass on to his customers. What was the condition of the trail leading to this lake or that peak? Seen people catching trout in a certain stretch of river? What about the deer, do you think they'll be moving down out of the park for hunting season? When do you think the contractor will finish the primitive road to Bear Lake, anyway?

By the time he had escaped from the outfitters McIntyre realized it was too late to start for Flattop. As long as he was already in town, he might as well stop at Murphy's grocery for a couple of tins of sardines and a couple of cans of tomatoes to take along on the trip. Mabel Murphy, who had seen him coming across the street, accosted the ranger the moment he came through the door.

"There's a coincidence for you!" she said.

Another one? McIntyre thought.

"What is?" McIntyre replied.

"One of Dottie's sons was here and not five minutes ago. She sent him to find you and say you were wanted immediately at your supervisor's office. And Tim?"

"Yes?"

"If this means you're transferred to the park they're planning to build at Death Valley, would you mind settling your bill? It's up to six dollars twenty-seven cents now."

Dottie came out from behind her desk, and a man McIntyre had never met stood up and approached him.

"There you are," Dottie said. "Ranger McIntyre, this is Professor Warren from the agricultural college. I told him you'd be able to help."

"Sure," McIntyre replied. "What's the problem?"

"Howard Warren," the professor said, shaking hands. "Very mundane, really. I believe you met my colleague, Wellington Lane? Very, very keen on studying the source of the mineral sample you sent. Very keen. The thing is, Lane telephoned to ask if I would care to accompany him up this mountain of yours. I caught a ride with a graduate student who was coming to the village, but by the time I got here I had forgotten where Lane said he was staying."

"Bear Lake Lodge?" McIntyre suggested. "I'm meeting him there tomorrow morning."

"Oh, dear! Bears? I'm very nervous about bears. A pair of bears accosted me, you know. It was while I was collecting *Zizania* specimens at Yosemite."

"It's just the name of the lake. Somebody back in the 1800s probably named it, so you can relax. The lodge has never reported a bear problem."

"Very good. Yes, very good. And Professor Lane will be there, you say? Now, I'm afraid this leaves me with a couple of problems."

"Such as?" McIntyre asked.

"How to find transportation to this Bear Lake place. And secondly where to purchase hiking boots. I seem to have forgotten to bring mine along."

Dottie was listening to the conversation, smiling in amusement. McIntyre glared at her. Thus far he had rescued a crazy lady covered in deer hide and he had promised to take an engrossed geologist to look at some white rocks; now he was expected to act as a shopping companion and taxi driver. Dottie simply smiled and returned to her desk.

"Unfortunately," she said, "the lodge station wagon is out of order this week. But the ranger will be happy to drive you."

For the next hour at the outfitters the ranger grumbled and frowned and browsed through the guns and fishing gear while Professor Warren tried on one pair of boots after the other. Then he spent an hour in Murphy's grocery watching the professor examine each can, tin, and package for suitability. It was nearly suppertime when the ranger finally led the professor to his pickup truck for the drive to Bear Lake. McIntyre had already decided one thing: he was going to eat his supper at the lodge and he was going to bill it to the park service. He was also going to stop at the ranger barracks and fill his pickup with government gasoline.

"Small Delights?" Professor Warren said when he saw the truck. "It is a species of advertisement, I presume?"

"Got the truck from a lodge when they went out of business," McIntyre said curtly. "Haven't found time to repaint the doors."

Once they were on the road, Ranger McIntyre's attitude improved. Professor Warren seemed to take a real interest in McIntyre's various jobs and duties, even to the extent of expressing sympathy when the ranger recounted stories of minor frustrations.

"You mean there are tourists who actually steal old driftwood? And will walk right up to a grazing elk? Hard to believe."

"Happens all the time. They see a nice rock or a weathered tree stump for their garden and dig it up and take it. Last summer a kid was gored because his father wanted to set him on a bull elk for a photo."

"And now you have a person leaving rocks rather than stealing them."

"Seems to be the case. Are you a professor of geology?"

"Gracious no! Although I do have an interest in mineralogy as it affects plant growth. I teach horticulture at the college. Let me amend my language. Horticulture sounds rather grand. What I mostly do is teach introductory botany to students, mostly students who are required to take the course but have no interest in it. As a reward, I'm allowed to teach a horticulture seminar every other semester."

"I see," McIntyre replied. "Sounds like my job. I have to do daily patrols, inspect campgrounds, hand out brochures and parking tickets, sometimes pick up trash and extinguish campfires. Once in a while, as a reward, they let me visit the wilderness I'm supposed to protect and preserve."

When they reached Bear Lake Lodge the professor and the

ranger agreed to have supper together.

"And we are arriving early enough," Professor Warren said, "so Professor Lane won't have eaten. We'll persuade him to join us. Tomorrow the three of us shall set forth on our expedition, eh? It should be a 'bully' time, as Theodore Roosevelt would say. Nothing to compare with Roosevelt's explorations, of course, but far more interesting than watching the grass grow."

"I guess you don't have much to do in the summer," McIntyre suggested.

"No!" the professor said with a laugh. "I mean it literally. One of my research projects is seeing how various grasses thrive on various soil types. I wouldn't call it engrossing."

Ken was at his usual post behind the reception desk. He readily agreed to send McIntyre's meal tabs to national park headquarters; however, his good news ended there. The rest of his information for the ranger was not reassuring.

"First off," Ken said, "Professor Lane couldn't wait any longer. He hired a horse and took off for Flattop before midmorning. Then your female friend, the nature girl, she hired a horse. I didn't see her, but the wrangler said she rode off in the other direction. Up toward Bancroft Lake. But the Bancroft Lake trail joins the Flattop trail up there on top of the ridge. So I don't know where the hell she was heading for."

"Camp gear?"

"The wrangler says she had coat, hat, and gloves. A slicker rolled up behind the saddle. We always make sure there's a slicker on every horse. She had an oversized shoulder bag. And a couple of flour sacks tied together to sling over the saddle horn. Cook gave her bread and apples but he didn't know what was in the bags. And that's not the end of my news report."

"What else?" McIntyre asked.

"Weather. In case you didn't notice when you drove in, there's a helluva storm boiling over the Divide. I'll tell the waitress to bring me your bill. You guys find a table and she'll be with you in a minute."

The ranger and the professor watched him walk away. They went to the dining room to choose a table.

"Your friend seems rather curt," the professor said. "For a gentleman in the hospitality business, I mean."

"He's got a lot on his mind these days," McIntyre replied. "The National Park Service keeps hinting about removing places like this from the parks, to begin with. He's worried about bad publicity, too. A dead climber. A nature lady with an extra hole in her coconut. Rumors of marauding grizzly bears. Oh, and the road to the place still under construction. News reporters haven't exactly been nice to Ken, either. He's been losing business."

They sat down and placed their orders and tried to talk about more pleasant topics; outside the window, however, they could see the western sky darkening and the first signs of rain approaching.

"Horticulture," Ranger McIntyre said. "What does it involve? Designing gardens, landscaping, planting bushes?"

Professor Warren smiled.

"Those activities do come to mind with most people. Myself, I don't work at anything as interesting as garden design. Mainly I talk to farmers and fruit growers about propagation and cultivation. When I have time for research I have to spend it trying to stay ahead of the clients, mostly."

"Stay ahead?"

"You'd be surprised to learn how many farmers hear about a newly hybridized grain or pasture grass and they go ahead and plant it without first investigating. After it sprouts they call me, or the extension agent, and say 'Hey! This weed's choking my irrigation ditches!' Last year I had a farmer who planted a 'new' kind of corn crop. Turned out to be popcorn. Cows wouldn't eat it, and he had no place to sell all of it. He decided to 'hog it down' by turning pigs into the field to consume the unwanted plants. Much of the popcorn seed, however, passed through the swine and ended up in the manure; this provided ideal nourishment. This season the popcorn came up again."

"People," McIntyre said, picking up his soup spoon.

"As you say," the professor replied. "At least my clients are not likely to require my help by becoming stranded in a snowstorm on the Continental Divide. Do you think we'll be able to make a start tomorrow?"

"I don't know. From here it looks like a two- or maybe three-day storm system. If Professor Lane has a tent or a tarp he should be okay. Cold and miserable, but okay. I'll probably go look for him tomorrow, even if it's raining. You don't have to come along, though. It's my job."

"No, I'll accompany you. I'd have nothing to do if I stayed in the lodge. I did bring a book to read, but accompanying you will be much more interesting than studying the propagation of popcorn."

Ranger McIntyre tasted his soup and helped himself to a dinner roll.

"Tell me," he said, "you mentioned gathering specimens at Yosemite? What took you to Yosemite?"

"A wild goose chase, I'm afraid," Professor Warren replied. "Some person or other, I don't know who, some amateur botanist, reported discovering a new species of wild rice growing in a marsh. A chap I know at the University of California wrote and asked if I would be interested in accompanying him to investigate. Total waste of time. Turned out to be a fairly common sort of wild grass, which the unusually rich soil in the marsh had caused to grow to a large size."

"Too bad," McIntyre said. "And the trip also left you afraid of bears."

"Yes and no. My phobia began much earlier. When I was a very small boy my father took me with him on a hunting trip to Montana. We arrived at a lodge not unlike this one, and while Father took care of checking in and putting the bags in the room I went exploring the place. As boys will do. Little did I know that some hunters had killed a large bear and wanted its hide for a trophy. I came around the corner of an outbuilding and ran smack into the skinned corpse hanging from a beam as if it were standing on its hind legs. Have you ever seen a skinned bear, Ranger McIntyre?"

"Yes, I have."

"You can appreciate how much a skinned bear resembles a human covered in blood. My father found me there where I had fainted. I saw the naked corpse hanging and I passed out cold."

"Awful experience for a kid," the ranger agreed, silently wishing he hadn't ordered the prime rib special.

CHAPTER SEVEN
WAS IT THE ALTITUDE?

McIntyre was awakened the following morning by the sound of rain beating heavily on the roof and slashing at the windows. When he pushed aside the covers the room felt like an icebox. Outside, the tall pines swayed and danced as the wind drove curtains of rain against them. When he went to his front porch for an armload of firewood he saw waterfalls cascading over the edge of the roof; when he went back inside he had to lean his weight on the door in order to latch it against the wind.

There would be no trek to Flattop Mountain this day.

The ranger built up the fire and thought about breakfast. Oatmeal sounded like the right thing on a morning such as this. Oatmeal and maybe some bacon. And coffee. While the water was heating he sat down at his desk to phone Bear Lake with a message for Professor Warren: they weren't going anywhere until the storm let up. But all he heard in the earpiece was a dead silence. The lines must be down.

McIntyre never minded being in his small log cabin alone. In fact, he usually found it very comforting, a nice, quiet, relaxing place to be. Relaxing, that is, unless he was being forced to stay inside. Being shut in by deep snow or a rainstorm made him as nervous as a cat in a dog kennel. After cleaning the breakfast things he swept the floor and made the bed, then hung up a couple of uniform shirts. They had come back from the laundry wrapped in brown paper and had been lying on a chair for over a week. Speaking of postponed tasks . . . he sat down at his desk, picked up a pen, and finished two reports for the S.O. He also read a half-dozen memos and directives he had been ignoring. One of the directives instructed rangers to monitor the fire danger in their district. *Okay,* he thought, *I'll go out there in the rain and see if there's any danger of the forest catching fire.* After finishing the paperwork he filed the memos and straightened the desk. As he carefully placed the inkwell on one corner of the desk pad and the notepad on the other corner, then arranged three pencils and a letter opener, he thought about Vi Coteau and her desk at the FBI office. He had never seen clutter on it, not so much as an empty envelope. The memory of the day he had met her made the confinement of the cabin that much worse.

He got up and began to pace the cabin, then stopped. Starting to pace back and forth meant it was time for him to get outside. He donned his rubber poncho and went out to the stable to check on Brownie.

The creek behind the stable, ordinarily a tiny trickle, had turned into a fast torrent. Fall River was probably out of its banks by now. The trail up Flattop Mountain would no doubt be a river of silt instead of a trail. For what seemed like the hundredth time, McIntyre hoped that the geologist was under shelter and had food. Or that he'd made it back to the lodge.

By noon the storm had subsided. McIntyre had taken a nap—an unusual thing for him to do—and when he awoke and looked out the window he saw that the rain had turned to mist. He tried the telephone and found it still dead. He checked on Brownie again, built up the fire, and laid out a jigsaw puzzle. While snapping a bit of puzzle border into place he thought about the crazy lady, Fannie Painter. She might also be in trouble out there in the wilderness. Now he pushed pieces aimlessly, sorting them according to color or shape, while his brain went over and over the bits of the Flattop thing. He didn't believe the part about a grizzly. He didn't even want to believe the dead guy's mumbling about a small person with a stone spear, except half of the spear point was lying over there on McIntyre's desk. He didn't want to believe the guy had been forced over the edge of the cliff, either, but hadn't he and Jamie found all his equipment strewn in the trees? But even if he did surprise a vandal in the act of placing rocks, why would the person try to kill him and throw his stuff over the side of the mountain? Maybe the same person had put on a grizzly costume to scare Fannie Painter away. Not likely. Highly unlikely. Or . . . McIntyre had once seen a man with a trained grizzly bear in a circus. Maybe the rock hauler had a trained bear. Or maybe Fannie imagined the whole thing.

Or maybe, she made up the bear story to keep me from going and seeing what was really happening up there.

The evening gloom and the first deep shadows of night finally came crawling through the rain-bent meadow grass. The ranger stopped shoving puzzle pieces here and there and lit a second lantern. He took the pot of stew from the icebox and set it on the stove. When he tried the phone he found it working again.

"Ken?" McIntyre said. "Glad to hear your voice. My phone's been dead all day."

"Oh?" Ken said. "Ours has been okay. Weather's rotten, though. What's up with you?"

"Not much. Listen, Ken, no matter what tomorrow's is, I think I'd better go look for the geologist. Could you give a message to Professor Warren for me? Tell him I'll be at the lodge at first light. If he wants to go up Flattop Mountain with me he'll need to be ready."

"Okay," Ken replied. "I need to tell you something. Might be bad news."

"Like what?"

"Professor Lane's horse came back last night. Saddle had

slipped sideways and the reins were broken off. It looks like he'd been tethered and broke loose. We're guessing he was spooked by something, maybe a bear. Or maybe the storm yesterday, maybe thunder made him break his reins and run away."

"Damn," McIntyre said. And immediately remembered you're not supposed to cuss on the telephone or the phone company will cut you off. "I mean, darn it. Any pack or equipment on the saddle?"

"Nope. Nothing except the saddle."

"Might be a good thing. Might mean Professor Lane had unloaded his tent and food and has them with him. Ken, I guess your wrangler ought to have another horse ready for me when I get there. I'll take it with me and go look for him. And Warren, too, of course, if he wants to go."

McIntyre settled down to his stew and bread. He opened Jack London's *White Fang* and propped it against the oil lamp so he could read while eating.

He now became the enemy of all things, McIntyre read, *and more ferocious than ever.*

Is it really possible, the ranger wondered, to drive any creature, man or wild dog, to the point where he hated everything around him?

Two figures rode away from the lodge. They went in single file with a riderless horse following behind. They wore slickers large enough to cover man, saddle, and much of the horse. With rain dripping from their broad-brimmed hats they looked like a pair of timeless cowboys riding off into the drizzling fog. There was no conversation, only the steady plop-plop-plop of the horses' hooves carefully stepping along the muddy trail.

The higher up the mountain they rode, the thinner the cloud cover seemed to become. By the time they arrived at McIntyre's earlier campsite they were seeing faint blue patches of sky above the Divide. Both men dismounted, stretched gratefully, removed their slickers, and shook the rainwater off before draping them over the scrub brush to dry. The ranger had hoped to find Wellington Lane there, since the little clearing in the krumholtz offered protection from wind and rain. Not enough protection, but the best available. The campsite, however, was empty. And there would be no tracks, not with the deluge they had been through. No man tracks, grizzly tracks, no tracks of dwarf men with spears or women dressed in deerskin.

"We'll let the horses rest here," the ranger said. "In fact, we might camp here. There's only a few hundred more yards of trail before it's too steep and rough for horses. Maybe you can see if you could find dry firewood? I'm going to hike on up the trail a ways."

"I'm coming with you," the professor stated flatly.

McIntyre was glad to have Professor Howard Warren along. He was turning out to be the kind of man McIntyre liked, the sort who didn't ask a lot of questions, who kept to himself and did whatever needed doing. McIntyre had been favorably impressed when he arrived at the lodge early and found the professor packed and ready to go with both horses saddled. It became obvious the man was an experienced trail rider.

"You were right," Professor Warren said as they hiked upward on the narrow trail. "This is no bridle path."

"It's bad," McIntyre agreed. "We've got plans to rebuild it, if the government gives us the funds. Probably make it so it would cut around under the east face cliff, take another route to the summit. We'd like for it to eventually tie into another trail, an old one that leads down the other side of the range. Hey! Look!"

McIntyre pointed. Up ahead was the flat space and rustic hitching rail where horseback riders would leave their mounts while making the final approach on foot to the top of the mountain. Both men saw the tarp hanging from the hitching rail; nearby, a yellow livery slicker was draped over a wind-twisted juniper. And a man wearing only pants and a shirt squatted in the center of a little ring of rocks. He was mumbling to himself.

"Wellington!" Professor Warren shouted. "Hey, Wellington! What are you doing up here?"

As they hurried toward him, they could see Wellington Lane shivering with cold. His eyes had a blank, unfocused look. He spread out his hands like a man warming himself at a campfire, only there was no fire. Nothing but damp rocks.

"Hello," he said. "Come to the fire. Cold here. It was hot earlier. Took off my coat but I can't find it. I've got a good fire. Look. C'mon up."

Wellington started to stand up as if to greet two strangers, but his legs crumpled under him and he fell to the earth. He propped himself up on one elbow and vomited.

"There," he mumbled. "Now I'll feel better. Feel fine now. Funny about these ol' legs. Worked fine a while ago. Got all stiff."

Warren had taken off his coat and put it around Wellington's shoulders. He felt Wellington's legs and tried to bend them.

"Spasticity," he told McIntyre. "Altitude sickness, makes the muscles get as hard as wood. It'll come and go."

"Gettin' hot again," Wellington mumbled. "Gotta get away from this fire, huh? Hey, I know you. You're Wellington, too. Name same, huh? Whatta ya think of my camp here, Wellington? Niffy, huh. Thash not a word. Nifty. Niffy."

He giggled and waved an arm toward the tarp hanging by one corner from the hitching rail.

"Got th' good ol' tent, see? Too warm in there, though. Is it bright out here? Oh, and look! Fireplace! Built it myself. Now listen to me. You take notes, now. Huh? Lookit these rocks I got. Ready? What'd you say your name was?"

He pointed to each rock as if lecturing to students on a field trip.

"There's granite, see. There's your obsidian, and quartz, and that one's brown. Or maybe gray. Too bright out here. Feldspar, chert, basalt . . . one's probably sentimental. Sedentary. Can't think. Head hurts like hell."

All the rocks were granite.

"Mountain sickness," McIntyre said. "Or you can call it altitude sickness. Looks like he has all the symptoms."

"Did this fire go out?" Wellington said, looking around himself at the empty ring of rocks. "I had a horsey but he ran away."

"What happened to the horse, Wellington?" Warren asked.

"Dunno. Oh! I know! He was here. Ran away. Thunder makes him nervous, you know!"

The sick man's voice dropped to a confidential whisper.

"Jus' between us, I think the little brown fellow startled my good ol' horsey, that's what I think," he told them. "Can't we go find my horse? I'd like to be home now. Head hurts! Feels like it'll split. In half!"

Wellington vomited once more before rolling onto his back to lie staring into the sky.

McIntyre stripped off his coat and layered it over Warren's.

"Stay with him," he said to the professor. "I think he'll start to feel better if we can move him to a lower altitude. See if you can persuade him to drink water, as much as possible. And you might try to wrap the tarp around him. I'm going down into the trees and get some poles to make a stretcher. Might be gone a while. Do you want my rifle?"

"No, you go on," Warren said. "I've got this covered."

Back where they had left the horses, McIntyre opened his pack and dug out his old Army sweater and the camp hatchet.

He made sure the other two horses were securely tethered and then stepped up into the saddle.

"Brownie," he said. "Go."

True to her many hours of training, Brownie moved down the stony, muddy trail like a dancer, moving as swiftly as it was safe to do. Within minutes she had carried her ranger out of the alpine zone and krumholtz, past the subalpine zone of stunted trees, and into the tall timber. McIntyre stood in the stirrups and searched the treetops, letting Brownie guide herself down the trail.

"There!" he said, reining her to the left.

The mare picked her way through low bushes and over half-hidden logs to the stand of lodgepole pine. McIntyre dismounted with his hatchet. It didn't take him long to cut down a pair of dead saplings and lop off the limbs. Shouldn't be cutting trees in a national park, even dead ones, but this was an emergency. He left the poles long, longer than necessary, thinking he might rig a travois with them later. Tying the thicker ends to either side of the saddle and leaving the thin ends to drag on the ground like a travois, he got Brownie lined out on the trail again.

Looking at paintings by Charles Russell or Frederic Remington, people might believe an Indian travois is a simple, efficient way to haul things behind a horse, but after making the long trip down the mountain with Wellington Lane, the ranger and the professor were of a far different opinion. For the first mile or more both of them had to walk alongside the poles, one on either side, to lift them over rocks and maneuver between trees; before long their backs were aching from repeatedly lifting the travois with the semiconscious Lane on it, not to mention having to walk sideways, crab-like, while doing it. Brownie behaved well, aware of her ranger's struggle with the load she was pulling, but the two livery horses seemed determined to put themselves at the head of the procession—when they weren't straying off to browse the occasional patch of grass.

Lane's body bounced with each bump in the trail even though McIntyre had lashed him to the poles. They had used the tarp and their slickers to make the carrying platform on the travois; three times it ripped loose and allowed Lane's weight to sag to the ground. No sooner had the trail become wider and smoother, two miles or more from the lodge, than one of the livery horses took it into his pea-size brain to tear his reins out of Professor Warren's weakening grip and make a dash for the stables. The ranger and the professor took turns on the remaining livery mount, one man riding while the other walked beside Brownie and kept an eye on their groggy cargo.

"He should have recovered, once we got down the mountain," McIntyre said. "I've seen altitude sickness before, with the splitting headache and muscle cramp, and it usually passes off when they descend to a lower altitude. I've never seen one with nausea this bad, though."

He and Professor Warren were slouched wearily in a couple of lounge chairs waiting for the waitress, who had volunteered to make hot chocolate for them. Hot chocolate and a piece of pie would go a long way toward making a man feel normal again. There was nothing more they could do for Wellington Lane: he had been wrapped in warm blankets and placed on a mattress in the back of the lodge station wagon and was on his way into the village to the doctor.

"Lucky for him they got the station wagon running again," McIntyre observed.

Ranger McIntyre smoked a pipe now and again, but didn't make a habit of it. Right now, however, he had a real craving for it. He looked over at Professor Warren, who was reading the journal they found in Lane's rucksack.

"Not altitude sickness, I'm afraid."

"What?"

"As I understand it," Professor Warren said, "and you may correct me if I'm wrong, altitude sickness is mostly pulmonary, brought on by a diminishing oxygen supply to the lungs and brain. Hence the headache, discoloration of skin, confusion, and muscular dysfunction. It could cause dizziness leading to nausea, but not so frequent nor so prolonged. Listen to what Lane wrote two days ago in his journal. *Medicine Circle camp, June 2. White rock loose dirt sampled, will dbl chk acidity at lab. Weather turning cold. Overcast. Visitor in camp, small oriental hiker. Odd brn cloak. Shared lean-to and soup. Rain let up. Oriental left awhile then rtrnd w/ wild onions/shallots?/ for soup. Much bowing, little talk. Left mid-aft. Not seen again.*"

"The little brown men again?" McIntyre said. "You're saying Lane was up there and feeling normal, normal enough to put up a lean-to, make a fire, boil soup, and write in a journal. It's darn odd. Altitude sickness usually smacks you as soon as you go too high. If you don't get it right away you usually get acclimated."

"When you went to find the stretcher poles," Warren said, "Wellington threw up again. I could see plant parts in the vomit. I went back to where he had thrown up earlier and found the same. He didn't have wild onions in his soup. He ate *toxicoscordion*. Death camas. It grows wild in these mountains. Looks like green onions but without any odor. Contains zygacine, which is poisonous."

"Kills cattle and sheep, I know."

"Right. They usually avoid it, but it's nasty stuff to have where animals are grazing. In a human it would cause the symptoms we saw—muscle spasticity, headache, lung failure, confusion, eventual paralysis."

"Doesn't look good for him, then?" McIntyre asked.

"No, it doesn't."

"I wish he'd written down more details about this 'oriental' in a 'brown cloak.' "

"Well, like me, Wellington makes quick notes to remind himself of anything he saw on a field trip. Later on, often the same evening, we'll use them to write out longer journal entries. Except by evening he wasn't well enough. Apparently."

"Nuts," McIntyre said with a deep sigh, taking out his own pocket notebook and a pencil, "it looks like I've got plenty to do. First thing to do is haul Brownie home and give her a good rubdown. On my way I'll stop at the S.O. and fill my boss in on what's going on. I could ask the secretary to contact Professor Lane's family."

"I'll do it," Howard Warren said. "Let me take care of contacting them."

"Sure I will. Thanks."

"I'll phone the doctor in the village, too. He'll need to know about the death camas."

"If there's any news, I'll be at Fall River Station tonight," McIntyre said. "I think I'll phone the FBI, too. In the morning I'm heading back up Flattop Mountain. I'll gather up whatever your friend might have left behind. And I'm damn sure going to look for tracks of this 'oriental' guy in the brown cloak."

"I'm betting he'd be long gone," Howard Warren said. "If he even exists in the first place. *Toxicoscordion* causes hallucinations. You saw how Wellington thought his pile of rocks was a campfire? I would find it easy to believe he saw a marmot. One of the animals might have wandered into his camp up there."

"Except he was still rational when he made his notes."

"You're right. Listen, how about if I go with you tomorrow? There's nothing I can do for Wellington here. And he's my friend. I'd like to know what happened to him. If he dug the death camas himself, perhaps I can discover where he found it."

"One request," McIntyre said. "We keep the poison plant theory as quiet as possible. It's bad enough to have newspapers writing about hordes of grizzlies. No reporters or photographers. Agreed?"

Professor Warren nodded and both men stood up to go. They shook hands across the table.

"Glad to have you along," McIntyre said.

CHAPTER EIGHT
A PUZZLE, A DEATH, AND UNEXPECTED VISITORS

By morning everyone at Bear Lake Lodge, not to mention half the people in the village, seemed to know about the unfortunate Professor Wellington Lane and his misadventure with death camas, despite the village doctor having sworn the telephone operator to absolute secrecy. He had left the operator a message to be delivered to Dottie at national park headquarters first thing in the morning. Keeping vigil over Professor Lane all night, the doctor had also ruled out the possibility of simple altitude sickness. Unfortunately, he let it slip that Lane's symptoms resembled those of polio. Alarmed tourists began packing their bags; alarmed villagers began boiling their drinking water.

Fannie Painter had returned to the lodge from her mysterious outing. Ken later told McIntyre that her mood seemed almost jovial, as if she'd received good news. Her happy mood, however, had changed very abruptly upon learning that the geologist was dangerously ill from something he had encountered on the mountain.

"She really took it to heart," Ken said, watching as the ranger unloaded Brownie from the horse trailer. "She was at breakfast. I was helping out, clearing tables and that kind of stuff, and she asked me what the other guests were chattering about. When I told her how the professor was brought down off of Flattop with something seriously wrong with him, she left her breakfast unfinished and hurried to her room. And she was sobbing, too.

One of the maids heard her. Hasn't come out since. I'd sure like to know what's going on with the woman. Her mood flies up and down like a railroad semaphore. Maybe, you know, she was a special friend to Professor Lane or something?"

"You might try and find out while I'm gone," McIntyre suggested. "I don't have time to talk to her. I need to go up to the mountain before the weather sets in again. Or before anybody can mess with whatever Lane might've left up there. Professor Warren's going with me."

Professor Howard Warren was no tenderfoot. Without being asked he checked the hitch on the packsaddle. After knotting the reins over the packhorse's neck he picked up the end of the lead rope, mounted his livery horse, and fell in behind Brownie. *The professor reminds me of Jamie Ogg. Knows what to do and does it. Reminds me of that sign on the wall of Officer Candidate School that said "Initiative is doing the right thing without being told." He's being awful quiet this morning for some reason. But I don't mind people being quiet. Probably he's worried about Professor Lane.*

They would leave the horses at McIntyre's first campsite in the krumholtz and climb up the final pitch on foot. The site had been used since McIntyre was there: a cooking fire had been built on a flat rock. After tying up their horses, McIntyre and Professor Warren separated to make a systematic search around the camp, the professor going in one direction and the ranger moving toward the little stream where he had found the fish trap. A half hour later they met back at the campsite.

"The fish trap I told you about," McIntyre said, "the one I sabotaged. It's still there. Somebody repaired it. Half a dozen little trout in it, which probably means it hasn't been emptied in the last couple of days. I guess nobody's been here for a while. You find anything?"

"I found where somebody threw their campfire ashes to the

wind. Like you said, there were kernels of burnt rice in the ash. And this."

He showed McIntyre a charred piece of wood he had sliced into with his sheath knife.

"Your phantom camper brought his own firewood. This is aspen wood. *Populus tremuloides?* Quaking aspen? Doesn't grow up here in the alpine zone. We didn't come through any aspen on the way up here, either. I'm guessing it comes from the north side of the mountain, down toward the valley over there."

"Makes sense," McIntyre said. "All the wood around here would be wet. Dead aspen branches would be about the driest wood you could find. Aspen burns hot and doesn't give off much smoke. If a guy wanted to keep his camp hidden, he'd want a smokeless fire. Why don't you grab your rucksack and let's hike on up to the medicine wheel."

"Can I make another observation?" Warren asked. "It's about death camas. If I were going to search for *toxicoscordion venenosum,* I wouldn't look here in the krumholtz. No. I'd start by looking for a well-drained open meadow near an aspen grove. Same kind of soil favored by *fragaria vesca,* your wild strawberry."

High mountains and untouched wilderness never failed to arouse in Ranger McIntyre a certain kind of calm marked by a sharpened awareness of his surroundings, a feeling of peaceful mental clarity. The level alpine summit of Flattop was no exception. He and Professor Warren had no sooner scrambled up the final incline and out onto the tundra than things seemed to begin to fall into place. In a strange way, McIntyre found it reminiscent of something that happened to him while playing a role in an amateur theatrical: one morning, after weeks of rehearsal, he had gone to the theatre for a book he had forgotten. The auditorium was empty and dark. A small window high in the back wall gave him enough light to make his way to the stage where he had left the book. And something very odd happened. In his mind he seemed to hear the play going on in the emptiness, seemed to see the actors moving here and there and all around him like phantoms of memory.

Now in the empty quiet of Flattop's summit, he was visualizing phantoms once again, only this time they were young Arapaho or Cheyenne vision-seekers sitting within the medicine wheel. Then things began to move as transparent actor images materialized in his mind: a rock climber poking around the rocks was being forced over the cliff edge by small figures in brown; Fannie Painter in her deer hide was being chased by a monstrous grizzly that left no track nor trace of itself; in his imagining he saw Wellington Lane's lean-to tent and small cooking fire with a soup pot simmering on it, saw Professor Lane lurching and stumbling, sick and disoriented, coming down off the summit dragging a torn tarp and rucksack.

"What are you thinking about?" Howard Warren asked.

"Hmmm?" McIntyre replied. "Oh, the whole thing. Mostly thinking about pieces I can't make fit."

"What pieces?"

"Well, the fact that two different men, both of them in shock and probably delirious, said there were smallish humans dressed in brown cloaks, humans who forced one man off the cliff and poisoned the other. There's a little bit of physical evidence—a broken spear point, the poison plants—but no sign of any little men, unless they were the ones who camped down there where we left the horses. Neither victim said anything about seeing a bear. Or any other animal. But the 'Eve' woman goes up there, doesn't see any little brown men, comes running down off the mountain with a story about a silvertip grizzly chasing her."

"Maybe one was. A bear, I mean."

"Not impossible," McIntyre admitted. "Unlikely, though. No

one else has reported any bears up here, especially not a rare one like a silvertip. I don't believe her. But I've been thinking about her story. I think she concocted the whole thing to keep me from coming back up here. She knew I couldn't leave her alone, you see, not with a rogue grizzly in the area, and she knew I sure as heck wouldn't try to bring her up here with me. If she had told me how two little brown men startled her and sent her running down the trail, I might have come up to investigate. Like I said, it doesn't fit. It almost seems as if she saw them up here, knew who they were and knew what they were doing, and went rushing down to head me off and keep me from interrupting them."

"Interesting hypothesis," Professor Warren said. "You seem to have a suspicious mind, if you don't mind my mentioning it."

"I blame it on the war," McIntyre explained. "One of my assignments was to fly over German lines and look for camouflaged artillery emplacements. Any neat-looking haystack or a barn with a tight new roof would make me wonder what was under it. Usually I was right, too."

"So now what?"

"I'm going to have a look down in the woods," McIntyre said, "on the other side of the mountain. Maybe find tracks of men or bears. Maybe find the tracks of our nature girl. Want to come along, or stay here?"

"I'll stay here," Warren said. "I'd like to sketch these alpine flowers and gather specimens."

"Okay," the ranger said. He handed Warren the short Winchester and a flat box of ammunition. "Here, you keep the carbine and extra cartridges. I've got my .45 if I need it."

The "other side" of the mountain was the north-facing slope of Flattop and, as anyone familiar with those mountains will tell you, north slopes are generally overgrown with dense forests of spruce and fir. Winter snow lingers there through April and May, creating perpetually damp soil beneath the towering conifers. The moisture and deep mossy ground encourage berry bushes and edible fungi, while the thick brush offers ideal places for newborn fawns to hide while their dams go searching for grass. Berries, mushrooms, and helpless prey. In other words, the north slope is prime habitat for bears.

Yet the ranger found no sign of bear. Not recent sign, nor old sign. No mushrooms had been dug up, no tree trunks had been marked by claws, no tufts of hair hung from wild rose thorns. In the open spaces, what few there are on a north slope, he expected to see paw prints and piles of scat; male bears, in particular, mark their territory, or their passage through another bear's territory, in very obvious ways.

He did find, however, a few very faint signs left by humans who had gone up the mountain from the northerly direction. Half a footprint here, from a shoe with no tread on the sole, part of a heel print there, a crushed spruce cone, bent grass and broken twigs. Looking at all the signs together, they made a clear trail from down in the woods up to timberline. Someone had come along there, several times, and not long ago. Maybe the same someone who made the secret camp down in the krumholtz.

McIntyre was a successful fly fisherman because he learned to think like a trout; now he cleared his mind and became the mystery person. He placed his foot in the quarry's track and visualized where he would step next, what route he'd take around that boulder and this thicket. He found a few more slight footprints—not much more than smudges—and in the damp sand beside a tiny trickle of a forest creek, he found where the hiker had set down what he was carrying. Probably to take a drink. The sand showed the impression of rough cloth, like a gunnysack or sponge bag might leave, and the impression was deep such as a cloth bag might leave if it contained something heavy. Like a large white stone, for instance.

Two indentations next to the mark of the bag could have been made by someone's knees. The man had knelt to drink from the water. McIntyre knelt in the same place, but when he looked back at where the toes of his boots would leave a second set of marks in the sand, he saw the quarry's toe marks were much closer to those made by his knees. Whoever had knelt there was short, possibly less than five feet tall.

McIntyre cupped his hands and drank from the spring. He sat back on his haunches and gazed northward, down into the thick wilderness forest. He felt he was looking at a corner piece of a jigsaw puzzle but couldn't quite figure out which corner it was.

In his imagination he saw one or two small men, Chinese-looking, wearing plain brown ponchos or capes, walking up this long-forested slope carrying a sack with a heavy load in it. Maybe it hung from a pole they carried between them. They were intent upon placing their stone in the medicine circle, but when they got there, the two small men discovered an intruder, someone camped at the circle. The intruder was using the cliff to practice his rock climbing. They chased him away, except he accidentally got tangled in his own ropes and died of exposure. One of them tried to pry the piton loose with a spear-like rock. To help the entangled climber? Or to make him drop to his death?

A week later the mystery pair came back. This time they found the geologist, Professor Lane, camped at the circle studying the rocks and dirt. How to get rid of him without attracting rangers or searchers? Answer is, make him sick. If he got sick or died, other men would come take him and wouldn't do any searching. It was easy enough to do: one of the little men ingratiated himself with Lane and gathered wild "onions" for the scientist to add to the soup. He would start to feel ill and he would leave. Or someone would come for him.

To McIntyre the most interesting figure in his imaginary picture puzzle was Fannie Painter. Where did she fit in? According to her own story, she had entered the park by way of the trail that begins at Longs Peak Inn. She wanted to live "naturally" like an Indian. Get her soul in touch with Mother Nature, be in harmony with the wilderness. And yet she prearranged a comfortable room at Bear Lake Lodge and had at least one large traveling trunk waiting in that room. It was as if she intended to start at Longs Peak and head directly for Bear Lake.

Like Charles Outman and like Wellington Lane, Fannie Painter claimed to have been frightened away from the medicine circle, except in her case she gave a bookish description of a silvertip grizzly. What did she do, rendezvous with the Chinese men there and agree to spread a story to keep people off the mountain? Were they trying to keep people away from the medicine circle? Why?

There was also the mystery of Fannie Painter's solo horseback ride. One of the principal rules of wilderness travel is that you always let people know where you are going. She told no one.

McIntyre couldn't spend any more time looking for tracks in the forest. He was starting to feel nervous about leaving Professor Warren alone up at the medicine circle. In any case, he had learned enough for one day and saw no real purpose in following the trail northward. He hiked back up through the tall trees, through the stunted forest to the Krumholtz, and emerged on the tundra to see Warren lying facedown next to one of the white rocks. He wasn't moving.

"Professor!"

The ranger ran the hundred yards even though the altitude made his chest burn with pain.

"Professor!" he called again.

"Yes?" Professor Warren sat up as McIntyre dropped to his knees beside him.

"You okay?"

"Certainly! This is most, most intriguing, Ranger McIntyre! Most intriguing. I can't thank you enough for bringing me along. I'm examining where the soil has been disturbed around this peculiar white rock."

"Peculiar?"

"Let us say 'out of place.' Scientists are always interested when something seems out of place or irregular. This rock, for instance, was obviously quarried. Look at the way the sides are fractured. Nor have they weathered, therefore we know the quarrying was recent. Granite stones in this circle show varying amounts of moss and lichen, but this one is pristine. It has not been here very long at all."

"We sort of knew that," McIntyre suggested.

"Ah, yes! But here's one thing I'll bet you did not know. Take my magnifying glass. Now kneel down very close to the ground and look at the loose soil next to the white rock."

McIntyre peered through the glass but didn't know what he was looking for.

"Dirt?" he said.

"Seeds, Ranger. Look for seeds."

Seeds they were. To McIntyre they looked like ant eggs, the kind you see when you kick open a hill of tiny black ants.

Warren pointed to a distant white rock.

"Over at that one I observed a green shoot coming up through the freshly turned soil," he explained. "Wondering what it could be, I excavated it and found a seed casing identical to the ones you are looking at. And at that rock, and that one, and that one. If you remove the dirt grain by grain, almost exactly one inch under the surface you'll find four of these seeds. I hypothesize they will be found on the south side of every single white rock in this circle. I found three that have sprouted. That one, that one over there, and the one where your carbine is. Sorry. I left your gun leaning on a rock. Rather awkward thing to lug around, you know. I prefer my pistol."

"It doesn't matter about the gun. Your theory is . . . ?"

"Only a hypothesis. There's a difference between theory and hypothesis. Or you could call it a suspicion. I suspect—no, I am reasonably sure—that some human has planted these seeds. Seeds don't plant themselves this way. Birds, animals, and wind can scatter seeds, but they do not plant them in tiny patches of tilled soil. Actually you would know that, since animal behavior is rather within your bailiwick. I presume the rocks are meant to offer protection and warmth for the seeds, since the south side of the rock would face the sun and be sheltered from prevailing wind."

"Why white rocks? Why haul them all the way up here?"

"I don't know. Possibly to reflect sunlight. But I suspect it has more to do with the mineral composition. We can ask Professor Lane when we get back, provided he has recovered. His notes and the specimens in his pack indicate he had an interest in learning the characteristics of the stones as well as the soil. I know your next question, but I cannot say for certain what these seeds are, what kind of plants they produce. I want to search for a larger specimen, a sprouted plant with *cotyledon*. New leaves, in other words."

McIntyre cast an eye at the clouds beginning to form in the valley west of the peak.

"Why don't you have a quick look," he said. "I'll hike down and collect Professor Lane's tent and stuff. Let's meet back at the horses in a half hour or so, okay? A storm's coming and I've got a feeling it's going to be a real doozy. We don't want to make camp here tonight. Not even down in the krumholtz."

"Dandy!" Professor Warren said. "I'll be as quick as I can. I'll take a bed at the lodge any day in preference to sleeping on cold rocks. Besides, I see no benefit in lingering through the night. If I find actual plants, analyzing them is going to take a week. Or more, if I have to force seeds into germination. And let me tell you, I'm awful excited to get back to the lab with them! Can hardly wait!"

McIntyre had seen men pepped up and bubbling over in nervous excitement before. It could happen after a narrow escape in aerial combat. Or after shooting a trophy-size elk, even after winning a Fourth of July foot race or a high stakes game of poker. But he had never seen a man as excited as Professor Warren. Not only had he found sprouted plants, oh, no! He rushed back to McIntyre cradling his hat in both hands. In the hat were two plants and a couple of quarts of dirt.

"Amazing!" he panted, breathless with excitement and altitude. "These have flowered and produced seeds! This bit of alpine meadow must be remarkably conducive to quick germination! I've never seen anything like it! Look at the maturity!"

McIntyre looked closely.

"Absolutely amazing!" Warren repeated. "I have a colleague who has done extensive research on germination and flowering of alpine flora following winter snow recession! Did you know that certain plants can actually bloom within two days after the winter snow melts to leave them exposed to sunlight? Wait until he sees these!"

"Where are the seeds?" McIntyre asked, looking closely.

"Aha!" the professor exclaimed. "Exactly! Either they have been eaten by some animal, or . . ."

"Or what?"

"Or they've been harvested. By a human. See how the tiny

pods have been snapped off? All except for several that have not matured. Are the horses ready? Can we be on our way back down to the lodge?"

"Take it easy, Professor," McIntyre said. "Heavy breathing this high up isn't a good idea."

Ranger McIntyre stood with Ken in the lodge parking area, thinking about the long drive back to Fall River Station, the rough road under construction, and the dark, chilly cabin waiting for him at the other end.

"You say there's more bad news?" McIntyre asked. "I don't need any more bad news."

"I wish there weren't," Ken said. "It's pretty indefinite. Might be nothing. Doc decided to take Mr. Outman's body down to the hospital in Longmont for autopsy. He phoned to ask if you were still here. Longmont's hospital doesn't have all the modern equipment, but the doctors who examined him think he had lots of adrenalin in him when you found him. They think he had possibly been in adrenalin shock. Something must have terrified him. And I've got more news, about the Painter woman. She's gone again and I haven't got a clue where she rode off to. Like she did before. Took food with her. And she was carrying a flour sack. Got a horse, rode north."

"So maybe Outman was in shock, is that what the medics are saying? I was afraid the poor guy might've been hallucinating," McIntyre said. "Saw a couple of cases of it in the war. Damn shame, the whole affair. Heck, all he wanted was to practice his climbing, spend a few days in the mountains. I wonder what he did for a living? Anyway, makes a man feel awful sad. I guess it's up to the doctor, maybe the sheriff to find out who to notify. Nothing more we can do about it right now. Suppose there's any chance of a bite to eat? Maybe a bed for the night? Suddenly I don't feel like driving back to my cabin tonight."

"Sure," Ken said. "We'll fix you up. There's a couple of empty beds in the employee barracks. You go ahead and take Brownie to the stables. I'll tell the cook to warm something up for you and Professor Warren. Then while you're eating I want to hear more about what's going on up there at Flattop. My guests are going to be asking if it's safe to hike again."

The following day dawned on what McIntyre would usually call a "delicious" morning, a sunny day off with no duties to do. On such mornings he would go outside in trousers and undershirt to feed Brownie. He would shiver slightly from the cold air and would stretch himself elaborately as the mare watched, and he would say to her, "Isn't this a delicious morning, Brownie? Makes you glad to be alive, doesn't it?"

But this morning he woke up feeling tired and without much enthusiasm for the day. He had dreamed about a man hanging from a cliff, swinging to and fro in the wind, and about a demon-like figure in a monk's brown robe grinning and waving a stone knife covered in blood. He awoke thinking about it, but the more he tried to remember the dream the more it subsided, faded, and left him. The cot in the employee barracks was narrow and the room was chilly; nevertheless, it was his day off and he had nothing to do, not even a horse to take care of since Brownie was at the lodge stable. He could curl up in his warm sleeping bag and keep dozing long after the morning light had come flooding through the windows.

It was probably the aroma of percolating coffee and sizzling bacon drifting up from the lodge that dragged him awake again. In the barracks a late-rising lodge employee dropped a boot. McIntyre continued to lie there absolutely motionless with only his nose and forehead out of the sleeping bag as he listened to his surroundings. He heard his stomach rumbling, warning his brain that enervation and fatal debilitation were imminent unless nourishment could be found. Preferably bacon and pancakes, although in this emergency biscuits and gravy might suffice. He heard the shower running in the anteroom and caught the scent of a hot woodstove, which meant the water heater had been fired up. To McIntyre, who had no hot shower in his cabin, the idea of a morning drench followed by a hot water shave went a long way toward making the day delicious again.

He was walking down the long, wide covered porch toward the dining hall, looking very official in flat hat, tunic, riding pants, and polished boots, when he saw the car in the parking lot.

"Can't be," he said to himself. He checked his wristwatch. "Not even ten a.m. yet."

The coupe was a spanking new two-door Marmon, yellow with wire spoke wheels and shiny radiator. Simply sitting in the parking lot it looked like it was going thirty miles an hour. Glamourous, sleek, streamlined, ready for speed and adventure.

"Gotta be her. Gotta be!"

As a hunter, fisherman, and warplane pilot in the Great War, McIntyre had learned how to remain calm in the face of excitement. And yet the sight of that fast-looking automobile still made his heart thump harder. He felt dampness on his palms and wiped them on his pants. And it wasn't because of the car.

When he reached the double screen doors he heard the laughter of her voice. He pushed open the doors and stepped into the dining hall and there she was, lovely enough to make a man stop and blink three times. Unfortunately, in McIntyre's point of view, she was sitting at a table with two young men. Two young men who seemed to McIntyre to be unnecessarily good-looking guys. One of them was Professor Howard Warren; the other was a stranger to McIntyre. McIntyre didn't like the way Warren was leaning on his elbows looking at Vi. He didn't like how she was laughing at something he said, either.

Both men politely stood up as the ranger approached. Vi Coteau looked up at him, took her time in giving his uniform an appreciative head-to-toe assessment, then gave him a smile to make his morning perfect.

"Good morning at last," she said. "You've cost me a dime, Mister Ranger."

She put her fingers on three dimes in the middle of the table and pushed them toward Professor Warren.

"A betting pool? What about?" McIntyre asked.

"Did you see my new car?" she said.

"Hard to miss it," McIntyre answered. "Very classy."

"We had a ten-cent pool going. I said you'd be here five minutes after you heard me drive into the parking lot. Howard said he had left you curled up in your sleeping bag like a worm in a cocoon and you probably wouldn't climb out until nature called you. This is Bob Daley, by the way. I've told him about you. He bet his dime you'd go fishing before you came to breakfast. Bob, meet Ranger Tim McIntyre."

McIntyre shook hands, pulled out a chair, sat down, and looked around for a waitress.

"I see you've met Professor Warren," McIntyre said.

"Yes!" Vi Coteau said. "I came into the dining room alone, looking for Mr. Daley, and seeing we were the only two people, Professor Warren introduced himself and offered to share his table."

I'll bet he did.

"I came up with Vi in her new car this morning," Bob Daley said, resuming his seat.

"And you survived," the ranger observed.

"Barely," Daley said. "Only two heart attacks. Thank God this stretch of road to Bear Lake is torn up. She actually drove very cautiously through all the construction."

"Vi Coteau, driving cautiously? I'd like to see that. What brings you all the way up here, other than a death wish?"

"Rice and alabaster. You see, once in a while I act as a Japanese interpreter for the FBI. This time, an FBI agent out in San Francisco had a case involving suspected peonage. At least a Japanese boy disappeared and it might be peonage. Or kidnapping. Evidence pointed toward Colorado so they called the Denver office and Vi called me."

The waitress arrived to take McIntyre's order.

"Interesting," he said. "How did you learn Japanese?"

"Familiar story. My parents were Christian missionaries in Kyoto. I grew up and went through school with kids who spoke nothing else but Japanese. My folks eventually retired to Denver—they inherited my grandmother's house on Logan Street—and here I am. I operate a little food store down in the Japanese district."

"Let's back up to the first question," McIntyre said, digging into his grapefruit. "Why come up here?"

Vi was the one to volunteer an explanation.

"Agent Canilly and I talked about your adventure," she said. "A day or two later we heard from San Francisco about a case of a missing Japanese boy. That's when I remembered your telling me about little men in brown, and how you found rice at a concealed camp, and I remembered the irrigation project north of the park."

"Haven't seen the project, but I know about it," McIntyre said. "They're using Chinese laborers. Blasting and digging a new irrigation ditch across the Divide."

"Japanese," Vi said.

"What?"

"They're not Chinese," she continued. "They're Japanese contracting companies. Usually out of San Francisco. A businessman gathers up a dozen or so men who need work, brings them out here. They sort of compete, one 'company' against another. Contrary to rumor, they are neither slaves nor felons. Except for Kiyoshi, maybe."

"Explain? Who's Kiyoshi?"

"He's the missing person. California state police list him as a juvenile missing person. If he was taken across state lines illegally, it's a matter for the FBI. According to his family, Kiyoshi is addicted to *pachinko*, a form of gambling. He'd been borrowing money from a man who contracts laborers to work on the shipping docks and roadways. We think this same labor contractor told Kiyoshi he could work off his debt in Colorado because he was young enough and strong enough for hard labor at high altitude. For a long time now the FBI has suspected these contractors of engaging in debt slavery—peonage, in other words—so when Kiyoshi's family went to the police and the police notified the feds, the Bureau saw an opportunity. They sent an operative up to the irrigation project. Predictably, nobody spoke English. Equally predictably, nobody had ever heard of Kiyoshi. The operative hauled one of the foremen all the way back to our Bureau office in Denver; we got in touch with Bob to talk to him, which is how we learned that Kiyoshi had left the project and had vanished into the mountains. With a bad guy. A very, very bad guy."

"Who?"

"His name," Bob Daley said, "is Tadashi. And from what the foreman told me, the other Japanese workers were damn glad to see him go."

Before McIntyre could ask any more questions the conversation was interrupted by Ken, who had come from conducting another couple to a corner table.

"Everything fine here?" Ken asked.

"Peachy keen," Vi said, giving Ken a smile to improve his entire morning the same way it had done for McIntyre's. "It's a lovely spot you have here. Too bad they're working on the road during tourist season, though."

"Well," Ken said with a sigh, "what can you do? We need the road. But business is definitely off. Between publicity about the dead hiker, the bear scare, the crazy Eve lady, and a mooching park ranger I'm running in the red. Having the road torn up doesn't help, either."

"Speaking of deranged women," said the aforementioned mooching ranger, "what's up with our Miss Painter? Is she here, or gone, or what?"

"Still gone. And one of our horses with her. Like I said yesterday, she'd been mooning around, getting more and more depressed. Wandering into the dining room, wandering into the lounge. The housekeeping girls said she seemed awful upset."

"Pardon me?" Bob Daley said. "Did you say 'Painter'?"

"That's right. Fannie Painter, believe it or not."

"A mystical sort of female, maybe late twenties, early thirties?" Daley asked. "Talks about Indian stuff a lot? One day she's dressed to the nines and the next day she comes out looking like she stole her wardrobe from a Goodwill trash bin?"

"Sounds like her," Ranger McIntyre said.

"If it's her, she's been in our Asian food store. Several times," Daley said. "I'm sure Painter is her name. I've seen her at local Japanese celebrations, too. Funny thing is, as I recall, she speaks fairly good Japanese."

"Horseradish!" Professor Warren exclaimed.

"No, it's possible," McIntyre said.

"No, no!" Warren exclaimed. "Japan! Asian food market! Japanese horseradish. *Eutrema Japonica!* I absolutely need to return to my lab and my reference books. Those seeds, Ranger. Remember the sheltering rocks? The choice of aspen for a campfire? Where to find the death camas growing? If my hypothesis is correct, the person we're looking for is a horticulturalist. And very possibly Japanese. If so, I think I might know what he's doing up there. I'll know more when I have these specimens back at my lab. Imagine! They might turn out to be a hitherto unknown species of *Eutrema*! Not species, of course, but you know what I mean."

"No idea," McIntyre admitted. "A new kind of horseradish?"

"Before we get too far off the track here?" Bob Daley said, "I'd like to finish answering Ranger McIntyre's first question. When Miss Coteau and I were talking, she said she intended to drive up here both to visit you and to gather whatever information she could about this possible case of wage slavery. We even hoped—both of us—you might have found Kiyoshi. He has family relatives living in Denver. I know them, you see. Not too well, but I know them. The Japanese community in Denver is very small. Anyone interested in things Japanese knows everyone else."

"Do you think he could have been who Charles Outman saw? The dead climber? This Kiyoshi kid gave toxic camas plants to Professor Lane?"

"You said they were two smallish brown figures?" Daley said.

"They were wearing brown capes or ponchos, according to the victims."

"The family said Kiyoshi might be wearing a brown coat, called *sashiko*. It's a kind of weaving they do in Japan. Looks coarse and heavy, but the cloth is woven very tight. Practically waterproof. Fishermen and firemen wear them. A workman's is generally plain brown. The least expensive color to make, you see. It pains me to think the boy might be involved with this *ijime-kko*, this bully named Tadashi. I wish I could stay here at Bear Lake until you find him. Or them. Unfortunately, I don't have the funds. I'm needed at my shop, too, but at least I can let Kiyoshi's family know that he may have been seen here and that a ranger is looking for him."

Might as well, McIntyre thought. *Nicholson's certain to order me to find Fannie Painter. I might as well look for Kiyoshi while I'm at it.*

"Excuse me," McIntyre said to the group. "I need to find a telephone and check in with my S.O."

After being assured that the ranger wasn't going to make any long-distance calls, Ken ushered McIntyre into his private office and let him use the telephone. The operator connected the ranger with the park headquarters, where Dottie instantly launched into a full interrogation demanding to know why he was eating and sleeping at a tourist lodge, whether he had arranged for someone to man the Fall River Station in his absence, and what kind of unexpected expenses were going to show up on his report.

"If you ever get around to filing one," she snapped. "I'll put Nick on the phone. He has a few questions for you, too, Ranger McIntyre."

"Boy, Dottie's in a fine mood today," McIntyre said to Supervisor Nicholson.

"You're telling me? I'm stuck in this office with her. What the hell is going on up there, Ranger? Can we expect to see you back at your duty station any time soon?"

Ranger McIntyre began at the beginning and told his supervisor every detail of the situation, including his suspicions and theories. And theories of Professor Warren. When he had finished there was a long pause in the conversation, but he could hear Supervisor Nicholson taking several deep breaths.

"Tim," he said at last, "I've got seven other rangers, plus four summer hires and six men on maintenance. If I sent any one of them up to Flattop Mountain to find out who the hell is hauling white rocks up there, they would find out who the hell was hauling rocks and put a stop to it and that would be that. But no. I send you instead. And now what is it? A case of murder and labor slavery and international god-knows-what and the FBI is involved and a scientist is poisoned and an egghead botanist believes the park is being overrun by horseradish. I'll say one thing for you, McIntyre. You keep me from becoming an alcoholic."

"How's that?"

"Because if I ever, ever let your shenanigans drive me to the bottle, I probably wouldn't stop. Besides which, I need to stay sober so I can see what you'll do next. Okay, here's your assignment. Kiss the glamorous FBI lady goodbye and send her back to Denver along with the Japanese interpreter. Tell Ken to phone Dottie and arrange for us to pay your lodge tab. And the feed bill for your horse. I've got enough publicity headaches without having the politicians find out my men are accepting room and board from local businesses. As for the crazy lady, tell Ken if she isn't back at the lodge by morning he's to phone the Colorado Mountain Club to send their people to search for her. Meanwhile you drive Professor Warren down here to the S.O. We'll see that he makes it back to the college. As soon as you've done that, Ranger, you haul your horse and your butt back to Fall River Station and wait there until I contact you."

"Yes, sir," McIntyre said. "But I was thinking. I ought to drive up to the irrigation ditch project and talk to the foreman. I think it's where the white rocks come from."

Another long pause ensued.

"Ranger," Nicholson said, with forced calm in his voice, "it's at least a sixty mile drive you're talking about, one way. The road follows a prime fly fishing river. Which means we wouldn't see you again until September. Don't tempt me to tell you what to do with your white rocks. Go home. Good ranger. Go."

McIntyre returned to the group at the table to relay Supervisor Nicholson's instructions, which he couched in more "official" sounding language.

"I know it doesn't seem like we're finished here," McIntyre told them, "but your help was really appreciated. It was really good of you to take the time and trouble. I'll be sure to let you know when there's new developments. And I hope you'll share any ideas or theories you might come up with. Anything at all."

"Glad to help," Bob Daley said. "But I do need to get back to minding my store, even if it means taking another thrill ride in Miss Coteau's coupe."

"I echo Mister Daley," Professor Warren said. "As much as I would love to return to the mountain and search for additional plant specimens, I am fairly champing at the bit to make a laboratory examination of the ones I have already."

"I suppose I should get back to Denver," Vi Coteau said. "If I'm gone too long, the FBI might discover that they can operate without me."

"Looks like I'm on my own," McIntyre said. "But I'm going to catch up with this Tadashi character, you've got my word on it. And let me say again how much I appreciate your help. The supervisor's right, though. There's no need to take up any more of your time. I need to back off, take a breather, let things settle down and sort themselves out."

He started to pick up his coffee mug to swallow the cold dregs but laughed and set it down again.

"Know what this reminds me of?" he said. "Fly fishing."

"Oh, surprise me!" Vi laughed. "I bet you're going to tell a story! And it's not even my birthday!"

"Smart aleck," McIntyre said. "No, I've been fly fishing with two, three other people in a group, see, and we move along the river and come to a fine-looking pool where we know there are going to be sizable trout. But everybody gets in everybody's way and everybody tries a cast and first thing you know, the pool is spooked. Nothing to do but step back, have a seat, and wait for everything to get calm again. Now after the trout have settled back into their natural feeding stations behind the underwater rocks . . ."

"I think I'll go put my things in your pickup," Professor Warren said, leaving the table.

"I need to check the tires on the Marmon," Vi Coteau said, following the professor.

"I wonder if they have any seasickness pills at the reception desk," Bob Daley said.

Vi Coteau took Ranger McIntyre by the hand and led him to the parking lot to see her new car, which gave them an opportunity to talk privately. She showed him the dashboard and steering wheel of polished walnut, the German silver door handles and knobs, and opened the long yellow hood to let him see the monstrous six-cylinder engine.

"You know I was hoping we'd have more time together," she told him. "I know I kid you about your long-winded stories, but you're still my favorite tree cop."

"I was hoping the same," McIntyre replied. "Seems like people keep getting in the way of life, doesn't it?"

She laughed and closed the hood.

"I can finagle a few days' vacation time," she said. "What are your plans?"

"My plans? My plans are whatever my boss says they are. Probably standing at the Fall River entrance station handing out maps and answering dumb questions until I'm an old man with a long white beard."

"I thought there was no such thing as a dumb question."

"Yes, there are."

"I suppose," she said, "there isn't anything urgent. Your friend Ken will probably call for a search party tomorrow to find the missing woman, the odd one who wears a deer hide. Professor Warren will be busy helping Professor Lane's family with travel arrangements, I'd imagine. I doubt if you'll hear from him any time soon. At least you won't be bothered by reporters."

"Probably not. Not unless they decide to maybe do a background story about Professor Lane. They might show up at my station to ask me about it. Again."

"You'd better keep your cabin tidy," Vi said, winking mischievously under the brim of her red leather cloche. "You never know who might show up."

"Oh, thanks!" McIntyre said. "Another little worry for me."

"Say!" Vi exclaimed. "I know one thing I could do to help! I told you how we had the construction foreman from the ditch, at the Denver office. He told Agent Canilly the ditch company had a telephone line. One of those dry cell setups."

"We had those in the war," McIntyre said. "They worked okay until an artillery shell or hand grenade hit the phone line. Hauling those batteries around was a nuisance, though."

"What if I look into it," Vi said, "and talk to the man in charge at the construction site? Save you a long drive up the canyon."

She stepped onto the wide running board and bent over to retrieve a notebook from the door pocket. McIntyre held his breath watching the hem of her pleated skirt rise past the backs of her knees.

"Now," she said, opening the notebook and clicking her automatic pencil. "What do you have in mind?"

McIntyre's response was succinct and immediate.

"Huh?"

"If I can talk to the foreman on the telephone," she said. "What do you want me to ask him?"

"Oh. Right. Well, ask if anyone has seen or heard anything to do with Kiyoshi and this bad guy, Tadashi. Missing food, missing tools, maybe odd sounds in the night, any suspicious stuff. Tell him the white woman from the lodge might be up in that area, too. Have his men keep an eye out for her."

"Shall I ask about the alpine plants? You know, the death camas and the one Professor Warren is fascinated with?"

"No, let's keep that in our pocket for now. But I'm awful curious about those white rocks and where they might have come from. Blasting powder might be a clue. Professor Lane found blasting powder residue on one of the rocks."

"Hey, you might have a good angle there!" Vi said. Her eyes were shining with excitement. "One of the more boring jobs at the Bureau is to file records of large purchases and interstate shipments of dynamite and other explosives. I could maybe hint to the ditch foreman how the irrigation company had failed to report a shipment of explosives and an FBI agent would need to do an audit. That'll make him cooperate!"

"Cute," McIntyre agreed. "Devious, but cute. I can see how a guy might need to keep an eye on you."

"I thought you were already doing that," she said with a wink.

CHAPTER NINE
OUT OF THE AIR AND INTO THE WOODS

The next few days dragged slowly by, like the wounded snake in the old poem by Alexander Pope. McIntyre spent his evenings fishing in Fall River or reading by lamplight or assembling one of his picture puzzles; during the day there seemed to be an endless stream of tourists with unanswerable questions. Will my car make it over Fall River Pass? Where are the bighorn sheep? Have you seen our friends from Iowa? Do you stay here all winter?

The ranger's day off finally came around again and McIntyre was determined not to waste a single moment of it. When Charlene "Charlie" Underhill, owner of the Pioneer Inn, raised the blinds that morning and unlocked the dining room door, she discovered McIntyre already standing on her porch, tall and good-looking in his civilian clothes and with a ravenous look in his eyes. Her chef was less pleased to see a hungry man early in the dawn hours: the chef liked to have his stoves warmed up and his kitchen organized before being handed a huge breakfast order. But he complied.

As for McIntyre, he relaxed into his favorite chair at his favorite table, the one with a window view of the entire village, the Fall River valley and the Front Range beyond. He loved to sip coffee, watch the sunlight slowly wash down the peaks and into the green forests, and smell bacon frying. But what's that? Up on the mountain? He sat upright and leaned toward the windowpane as if being a few inches nearer would help him identify the light-colored streak of gray on the mountain over six miles in the distance. Smoke? Was he looking at the beginnings of a forest fire?

He got up and went to the cashier desk where Charlie kept a pair of binoculars, good ones with more power than McIntyre's government-issue field glasses. Back at his chair he steadied his elbows on the table and scanned the light-colored streak that was showing against the dark forest.

"Whatcha lookin' at?" Mari asked as she set down his order of toast and butter.

"Thought it was a forest fire," McIntyre said with a laugh. "But it's not. It's only the way the sun's hitting a cliff up there. See? Looks like smoke, but it's a gray cliff."

When his sausage 'n' scramble and pancakes arrived, McIntyre dug in with gusto. He was going to enjoy a fine breakfast and not think about rangering. Afterward he was going to drive up the Thompson River to a certain stretch of prime trout water and not think about white rocks. He consulted his watch: perfect. He would be on the river by ten o'clock, in time for the first rise of the day. He soaked a piece of pancake in maple syrup and put it into his mouth as he mentally rehearsed what he was going to do when he got to the river. He would start with a mosquito pattern, maybe a size 14. Around noon, with the high sun making the lunkers stay down in the depths, he'd switch to a new grasshopper pattern he wanted to try.

As things transpired, he turned out to be correct about the Thompson River trout. In the morning light there were any number of ordinary-size fish coming to the surface for bugs, and they weren't terribly particular about whether those bugs looked like mosquitos or mayflies. Around noon he was getting a little tired of catching and releasing them. So he reeled in his line, propped his fly rod against a tree branch, and sat down to relax on the grassy bank. He smoked his pipe and watched the stream. The water was absolutely transparent, like looking through glass.

Which is why he was able to see it. A monarch among German brown trout. A bully lunker lazing insolently on the bottom of the current, keeping in place with slow sweeps of its broad tail. McIntyre wouldn't have spotted it, had the fish not drifted across a patch of light-colored stones. Against mossy pebbles and dark sand it would be nearly invisible. McIntyre lost sight of it again; he kept his eyes focused on the lighter place, however, and in a minute the giant crossed over it again.

He had no desire to kill the fish, nor was it the kind of fish he'd expect to rise to a floating dry fly. It had grown to its great size by staying down deep, by feeding on the tiny worms and insect nymphs the river current brought down. *I could sneak upstream,* McIntyre thought, *maybe twenty yards. Soak a grasshopper pattern to sink instead of float, let it drift down. Might work. Except a fish like that . . . if it did take the hook, I'd need to fight it to exhaustion before I could get the hook out again. Might kill it. And I don't need to.*

In the end he caught three full-bodied, firm trout for supper. As he was driving back toward his cabin, however, McIntyre kept thinking about the lunker and the light-colored rocks, which started him thinking about those white rocks on the mountain, a few of them heavy enough to make him think two men must have carried them slung from a pole between them.

Back at his cabin McIntyre left his creel and rod on the porch. He went inside, selected a topographic map from the basket, unrolled it on the table beneath the window, and picked up his measuring dividers and pencil. It looked feasible. From the approximate location of the irrigation ditch project it was slightly more than ten miles of steep slopes and heavy forest to the medicine wheel on Flattop Mountain. If they had an intermediate camp where they could rest and if they did it in two or three stages, two men could carry the rocks from ditch to mountain.

He cleaned his fish and carried the guts outside to bury them away from the cabin. In his mind he was still seeing the map, and the white rocks. Why did they need the rocks . . . or why would they move them . . . why move white ones and not any other kind?

Okay, McIntyre, forget about "why" they would lug rocks across through heavy forest and up a steep valley. Try a different picture. They found these white rocks, how? Working on the ditch project. Came to a ledge of alabaster, blasted through it with dynamite, white rock scattered everywhere. For some reason, one or possibly two of the ditch workers wanted those rocks.

The idea forming in McIntyre's brain was more like a picture than a carefully considered scenario. Like Hamlet, he was seeing through his mind's eye. In one corner of the picture was Supervisor Nicholson, nodding approval; the other corner of the picture was the airfield, where Polly, hands clasped, watched in thrilled admiration as he took the Douglas M-2 biplane roaring down the airstrip and into the sky. In front of him Vi Coteau gripped her cockpit's padded leather rim and held on for dear life while he gave her a taste of her own speed demon medicine. He carried her soaring above the clouds, made a steep power dive and pulled out of it almost at treetop level, and left her breathless with tight turns, searching the ground until he spotted the objective. He wrote down the position on the notepad strapped to his leg and ruddered the powerful biplane in the direction of its aerodrome . . . but no. Wait!

Since this was a fantasy anyway, why not bring along a picnic and land in some mountain meadow where they could be alone? She would look beautiful, of course, in high boots, riding pants, leather jacket, and flying helmet. He would land the plane and coast to a stop in the meadow. As he cut the engine she would look back at him and her cheeks would show the flush of excitement.

It made a lovely picture. He would borrow an airplane, fly a scouting mission over the mountains between Flattop and the irrigation project, and he would take Vi Coteau along with him. First, however, he would need permission. His telephone call to headquarters hit his flying fantasy with a bit of reality. Supervisor Nicholson was less than enthusiastic.

"Go ahead and try it, but if you crash and burn in those mountains, for God's sake don't let it start a forest fire. If it's burning, extinguish the fire before you die. And don't talk to any newspaper reporters."

"Before I die?"

"Before, after, I don't care. Just don't."

The second phone call was even less encouraging. Polly had left the airfield early, but whoever answered the phone told him to speak with Captain McKay of the Army National Guard, the officer in charge of the airplanes. The captain listened quietly to McIntyre's plan.

"Can you give me any map coordinates for this place?" the captain asked.

"Sure. I'm looking at the Geographic Survey Quadrangle for Medicine Bow. The coordinates are H-11."

"Wait a minute while I find my own map."

There was a delay of several minutes.

"Okay, got it. Now, what's your idea?"

"I need to borrow one of your planes so I can take a, uh, a representative of the Denver FBI office, to search for a possible murderer's camp and a kidnapped kid and a missing woman. Life and death, see."

"Are you a bachelor, Ranger?"

"Yes?"

"This FBI 'representative' wouldn't happen to be Vi Coteau, would it?"

"As a matter of fact, it would. Do you know her? I haven't told her my idea yet, but I know she'll want to go along."

"No can do," Captain McKay said.

"I can handle the plane," McIntyre replied. "I flew in France during the war. Nieuports. And a Curtiss Jenny, here in the States."

"Ever flown in the mountains?"

"No," he confessed.

"Whole new ball of wax. Besides, I can't let you do it anyway."

"Oh?"

"Rules. According to the rules, only an ANG officer can fly the plane. Which means me. It's probably the same where you are. The park service probably won't allow you to loan your government pickup truck to civilians."

"Dang," said McIntyre.

There went his lovely plan to lure Vi Coteau into an airplane and scare the pants off her. And impress her with his flying skills.

"Tell you what I can do," Captain McKay said. "My aeronautical chart is showing an airstrip next to the foothills near a little town called Lyons. Do you know the place?"

McIntyre did. The airstrip was nothing more than a long piece of ground that had been cleared, leveled, and planted with grass. The U.S. Mail Service maintained it for emergency landings.

"Yes."

"Could you meet me there, say at dawn tomorrow?"

"Sure! Thanks!"

"You'd better bring along a couple of rubber airsick bags.

When we hit those bouncy air currents over the mountains I don't want you vomiting all over my aircraft."

Two days later, Ranger McIntyre was picking up his gloves and heading for the cabin door when the telephone on his desk jangled. Brownie, who was hitched to the porch rail, impatiently chopped at the ground with her front hoof. They were supposed to be going on patrol across the Deer Ridge trail, not yakking into the black noise thing.

"Fall River Station," he said. "Ranger McIntyre."

"Good morning, flyboy," Vi said. "Have a nice flight?"

"Excellent flight, thank you," he replied. "And how are you on this lovely morning?"

"I'm 3F: Fit. Fine. Feisty," she said. "Bob Daly and I managed to contact the irrigation foreman yesterday. The connection was very poor, but I'm sure we got the facts. Such as they are. His crew was able to resume digging in late May after the road could be cleared of snow drifts. Within a couple of days, he said they encountered a 'reef' or 'shelf' of extremely unusual limestone but found it easy to blast. They didn't need the rubble to use as 'fill.' Instead, they dumped it in a pile and went on digging."

"He said it was unusual? Odd how?"

"We had a bad connection, but I think he was saying most of the rock in that area is granite. Except for 'way farther north where you find the white quartzite. Only this 'reef' thing looked like limestone, too soft to use as fill material on the ditch. It would wear away too fast. The Japanese laborers seemed excited when they found it. Awestruck, sort of. He didn't know why. Anyway, a few days after they blasted through this ledge of unusual white rock, the worker they call Tadashi started acting strangely."

"Did he say how?"

"I think Tadashi kept going missing. Lots of static in the connection. I gathered Tadashi had been sent out, with one or two other men, to cut trees ahead of the ditch workers and give the surveyors a clear line of sight for their measurements. Tadashi began quarreling with the others, seemed moody and nervous. He became excitable, when he wasn't acting sleepy and distracted. Apparently Tadashi would break for lunch and disappear into the woods and they wouldn't see him again until the next morning. Kind of like a park ranger I know. Except Tadashi didn't have a fishing pole."

"You are a riot, Miss Coteau."

"The foreman wasn't too certain about when, or else I couldn't hear him clearly, but after a week or two Tadashi apparently vanished altogether. At least he didn't show up for work. Soon afterward the boy, Kiyoshi, went missing. This made the Japanese contract foreman very nervous, since he did not know whether Tadashi and Kiyoshi were in the U.S. legally or not. If they weren't, and they went and got themselves arrested, the company could be in hot water with the government. I didn't learn anything else because the telephone line went fuzzy and died. Hope this much helps."

"You bet. I don't know what those darn rocks have to do with anything. But I think they're going to point the way to finding who's responsible for our 'accidents.' "

"Speaking of finding, did the Fannie woman show up?"

"No. The Colorado Mountain Club team searched all the logical places, but no. The horse didn't come back, either. Which is a little suspicious."

"Why? You think the horse maybe murdered her? And ran away? Maybe disguised himself as an elk and hid in the woods so he wouldn't get arrested!"

"I think I'll call the riot squad to arrest you, wiseacre. No, because it's a livery horse, see? Loose livery horses generally return to the livery. If a rider falls off, or doesn't tie the animal properly at night, it's likely to make a beeline for the barn. But it didn't come back and the searchers didn't even find a hoof-print. Between you and me, I think they were searching in the wrong place, but I can't seem to convince anybody of it."

"You didn't see any sign of the woman, or the horse, when you flew over the area, I guess."

"Nope. Didn't really think I would. Speaking of which, by the way, how do you know Captain McKay? In fact, how did you know he flew me up to the ditch site?"

"Bootleggers. Army National Guard is assisting the FBI looking for aircraft being used to run illegal liquor across the state. When you said you were a flier in the war, he phoned me to check and see if you were on the up-and-up. I told him everything about you."

"Everything?"

"Everything legal to say over the telephone. What did you find out yesterday?"

"I discovered that mountain flying is for the birds. Holy cow! When you're fly fishing you learn to be sensitive to air currents. They're always moving up or down or across a stream. But in a light airplane up above the mountains you feel like a cork in the rapids. Updrafts, downdrafts, side winds. That Douglas is a heckuva machine. Twelve cylinders. Solid, streamline body."

"Did you see anything?" Vi asked.

"Saw what I was looking for. We flew right up the river, hit a good updraft almost at timberline. I could feel the plane losing power and lift, but Captain McKay found enough updrafts to keep us in the air. It was like riding a wobbly roller-coaster. We spotted the irrigation ditch project and followed it. Saw the workmen waving to us. I signaled the captain to head toward Flattop Mountain, we dropped back below timberline, and I saw what I thought I would."

"Being what?"

"A pile of white rocks, down in the trees, a mile or more from the irrigation ditch. You see, I came up with a theory while I was fishing. Well, fishing and having breakfast and seeing what I thought was a forest fire."

"Tim?"

"What?"

"If you're not going to make sense, I'm going to hang up."

"Sorry. Here's my idea. One man carrying one of those rocks, or two men carrying one slung on a pole between them, they couldn't carry it more than halfway to Flattop from the ditch. I think they started by using their lunch break to lug rocks back into the trees where nobody would be tempted to try using them as fill material. Flying toward Flattop Mountain we spotted another pile of rocks about halfway between the ditch and the medicine circle. I think those two Japanese guys went AWOL from the excavation crew and transferred rocks to this second location. They probably camped there while they moved rocks on up to the circle."

"Why leave piles of them behind? Why not move all of them?"

"Dunno. Maybe they intend to. Maybe it's a stockpile they're saving for later, for some reason. I'm beginning to think those limestone rocks have a religious significance for the Japanese. Anyway, my next move, as soon as I can get my supervisor to approve of it, is to head up there on horseback and see if I can find it. And maybe their camp. I think they're camped up there waiting for things to calm down. I plan to pretend like I'm on routine patrol. I'll set up my tent, wander around with notebook and field glasses, make it look like a ranger doing a wild game survey or maybe inspecting the watershed. Just between you and me, I think I'll find the Painter woman camping with them. Call it a hunch."

Vi Coteau wished him well, said she would stay in touch, and rang off. And she was true to her word: that same evening McIntyre's telephone jangled and it was her again.

"Have a nice day?" she asked.

"Is this your idea of staying in touch?" he asked, smiling at the telephone mouthpiece. "Calling me every morning and afternoon to find out what I'm doing?"

"Sure. Have a nice day?"

"Grand, simply grand. Had to spend it in full uniform, gun belt and all. Rode the whole Deer Mountain trail, talked to four groups of hikers, got my picture taken twice, ate my bologna sandwich and an apple at the summit, dragged logs to block where hikers have been taking a shortcut down the mountain, and interviewed a family of ground squirrels. The squirrels reported two chipmunks begging treats along the trail. Let's see, what else did I do? The deer population looks healthy, no sign of elk. No sign of mountain lions, either, but the coyotes have been doing their job. Keeping the deer in check, I mean."

"And nowhere to do any fishing up there? But listen, I had an idea."

"No kidding? Let me sit down."

"Such a humorous ranger you are. Why don't I go along with you on your camping trip?"

"Must be a bad connection here. Did you say you were going shopping for dresses and hats while I was out in the woods?"

"I told you I've never done it. I could take a few days off and you could be my teacher. Show me all about backpack camping."

"My feet are under my desk," McIntyre told her, "so I can't see them. But I'd swear I can feel my leg being pulled. Your girly-girl flirty thing is old enough to grow whiskers. 'Oh, teach me to ride the horsey' or 'oh, teach me how to fish' and you can throw in skiing, ice skating, and rifle shooting for good measure."

"I'm not kidding you," Vi said. "I slept in a tent a couple of times when I was a girl, but never learned how to camp."

McIntyre leaned back and considered.

Vi Coteau, offering to spend several days in the mountains with him. A woman whom people might call "pretty" if they didn't know the word "gorgeous." Full of energy, fun, full of life, sharp as a new knife, intelligent. End of consideration.

"Okay," he said.

"Gosh, your enthusiasm overwhelms me. Well, what shall I bring? I've got sturdy boots, twill pants, a heavy coat and poncho. What kind of food? Oh, and shall I bring a nightie?"

"Uh . . ." McIntyre stammered. "A nightie? You mean a nightgown? Golly, that's a new one. I generally sleep in my long johns. Although another school of thought says when you're using a sleeping bag in a tent you should be . . . you know . . . bare. Naked? The body tends to sweat inside a sleeping bag and you end up with damp clothing, which can be colder than no clothes at all."

"See?" she said. "This is already educational! We're going to have fun!"

"Fun's not the idea of the trip," McIntyre said in his best Serious Ranger voice. "We're looking for a woman, possibly dead, and at least one murderer."

"I'll bring my revolver. I'll even sleep with it, if it will make you feel better."

"You'd better pack a little kit of . . . uh . . . personal things. You know, soap, tooth powder, aspirin, stuff like that. I always like to have a couple of extra handkerchiefs along, too, the large red kind. They're good for all kinds of things. I'll scrounge up a couple of packs and canteens, plus an extra mess kit. And a sleeping bag for you. Jamie Ogg won't mind me taking his. I'll contact Ken, too, and have him pick out a good horse for you, plus a packhorse to carry the tent and equipment."

"Make my horse a light tan buckskin, if he has one," Vi said.

"Buckskin?"

"To go with my outfit."

The ranger groaned.

"While you're picking your outfit," he said, "keep the leather down to a minimum. And as little cotton as possible."

"Why?"

"If it rains, and it probably will, cotton stays wet and cold. Wool gets wet, but it's warmer when wet and dries quicker. Wet leather, like a suede jacket, is pure misery. You need wool pants, a linen or flannel shirt. Wool jacket. And a sensible hat, if you own one."

"You'd be surprised how many hats I have."

"No, I wouldn't. Goodbye, Vi," the ranger said.

"Talk to you later!" Vi Coteau said.

When Ranger McIntyre parked his truck and trailer next to the lodge stables he spotted the bright yellow Marmon sitting across the yard. Ken and the wrangler helped the ranger unload Brownie before giving him a hand with the camping gear and the packhorse.

"By the way," Ken said, "would you mind if we unhitched your trailer and put it behind the stables? We might need the room for cars. There's a wedding party coming."

"Sure," McIntyre said. "And I'll leave the key in the ignition, in case you need to move the truck."

"Good," Ken said. "Thanks. Miss Coteau did the same thing."

"Any word of Miss Painter?" the ranger asked.

"Nothing. Two guys from the Mountain Club went out again but didn't find anything."

"You're keeping her room for her?"

"Sure. It's all paid up for the season. The cleaning lady, she found one odd thing. You said to watch for anything out of place, remember?"

"Yes."

"Well, the cleaning lady, Janet, was dusting Miss Painter's room and moved the steamer trunk to dust behind it. Guess what she found."

"Dust? Mice? I don't know."

"Not mice. Rice. Grains of rice had dribbled out of the trunk. She must be carrying her own food in her luggage."

Or supplying it to somebody, McIntyre thought.

"And that's not all. Janet went back into the room two days later. It looked like the trunk had been opened. You know how those things stand upright and swing open like an icebox? The lid scratched a line in the fresh floor wax. I talked with our night man, Pendell. I don't usually see him because he sleeps most of the day. But he walks around the place at night, keeps an eye on the front desk and the lounge. He said he saw a person, thought it was a woman. Saw her ride up to the stable, tie her horse to the rails, go inside the lodge, and come back out. She had a backpack with her and a white sack. He figured she was one of the guests who went out on an overnight trip and had forgotten something. It seemed that way to him, anyway."

"She wasn't sneaking around?"

"Nope. Pendell says he didn't think much about it. She came like she was staying there and knew the place, went upstairs, came back in a little while, left again. Didn't try to hide, didn't act sneaky at all."

"He didn't talk to her?"

"No. According to Pendell, she didn't even see him. Say, speaking of women! Here comes your lady friend."

This time Vi Coteau was wearing a man's hat, a narrow brim Stetson. Her thigh-length wool jacket with wide pockets below the belt was buttoned and belted. Her white shirt was unbuttoned at the throat and she was wearing her necktie loose, sailor-fashion.

"It ain't fair, is it?" the wrangler said.

"What ain't?" McIntyre asked.

"Well, a man puts on his riding boots and his hat and jacket and he looks like a man about to go to work. A woman, she can put on the same darn thing and looks like she's going to a posh place for lunch. Anything they put on, women always look classier than men do. Even if they're wearin' the same thing. Ain't fair."

Vi gifted each man with a separate greeting and smile. As she handed the wrangler her backpack to hang on the packsaddle she looked up at the bright blue morning sky. With her hands on her hips she tilted her head back and filled her lungs with cool mountain air.

"Beautiful!" she said.

Three males agreed. Silently. But sincerely.

Having the packhorse walking along between them as they rode made for difficult conversation. Vi had agreed to let McIntyre take the lead because he knew where they were going. The packhorse was right behind him because he had experience leading a horse. To Vi it seemed her only function was to trail along behind and pick up anything that might fall off the packsaddle. She asked a few questions, but shouting them at the ranger's back was awkward, to say the least.

McIntyre didn't mind not talking. For one thing, he was a little bit miffed—okay, a little bit jealous—because Vi had been paying attention to Howard Warren, the horticulture professor. He was also quiet because he seemed to think better when he was in the saddle. Like standing at a trout stream with a fly rod in his hand. As he had told Supervisor Nicholson, given a little saddle time or a few days with a fly rod and he was sure he could figure out what—or who—had caused the two deaths. In order to do it he needed to solve the riddle of the white rocks. While saddling the horses, Ken had told him about a lodge guest who had gone up Flattop and reported seeing new white rocks added to the circle.

He halted at the trail junction. Vi Coteau rode up beside him.

"The sign says 'Flattop Mountain thataway,' " she said, pointing.

"Park service signs do NOT say 'thataway,' " McIntyre replied. "Besides which, we're going thisaway."

He pointed north, where a rougher and less-used trail led into the dark shadows of the forest.

"Why? Is there a better trout stream thataway?"

"Perish the thought. Like I told you, from the air the other day we spotted what looked like a stockpile of white rocks. It's in a clearing in the trees down there on the north side of the mountain. You and I are going to set up camp nearby and see if we can't map out the route they took from the irrigation project to Flattop. I found part of it already. They couldn't help leaving tracks. Couldn't help it."

"I understand. But I'm not sure I see the point of finding their tracks."

"It's like hunting mountain lion," McIntyre said. "Or bear. Let's say a rogue has been killing livestock and a ranger needs to stop it. There might be several lions in the same area, and you need to be sure which one you're dealing with. You scout around until you find where the rogue left his kill, or where he ate from it, and from there you try to figure out his pattern, how he goes from den to the herds and back. Once you know his routine you can pick your spot to ambush him. But if you wander around without a plan and take a shot at the first preda-tor you see, you probably won't ever see your perpetrator."

"Scary," Vi said.

"You're scared of stalking these Japanese guys?"

"No, no. What scares me is beginning to understand how you think. Wow. If you're so good at stalking lions and bears, what would you do if you fell hard for a certain woman and wanted to catch her?"

He did his best to ignore her fake wide-eyed innocent look of curiosity.

"Why don't you fall back into line where you belong and we'll head up the trail," he said. "Watch out for overhanging branches."

"Here's our spot," he announced. "Ready for a camping les-son?"

The clearing, deep in the conifers on the northeast slope of Flattop Mountain, was fringed with white aspen trees and dominated by a dead pine, still standing, of enormous size. Nearly devoid of branches, it pointed skyward like an obelisk.

"Lightning," McIntyre explained. "But a long time ago. I'm only guessing what happened, but probably thirty, forty years ago there was a thick stand of pine here. There was a storm. A bolt of lightning came down and hit the tall old veteran there and set fire to it. The fire spread all over this place, burned trees, stumps and roots and all. Probably smoldered in the duff and roots for weeks until snow or rain put it out. Afterward the aspen took hold, like they usually do after a fire. But now these aspen are near the end of their life span. They're dying off. The grass will take over for a while. Eventually the pines will come back."

"Where's this pile of white rocks you saw from the airplane?"

"That direction," McIntyre said, pointing west. "I think it's about a mile. We'll camp here and make it look like we're not interested in the white rocks. Pretend we're doing a forest survey. Come on and help me set the tent up."

He took out his pocket compass and consulted it carefully.

"Are we lost?" Vi asked sweetly.

"Not hardly. No, I'm taking a compass heading on the sunrise. Checked it the other day at my cabin. The sun rose at about sixty degrees, a couple of points north of due east. Which means, Miss Smart Aleck, we'll put the tent right over there. On the edge of the clearing. You want to be near the woods to break the wind, but you need to avoid any trees that might blow down on your tent. Don't camp under heavy dead branches, either. Now, it's very cold in the morning at this altitude, so we'll put the tent where the first morning sun will hit it. Otherwise we'll be shivering in shadows for another hour or two. That spot is good for the way it rises a little, too. Drainage if there's a thunderstorm."

"Gee," she said. "Thunderstorms, wind, falling trees, freezing nights, hard ground. I can see why you enjoy camping. I read somewhere that you should dig a ditch around the tent in case it rains."

"Where did you read that? In your *Woman's Home Companion*? For one thing, digging a ditch and having it drain efficiently is lots harder than it sounds. And it makes a terrible mess of dirt and mud, especially if it rains. And for another thing, it doesn't work."

"What about laying your lariat around your sleeping bag to keep rattlesnakes from crawling over you?"

"Oh, boy!" McIntyre exclaimed.

"Look again," Vi suggested. "I'm not a boy."

"That lariat trick's an old gimmick from dime westerns. Number one, any snake worth its hiss crawls over sticks and thorns all day. A rope won't stop it. Two, they don't crawl around at night looking for sleeping campers to bite. And three, we don't have any. You won't find any poisonous reptiles at eight thousand feet of altitude. C'mere and help tie up these horses."

After they had strung up a picket rope for the horses and moved the saddles into the shelter of the trees, Vi thought she would like to sit and enjoy the sunshine or else stroll among the meadow flowers. McIntyre, however, untied the camp axe from the packsaddle and beckoned for her to follow him.

"We'll find tent poles in the aspen," he said. "Dead and standing saplings would be ideal. Six of them, approximately eight feet long should do nicely. And while we're at it, we'll start collecting firewood."

Once they had selected their poles and had gathered a pile of firewood, he sat back against a tree, lit his pipe, and issued directions to Vi Coteau.

"Clear your ground carefully," he said. "Be sure you find every pine cone and rock and stick. Otherwise they have a habit of crawling under your sleeping bag in the night."

Vi went over the tent site removing pebbles and pine cones, being careful not to kneel on the ground in her clean new riding trousers.

"Now unroll the tent and find the back wall of it. The stakes are rolled up in the canvas. Put one stake at each corner, to begin with. You can use the camp axe to hammer them, or you can use a rock."

He could have helped her with the stakes, but after all, he thought, she had said she wanted to learn from this trip.

"Shelter," he said. He was watching her pound the last corner stake into place. "The Big Three of camping. Shelter, fire, water. Take care of those first, and in that order. Before you go picking flowers or sunbathing, make sure you've got a shelter and a way to have a fire."

"Where's the water?" she said.

"Probably down in those aspen trees. Aspen like to grow where there's water, so there's bound to be a little creek there. We'll go look after we stretch the tent. I guess I'd better get up and help with the front poles. You go fetch the longest one. And while you're at it, bring the two poles with the forked branches at the top."

She rankled at the command to "fetch" but during the next quarter of an hour, Vi Coteau learned how to place the upright poles and how to tether them so they wouldn't fall down. He explained how canvas can sag and get loose after a while and showed her the way to tighten the tethers using what he called "canoe knots."

The lesson included standing behind her and covering her hands with his while he showed her how to form the loop for the knot.

"There we go," he said when they had erected the back wall and had stretched the tent with the remaining stakes. "A couple more stakes to hold the front awning poles and we're finished."

"Speaking of which," she said, "where is the front wall? It's only got three walls."

"We can drop the front awning, if we need to. Most of the time I leave it up to protect the fire. In case of rain. The heat will reflect into the tent. Cozy. Called a 'baker tent.' "

"Named after a Mr. Baker, who didn't care much about

privacy, I take it?"

"Nope. Because it's shaped like a campfire baking oven, see? A small fire under the edge of the awning and we'll be warm as toast in there."

"Oh, goody."

With the tent up and firewood stashed where it would stay dry, McIntyre handed Vi Coteau two of the gallon-size canteens and suggested they take a stroll in the direction of the white stone stockpile he had spotted from the air. They would find water on the way. She slung the straps over her shoulders.

"You're not bringing the other canteen?" she asked.

"It's still full. Besides, I need my hands free to carry the carbine. C'mon."

They made their way into the aspen grove's white columns and discovered a miniature brook barely wide enough and deep enough to submerge the canteens, but clear as cut glass and pure as snow. Having filled the canteens they crossed the brook and entered the thick shadows of a spruce forest, finally emerging into a tiny mountain meadow. There, hidden from view in a tangle of chokecherry and wild rose bushes, they found the pile of white rocks.

"Good," McIntyre said. "Right past the aspen grove and due north of that rock knob. They were careful to camouflage their stack of rocks in the bushes, but when you look straight down on it from the air those white rocks really stand out. Now we know where it is. We'll come back tomorrow and see if we can figure out these guys' movements. I already noticed something which bothers me a little. Did you see them?"

" 'That' bothers you?" she suggested.

He ignored the grammar correction.

"Hoofprints. A horse was here, a horse with practically new shoes. Livery horses are shod every six weeks or so."

"So?"

"Fannie Painter didn't come back to the lodge, not after the night she returned for something from her room. Her horse didn't come back, either. It doesn't make sense for her to be riding back and forth through these woods for no reason. But if she took some rice to these Japanese guys and then they decided they needed her horse to haul their rocks . . ."

". . . they might kill her and take it?"

"Bingo. Which means their supply of rice has been cut off. Which in turn means our prey might be hungry and need to spend more of their time gathering food. Maybe they'd try to steal it from the construction camp. Or, there's a good-size creek down in that valley over there. Maybe they built another fish trap. Tomorrow we'll scout around and see."

"Want to hike over there right now? I'm not at all tired," Vi said.

McIntyre looked toward the sun sitting a few degrees above the western range of mountains.

"There's not enough daylight," he said. "Here on the north slope the sun goes down behind the mountains early. It'll be chilly here in about an hour. No, I think we need to go back to camp, build up the fire, check the horses, and see about making supper. Before dark I'd like to have the cooking stuff cleaned up, the food bag hung in a tree, and more firewood collected in case we want to sit up late and chat. Let's go."

"Would you like to carry one of these canteens?" Vi suggested.

"Well," he explained, "like I said, I've got this carbine to carry, see? Besides, if you have one canteen on each shoulder it gives you better balance. Carrying both of them you're less likely to trip on something and fall down."

"Oh, brother," she answered, "you really do win the cakewalk. Just for that, Mister McIntyre, I'm not going to change into my evening gown for supper. So there."

"Darn," he said.

CHAPTER TEN
A DEAD HORSE AND A FRESH GRAVE

Vi Coteau woke to find dazzling morning sunlight warming her face. She also had a hissing noise in her ears. Outside the lean-to tent, Ranger McIntyre was fully dressed, sitting cross-legged by the fire. The hissing was coming from a little camping stove no larger than half a loaf of bread. The fresh coffee smelled heavenly.

"Good morning," she said, rising on one elbow in her sleeping bag and blinking into the sun.

"Hi there!" McIntyre replied. "Did you sleep okay?"

"Slept like a log," she said. "I did wake up a couple of times, but dropped off again."

"Friend of mine used to say she slept like a log and woke up feeling knotty."

"What's for breakfast?" she asked. "Besides cornball, I mean?"

"Coffee. It'll be ready in about five minutes," he said, pointing to the pot. "I'm going to go check on the horses while you put your clothes on and wash your face or whatever. We'll grab a quick cup and go back to playing at being forest detectives."

A quick cup of coffee for breakfast? Nothing more?

The ranger returned to find his tent partner fully clothed and brushing her hair. She had nothing to say to him, but the way she was savaging her hair with forceful brush strokes conveyed a clear message. A silent ten-year old girl brushing her hair that way would be called petulant. McIntyre set the food bag next to the fire.

149

"Hung our food in a tree last night," he reminded her. "It's supposed to keep the rodents from getting into it. Or bears. Hey, why so quiet? Didn't you know I was kidding about no breakfast? I'll make you a deal: you drag out the sleeping bags and spread them on the ground to air out and I'll whip you up some fried eggs, bacon, and trail bread. How's that sound?"

"I hope you don't mean you found bread lying on the trail."

"Hah hah. Now who's being funny? No. I'm not sure why they call it trail bread. I guess on a longer camping trip you'd bring flour along and bake your own bread at the fire. On a short trip I prefer the kind I can get at the grocery, those lumpy loaves. Tough enough you could use them for a pillow. Although if you did, you might have a crumby night."

"I'm warning you," Vi said. "Don't do that again. I hate bad jokes early in the a.m. Or any time. I'd shoot you if I had my .38 on me. Where did I put my gun, anyway?"

"I've often wondered the same thing, but I think I'm not supposed to know."

McIntyre had seen Vi Coteau holding a stubby .38 revolver, but where she kept it when it wasn't needed, he had never learned. The whereabouts of her pistol on her person made an ongoing private joke between the two of them.

Vi Coteau and Ranger McIntyre had known one another ever since they met on the Case of the Unmentionable Murders where she learned about the tragic death of his one and only love, about his penchant for huge café breakfasts, and his aversion to carrying a gun. He, in turn, had become aware of her fondness for fast cars, egg salad sandwiches, nonpareils, and three-point symmetry; however, he had not yet had the opportunity to learn about Vi's various pet peeves, high on the list of which was any person—in this case a grinning forest cop—who tried to be cheerful before she had had her morning coffee.

★ ★ ★ ★ ★

"Did you have enough breakfast?" she asked. "Don't you usually pack away enough for two people?"

They were in the saddle now, the ranger in his flat hat and uniform tunic and the FBI secretary in her trim Stetson and her tweed jacket, retracing the route back to the cache of white stones.

"Funny about that," McIntyre replied. "Cooking for myself in the cabin, I'm content with a few pancakes and a couple of eggs. Out here in the woods I can go all morning on a bowl of oatmeal or bacon and eggs, maybe an apple. But in a good café with a menu I eat like a pig."

"Now, there's a charming picture," she said.

When they reached the cache of stones they rode around it in widening circles, searching the ground. It was easy to see traces of where the mysterious stone haulers had walked, apparently leading the shod horse. As McIntyre had expected it would, the trail led to a primitive campsite. It was nothing more than a very small fire ring and a rustic lean-to of tree branches, but it had been used recently. McIntyre dismounted to study the ground. Vi Coteau did likewise, although she wasn't one hundred percent certain she knew what she was looking for.

"Here!" McIntyre said. "Looks like they were here a while."

She went to his side and looked down. There seemed to be nothing to see: McIntyre pointed at a pile of curled-up dry bark peelings and a scattering of stone chips.

"Not good," he said, picking up a stone chip and looking at it.

"Explain?" Vi said.

"They sat here chipping flint. To make spears. Or arrows. My guess is spears because none of the wood around here would be any good for making a bow. These chips are chert, also called flint. They sat here and chipped at least one flint spear point.

They stripped a green sapling to make a shaft for it, too. See the bark peelings?"

"Yes. And what do you make of it all, Mister Holmes?" she asked.

"Well, Doctor Watson, I'll tell you what I make of it. It makes me nervous. These two characters are obviously working as fast as they can to lug rocks up to Flattop, God knows why. They're in a hurry. Yet they take the time to stop here and make a spear. Or two. Which tells me they don't have a firearm but that they feel a need for a weapon. One minute they're only carrying rocks, but now they carry a spear, too. Which would be awkward. Maybe they spotted a deer and hoped they could kill it for food. Maybe a bear scared them. Or maybe they think they might need to attack somebody or defend themselves from somebody. Either way, it makes me nervous to think about sneaky little guys in drab brown cloaks lurking in the woods with stone spears."

They resumed their careful search, walking and leading the horses. McIntyre was out of sight behind a thicket when he heard Vi Coteau's bloody shriek and ran to find her fighting to control her horse. The animal's eyes rolled back wide with the whites showing. The nostrils were flared, the ears laid back as it struggled against the reins. Brownie smelled the death gore, too, and she pulled back snorting and staring. But she stood fast.

They had discovered the livery horse. It was not a pretty sight.

"Broken leg, is my guess," McIntyre said. "Must have cut the animal's throat and left it to bleed to death. C'mon. We need to move our horses away from the smell of it."

A few minutes later Vi saw another brown shape lying in the trees a little ways off the track, but when she and McIntyre cautiously investigated, the thing on the ground turned out to be nothing more than a discarded saddle.

"Cinch is torn in half," McIntyre observed. "Probably why they ditched it. And look how the leather on the seat is all scratched up. Our Japanese boys were probably trying to use it to haul rocks. See those little bits of white stuck in the gouges? I imagine it would be hard to do, lashing a heavy rock onto a riding saddle. I don't like the looks of this, Vi."

"Because they had an accident with the horse?" she asked.

"Nope. It's the fact that they had the horse. Her horse. That's what I don't like. It's a long hike back to the lodge from here, even if she didn't go back the way we came. She could have gone on in this direction to the base of the Flattop cliffs and walked down the trail from there. It's still a tough hike from here to there, though. If she knew how far she'd have to walk, and how steep the trail is, and we can be sure she did know, why would Fannie Painter let her Japanese cohorts use her horse to haul their rocks?"

"Yes," Vi said. "Why would she? Unless she couldn't prevent it. Unless they simply overpowered her and took it. But what would they do with her . . . body?"

"Good question," McIntyre said. "They wouldn't want her walking back to the lodge. Or lurking around their camp waiting for a chance to steal back her horse. Won't surprise me if we have to chalk up another killing to these clowns in brown. Wouldn't surprise me at all."

"The poor woman," Vi said. "She's nuttier than a bag of almonds, but you've got to feel sorry for her being on foot and hungry out here. And like you say, maybe murdered. Anyway, what do we do now? We've got horses and we've got guns. I say let's go after them. Right now."

"I don't think we should," McIntyre replied. "I don't mean to startle you, but I'm fairly certain I caught sight of at least one of them watching us. From a distance. I've seen little glimpses of movement way out in the trees. Brownie's acting nervous, too. Let's keep acting natural and put distance between them and us. I'm not ready to try and catch them, not until I can pick my own place and time. One of us, or one of them, could end up seriously hurt if we go crashing through the forest chasing them, which would leave us with an injured person to take care of. Or they might hear us coming and take off for the high timber and we'll have to find them all over again."

"Oh, c'mon, Ranger!" Vi said. "At least let's follow the tracks a ways. Or here's another idea: we could casually wander off into the forest and maybe sneak around behind them."

"You do know what they say about trying to argue with a Scotsman, don't you?" he said. "Besides, this is my district and my responsibility. We'll look around from here, pretend to make notes, maybe take a few compass sightings. We'll amble up to the top of the ridge, over there, in the opposite direction from Flattop, maybe make it look like we're measuring trees. Afterward we'll eat our lunch and head on back to our camp."

"But they'll get away!" Vi said.

"I doubt it. Let me tell you a story about tracking a wounded mountain lion."

"Oh, God," she said.

"What?"

"I said 'oh, good!' Another tree cop story!"

Aware that the mysterious Japanese might be watching them, McIntyre and Vi Coteau made a leisurely progress back toward the little clearing in the woods, sometimes riding, sometimes walking, often pausing while the ranger consulted his pocket compass unnecessarily or pretended to write in his notebook. They took a detour to ride up the bald ridge where they would be in plain sight of anyone in the forest below; there they dismounted and made a show of pointing one direction and another.

He didn't bother to embellish the mountain lion story, but the point of it was this: an experienced hunter looking for a wounded lion, or even a wounded elk or bear, would not rush after it hoping to make a quick kill. He would know that a spooked and wounded animal, nervous and frightened, could either ambush the hunter, or make a desperate escape and end up lost and exhausted where he couldn't find it to put it out of its pain.

"It's kind of like disturbing a good fishing hole," McIntyre explained. "You go about your business, leave the animal alone, and it will try to return to its familiar routine even if it's wounded. It will still go back to its lair, if it feels safe. After lying up and recovering a little it might actually try to make its daily rounds, marking its territory, visiting places where it's found food before. So instead of chasing around after these stone-carrying characters, now that we know their route and at least one of their camps, we'll get up early in the morning and go wait for them. If you're not scared. If you're too scared I can take you home instead."

"Fat chance!" Vi replied vehemently. "I'll probably get in trouble for missing another day of work—again—but I simply must see how your strategy plays out. Besides, remember how I invited you to Leup's formal dinner party? And you bravely donned a tuxedo and fearlessly faced a deadly array of silverware and glassware, not to mention how courageously you maneuvered among all the low-cut evening gowns? If you can show such bravado at that, I can certainly risk being ambushed by a spear-thrower."

He laughed. The memory of that night always made him shake his head and grin. Vi Coteau had told him that his tuxedo had made a striking impression on the wealthy assemblage, especially among the women. Oddly enough, however, he had hardly noticed any of the individuals at the dinner party. It was mostly a blur of faces. What he remembered clearly was how glad he felt when it was over and they could leave.

"And another thing," she continued, "you're supposed to be showing me how to be a better camper. As long as we're pretending to act normal, maybe we'd better resume my lessons. Whatta y' say, coach?"

The first camp task was to lead the horses to the creek where they could drink their fill of water. The ranger brought along his carbine and also his special fishing pole, the five-section bamboo rod he had built one winter. Whereas most fly rods were two or three sections, he had made his in sections short enough to hide in a rucksack. The reel was equally compact. His fly wallet held a small selection of dry flies and simply looked like an ordinary gentleman's wallet, or a tobacco pouch. Anyone noticing a uniformed ranger with backpack hiking toward a trout stream would assume he was on an important mission for the government. But more likely than not, as McIntyre's supervisor knew all too well, he might be going fishing.

They tethered the horses to graze at the edge of the creek while they went upstream. The job of carrying the water bucket fell to Vi Coteau, since the ranger had to carry both his fly rod and the carbine.

"Know how to dip water?" he asked.

"Do you know how to dodge a water bucket thrown at your head?" she replied sweetly.

She plunged the bucket deep into the icy current and brought it up dripping and full.

"City girls," McIntyre said. "Think they know everything."

He took the bucket from her and carefully poured the water out onto the ground, then showed her the fine sand and waterlogged aspen leaves left in the bottom.

"Pushing the bucket straight down like that stirs up the bottom. And besides that, you dipped upstream. Anything floating in the current would flow straight into the bucket."

He got down on his knees beside the creek. She felt a funny urge to push him in.

"Watch," he said. "You dip downstream, see? And off the top of the current. That way you don't end up with sand and leaves and junk in your morning coffee. You're aware, of course, why we came upstream of where the horses are? And we got our water before we tried to catch fish, which can also stir up sediment. Okay, now we have our water. Let's see if we can catch some trout for supper."

"You didn't scare the fish away?"

"Not for long," he said. "It's like with the mountain lion. Leave them alone a few minutes and they go back to their business."

He took the wallet from his pocket and Vi heard him humming softly to himself as he selected a dry fly from it.

The night sky was clear, lovely, and endlessly deep. A nearly full moon floated on a blanket of stars stretched from mountain peak to mountain peak. Ranger McIntyre brought the horses to the tent and picketed them there lest the Japanese rock-shifters might get the bright idea of helping themselves to one. The ranger sat up late with the carbine beside him, feeding sticks into the fire. Vi slid into her sleeping bag and propped herself up on one elbow, valiantly trying to stay awake and talk to him, but the cozy warmth of the bag and the silence of the night, punctuated only by the snapping and crackling of the fire, eventually lulled her into dreamland. McIntyre watched her sleeping. Crazy as it may seem, despite knowing a killer with a spear might be lurking and waiting for him to get drowsy, McIntyre was fully content with life at that moment.

During the Great War, McIntyre had been a daily witness to

death, whether it was watching a doomed biplane corkscrew into the earth or looking down from his cockpit at khaki shapes sprawled grotesque and motionless in the mud. The thought of dying on foreign soil was the thing he hated most about being in war-wasted France. Every day as his Nieuport biplane lifted off the ground he said a simple prayer: "please, dear God, let me die in my own green mountains. I ask nothing more."

Morning found them riding back toward the low, bare ridge overlooking the route of the rock movers, back along the forested valley where they had found the dead horse and the ruined saddle. They had the packhorse with them, carrying their food and nearly everything except for the tent and sleeping bags. "We'd better bring it with us," McIntyre had explained. "There's probably three people out there," McIntyre explained, "maybe hurting for food and maybe willing to make off with a horse."

Near the top of the treeless ridge they dismounted. They tied the horses and crept cautiously forward to crouch behind a rock that offered them a view of the valley below. Vi Coteau held the carbine, while McIntyre scanned the forest with his field glasses. After what seemed like an hour of lying on the hard ground with the sun beating down on her back, Vi rolled over and pulled her Stetson down over her face.

"Let me know when you see anything," she said. "This warm sunshine is making me all drowsy."

"Some help you are," he said, looking at her and smiling. "Nodding off on the job."

"Hey, I didn't sleep too well last night," she said, although she was fibbing. "There was a ranger sitting in front of my tent humming to himself and breaking twigs. Besides, there were pebbles and sticks under my sleeping bag. Tonight why don't we cut nice soft fir boughs and put them under the bags? I read in a Boy Scout book it makes a nice bed."

"Only if you don't mind tree sap all over your ground cloth and sleeping bag. And you'd feel all those little sharp twigs from your boughs sticking you in the back all night, believe me."

"Pooey," she said.

"Hey! There's our quarry. See? He's moving. Down there!"

The field glasses showed a lone figure among the trees, headed in the direction of Flattop. On his back he bore a crude pack frame, apparently lashed together from willow or aspen, supporting a white rock the size of a man's head. He wore a brown cloak like a poncho. His long walking staff was a primitive spear. McIntyre watched him trudge along, in and out of the shadows and around the trees, until he vanished over a rise of ground.

"I think he's alone," McIntyre said. "At least I don't see anybody helping him. Let's sneak down the hill—he won't be able to see us if we go down that draw over there. See it? We'll follow him. If the other two are nearby we might be lucky and see them before they spot us. Or we might get even luckier and nab 'em."

Vi didn't exactly credit the notion that a ranger, a woman, and three horses could sneak through the forest unseen, but the Japanese man seemed awfully intent on carrying his load. He was far enough up the valley that he wouldn't notice them unless he turned around before they could reach the cover of the trees.

"Now I feel better," she whispered as they stopped in the shadows.

"Me, too," McIntyre admitted. "We'll keep our distance until we're sure he's alone."

"Going to make an arrest?"

"We need to catch him first," McIntyre said. "Besides, we don't actually have any real proof that he's done anything illegal. Except for littering and tampering with nature. But I darn sure want to keep hold of him until we find out what's been going on. Might need to call on your Japanese interpreter friend."

They rode at a slow walking pace for another half mile before they arrived at the edge of a wide-open clearing in the forest.

"Better not take a chance of riding out there," McIntyre said. "Let's take to the woods, stay in the shadows."

The shadows, however, held a surprise for them. In a particularly dark, particularly damp spot guarded by three sky-touching spruce trees the pair came upon another pile of stones. Only this pile was of ordinary rocks. It was a rectangular mounded shape, a cairn a foot or two longer than the average human body. McIntyre dismounted to have a closer look.

"It's fresh," he told Vi. "The ground is torn up where they yanked rocks out of it. There's dirt on the rocks. I'd say it's been here a week or two, not much longer."

"It's a grave, isn't it?" Vi said.

"Sure does look like one," McIntyre said.

"Whose, do you suppose?"

"My best guess is Fannie Painter."

"Not the other Japanese boy, Kiyoshi?"

The ranger didn't answer, but stood there studying the pile of rocks as if trying to see through it.

"It looks like the work of two people," he said. "One man all alone, he wouldn't hunt up so many rocks, wouldn't do as neat a job as this. I can imagine two people working on it. That puzzles me. How carefully built it is, I mean. Why would they take the time, since they're in such a big hurry to move white rocks to Flattop?"

"Should we open it and make sure?"

McIntyre walked around the burial cairn with his lips clenched and a furrow across his brow. Finally he came back to Brownie and patted her neck and scratched her ears.

"I don't think so," he said. "Not right away, anyhow. I think we ought to keep up with our Japanese man and see if we can detain him before midafternoon. But we're going to be even more extra careful. I don't suppose there's any point in asking you to stay behind while I ride ahead and catch up with him?"

"No point at all," Vi said. "And before you start arguing about it, I want to tell you that you don't have to be a Scot to be stubborn."

"Okay," McIntyre said with a grin. "Okay, okay. You win. But I'm assuming he's a murderer and he's dangerous. Plus, from the little clues he's left behind, I'm also assuming he's very sneaky. If I signal you to stop, or take cover, do it."

Once he was back in the saddle Ranger McIntyre slid the Winchester carbine from its scabbard.

"Here," he said, handing it to Vi Coteau. "I'd feel better if you had more firepower than that hidden .38 pistol of yours. Where the hell do you hide your peashooter, anyway?"

"If you were more observant, you'd probably know. I've been dressing and undressing for two nights now. Not that you would sneak a peek!"

"I'm shy," he said. "C'mon, let's go."

They returned to the faint trail of footprints leading upward along the valley in the direction of Flattop Mountain. They had not gone very far, however, before McIntyre saw Brownie twitch her ears. The Japanese was nowhere in sight. McIntyre signaled Vi to stop—and was glad to see her actually follow orders— while he dismounted and crept forward with the field glasses.

Nothing. In all the shadowed forest the only living things seemed to be themselves and the three horses. Maybe Brownie had only caught the scent of a dead animal back in the trees.

The park ranger could have been the next forest fatality, had it not been for those field glasses. As McIntyre picked up

Brownie's reins and got ready to mount, he thought he would put the field glasses back in the saddlebag rather than have them slung around his neck. He was facing the saddle, bending down to set the stirrup in position for his boot. But, bothered by the dangling field glasses, he straightened up and turned toward the saddlebag instead.

"Eeeeeeee Aieahhh!!"

Tadashi aimed the thrust of his stone-tipped spear for McIntyre's spine but it glanced along his back instead, slashing the green tunic. The small man screamed again like a demented demon or an adrenalin-crazed warrior. Brownie jerked away. The packhorse reared and tried to tear loose. With another scream the Japanese poised his spear to thrust again and McIntyre saw that his eyes were as wild and as insane as his screaming. The ranger's reaction was to grab for his revolver, but his arm seemed heavy as lead and his fingers felt thick as they fumbled the leather flap of the holster.

Luckily for the ranger, Brownie was a ranger horse. Through and through. McIntyre and Jamie Ogg had taught her many maneuvers, among which was "break it up!" Given the command, Brownie would charge into any bunch of troublemakers, from a small single black bear threatening a tourist to a gang of armed poachers. Now, without needing any command, the mare turned on Tadashi with her head and chest held high and her front hooves chopping at the ground. Tadashi wisely retreated, backing warily into the shadows.

"Good girl!"

McIntyre briefly considered running after his attacker but then thought better of it. Tadashi was going through the forest at almost nonhuman speed, stumbling over logs and crashing into bushes like a frantic crippled deer. If McIntyre followed him into the trees the little maniac might possibly circle back around and grab one of the horses. Or try to impale Vi on his spear. He seemed deranged enough to try anything. No, the safe thing to do was to stay with Vi and the horses.

"Wow!" He leaned against Brownie's shoulder to get his breath back. "Good girl, Brownie. Good girl! We sure didn't see it coming, did we?"

"Are you okay?" Vi asked. "It looks like he ripped your coat. He didn't draw blood, did he?"

McIntyre reached back and felt around for damage. His fingers touched the torn place, but he didn't feel any blood. He brought his hand back around and looked at it.

"I guess not," he said. "But there goes this season's uniform allowance."

"I'm glad you're not hurt. That was scary," she said.

"I don't like to criticize," McIntyre said, "but weren't you supposed to shoot him? Or something?"

"Had you been paying attention, you'd have noticed two horses and a ranger between me and the wild man with the spear. And, wise guy, the packhorse was going crazy and my own horse was dancing around. Shooting off a gun didn't seem like a very smart thing to do at the moment. Besides, I might have hit you instead of him. And how would I explain to your supervisor why I plugged one of his rangers, hmmm?"

"He'd probably give you a reward. And maybe give you my job."

Vi Coteau took three deep breaths and allowed her shoulders to relax.

"I don't want your job," she said with a smile. "It's not interesting enough. Anyway, what do we do now? Obviously Tadashi knows we're following him."

"Interesting puzzle, isn't it," McIntyre said. "I don't think it's advisable to go back to our tent. We haven't accounted for the other Japanese, the young one. Either one of them could sneak up on us in the dark and take the horses. Maybe spike us to the ground with a stone spear."

"I agree."

"It's still early in the day," he said. "We can ride on up this valley to the Flattop trail and take it down to the lodge. Plenty of daylight left. I think we ought to keep on going, if it's okay with you. We'll need to stay alert. But keep on toward the lodge. It's like one time when I was tracking a rogue bull elk. A novice hunter had wounded it and it ran away into the park, so my job was to track it down and finish it. Well, I was following the blood trail in the snow and out of the blue this big enraged elk turned on me . . ."

"Tim?" Vi said sweetly.

"Yes?"

"Did the elk kill you?"

"No."

"Then can you spare me the story? Will you? Just this once?"

McIntyre smiled as he slid his field glasses into the saddlebag. She studied his broad back while he bent his knee up to put his foot into the stirrup. She admired the smooth motion of his other leg swinging across the saddle.

"Hey!" Vi exclaimed. "Wait! Climb down!"

He dismounted, dropped Brownie's reins, and hurried to her side.

"What is it? Did you see him?"

"No," she said. "You'd better mount up again."

Shaking his head, the ranger once again set his boot in the stirrup and put his leg over the saddle. Vi rode up next to him.

"What was that about?" he asked. "Did you see him or didn't you? What was it, anyway?"

"Oh, nothing," she said, smiling her wide-eyed innocent smile. "Nothing! I simply enjoy watching how you mount your horse. Would you mind doing it again? For me?"

McIntyre replied by kicking Brownie into a trot, taking the

lead with the three animals in line again, the packhorse in the middle, the smart aleck Coteau bringing up the rear. He kept his back to her so she wouldn't see him smile.

Despite the banter, his mind kept replaying the attack, the way Tadashi's eyes looked when he came at him with that spear. Wild eyes, huge black pupils in blood-red circles. The guy must have been eating his own dope. It's got his mind screwed up to the point where all he can think about is hauling another rock to the top of the mountain. Possessed, that's what he is. And dangerous. If he thinks we're going to interfere with his rocks he'll probably try to kill us. Again.

"Stay alert, Brownie," McIntyre whispered.

The brown mare needed no reminder. Her species already carried a deeply imprinted sense of caution when it came to brown predators leaping out of the trees.

The valley ahead became narrower and its sides became steeper as it rose toward timberline. Through an opening in the trees McIntyre saw a blind corner coming up, a place where the forest of spruce was too thick to ride through and where they would need to stay right up against a rock ledge, a kind of low cliff about twice the height of a man on horseback. McIntyre remembered another place in the park much like this one, where a high rocky ledge loomed over the trail. He and Jamie Ogg had been tracking a mountain lion at the time, Jamie in the lead, when McIntyre happened to look up to see the cat lying on the ledge, perfectly relaxed, watching Jamie with intense curiosity.

CHAPTER ELEVEN
UNEXPECTED DEATH AND A LECTURE

The ranger turned in the saddle, hand raised, signaling for Vi to stop and wait. She got the message. Vi had also seen Brownie's ears stiffen forward. She reined her horse into the shadow of a spruce tree and sat there motionless. McIntyre handed Vi the end of the lead rope before he drew his .45 service revolver from its holster and urged Brownie forward. The mare seemed worried. McIntyre didn't like it. She kept looking to one side with her ears flicking back and forth, trying to locate the source of a sound.

Once they reached the foot of the low cliff, McIntyre became less nervous now that he had a protective rock wall on one side. Brownie walked slowly, putting each foot down delicately, "sneaking" as she had been trained to do. They stayed in the shadow of the cliff, skirting bushes and boulders, until the faint trail began to open up again and McIntyre could see fifty yards or more up the valley ahead. Nothing moved. Wherever the Japanese man was, he didn't seem to be ahead of them.

Vi Coteau was about to start forward to join McIntyre again when, out of the corner of her eye, she caught a glimpse of movement. The Japanese had crawled out of the trees on top of the cliff and there he stood, directly above the unsuspecting McIntyre. His hands were raised high above his head, holding a large, heavy rock, which he was on the verge of throwing at the ranger's head.

Vi didn't hesitate. Quickly and with calm precision she

166

considered her target and was making her choice even as she was bringing the Winchester carbine to her shoulder and levering a shell into the chamber. She did not know the gun, didn't know what distance the sights might be calibrated for; she would have to let instinct do the aiming. Her mind raced through the situation. Her target would have to be the rock the Japanese was holding above his head. To hit him in the body might make him drop the rock and hit McIntyre; if she shot him in the leg he might topple forward and also fall on McIntyre. She needed to put the rock out of the equation. She focused all of her concentration on that gray shape and when instinct told her that the carbine was aimed perfectly, she squeezed the trigger. The explosion made both horses jump and whinny, but Vi held them in check.

The ranger heard the rifle shot and Tadashi's scream simultaneously. Brownie didn't wait for a command but plunged forward to carry them to safety. Brownie's move, however, was unnecessary: the danger had been eliminated.

Vi's aim with the .30-.30 had been as true as her instinct. The heavy rock dropped to the ground. The small man dropped to his knees, slumped as if he was very, very tired, rolled to his side, and lay there unmoving.

McIntyre reined Brownie to the right and up the hill they went, circling around the end of the rock cliff, scrambling up the steep slope with Brownie's strong shoulders pulling them along, the ranger riding with revolver in hand, watching everywhere for the other man while heading for the one Vi had shot. When he drew Brownie to a stop at the flat summit of the cliff he realized the figure on the ground was no longer dangerous. In fact, he looked dead.

Vi Coteau arrived a few minutes later, by an easier way up the hill, still leading the packhorse. She was not prepared to find the Japanese man dead, but dead he was. McIntyre had dismounted and confirmed it.

"Stay on your toes," McIntyre told her. "Keep your eyes on the forest. And the hillside. The other one could be anywhere out there. This one's done for. He's dead."

"But I only shot at the rock!" Vi protested. "I know it! I know I hit it, too. He was holding it up over his head, like this, with both hands. He was about to throw it down on you. Where is that rock? Find it. I'll bet anything there's a bullet mark on it."

The rock lay near Tadashi's body. Rough granite, good and hefty, heavy enough to knock a man unconscious if it was dropped on his head. Or kill him. Vi was right: there was a fresh new streak of lead where the carbine bullet had struck it.

McIntyre knelt down and looked closely at the dead man's head.

"Ricochet," he said. "You hit the rock all right. Dead center. But the bullet glanced off and went right down into his skull."

"Damn," she said. "Now what do we do? Where do you suppose the other one is?"

"I don't know. I haven't seen any sign that he's anywhere around here. But be careful anyway. Can you go back down to the trail and bring the packhorse up here?"

"You bet," Vi said.

"Okay. Meanwhile I'll scout around for his belongings."

He found Tadashi's crude pack frame along with his homemade rucksack a dozen yards or so up the hill, but the sack contained very little. Vi Coteau came back with the packhorse and saw that McIntyre had arranged the rucksack's contents on the ground. He was looking at the assortment with the face of a man studying a jigsaw puzzle. There was a crude knife with a stone blade, a small blanket tightly rolled, several oilskin packets containing rice, a small tin teapot, and three live seedling plants with their roots bound up in oilskin.

"I didn't see anyone when I went for the packhorse," Vi Coteau said. "Nothing moving down there. Not even a new footprint or anything."

"I'm not surprised," the ranger replied. "It looks to me like he was working alone. I think his two confederates deserted him. He's been working hard, too. Almost frantically. Hasn't even taken care of himself. Fingernails, toenails all broken and dirty, sandals almost worn out. Looks to me like he's been in a rush to finish whatever it is he's been doing."

"He's Tadashi, obviously. What's happened to young Kiyoshi, do you suppose?"

"I don't know, but I've been thinking about it. Sitting by the fire all night gave me a chance to piece together a picture of what they've been up to. Maybe I've got most of it figured out. Or a theory, at least. There's one thing I can't seem to get straight, though."

"What's that?" Vi asked.

"That burial cairn back there. It's wrong. I can't imagine Tadashi taking time to make it. Everything points to the fact that he's obsessed with taking plants and white rocks up to Flattop—or at least he was—and it doesn't make sense that he would spend most of a day carefully building a burial cairn over Fannie Painter's body. Maybe the kid—Kiyoshi?—maybe he covered her body all by himself. But it's too carefully built. Too thorough. From the condition of that dead horse we found, I'd say Tadashi didn't care about anything except his rocks and plants. I can believe he killed Fannie Painter in a rage or else in a fight over her horse—like he attacked the two men who were unlucky enough to run into him up there on the mountain—but what I can't believe is how he could take the time and have enough decency to build a stone cairn over her. And another thing: he didn't even take proper care of that poor horse."

"So you're thinking maybe it was the boy, Kiyoshi, who carefully buried her? And now he's run off and deserted Tadashi?"

"Looks like it to me, yes."

"And what else did you say you figured out?"

"What it all boils down to is a certain spot he's willing to kill to keep people away from, plus seeds and plants he's been moving to that same spot, along with white stones. Soft ones, like limestone or gypsum. Professor Warren thinks Tadashi lived in Japan and knew his plants. What does it all say to you?"

"He was building a garden?"

"Yeah. I know it sounds weird, but it's the only thing that makes sense. Those pieces of stone have something to do with those plants. So does that wide-open stretch of tundra on top of the mountain."

"The stones were special. To him, I mean? The key to the whole thing?"

"Right. Maybe he was with a crew of men who were laying out the route the ditch was going to take. Clearing trees, building an access trail. Maybe Tadashi stumbled across these plants. They looked like plants he had known in Japan."

"Together with the white rock, you suppose?" she asked.

"There's an idea! A good idea, too. Should I make a wisecrack about you being more than just a pretty face?"

"Please don't. I'm not in the mood. Girls with pretty faces don't go around shooting people."

"Maybe," McIntyre continued, "maybe these particular plants grow where the ground has the limestone. It's possible that he discovered them, saw how valuable they might be, and from experience he knew the connection to limestone. Let's say he harvested some seeds, tested them on himself, and sure enough, discovered they're potent hallucinogens. He decided to move them away from the ditch route to some place safe."

"Why so far?"

"Maybe the building of the ditch was going to destroy them?"

"Or to give himself easier access?"

"Hey, you're right again! It's a long, tough road to the ditch. And when the ditch is finished and open for business there would be patrols watching it. But in the national park he could come and go any time. Plus, the park itself would protect his 'garden' for him."

"I bet he's also worried that one of the other Japanese workers would recognize the plants. Another reason to move them far away from the irrigation project."

"Miss Coteau, you are a genius. I think I'll ask my boss to hire you as my assistant so we can do this kind of thing all the time together."

"Oh, goody gumdrops," she said.

"Now," McIntyre went on, "with ditch construction coming closer and closer to where the plants grew, he got more and more frantic. He roped the kid Kiyoshi into helping him. Maybe it was Kiyoshi who had made acquaintance with Fannie Painter and persuaded her to bring them food and stuff."

" 'Made acquaintance'? What kind of books have you been reading in those long winter nights?"

"Come to think of it," McIntyre said, "peddling a natural drug would be right up her alley. Nature girl? New experience, mental enhancement? Seems like exactly her sort of thing. She could reserve a room at Bear Lake Lodge near the medicine circle, bring in a trunk load of rice, haul it up the mountain to the Japanese guys, and they'd pay her with enough seeds to make her wealthy. Or . . ."

"Or what? And aren't you getting a little carried away with this notion that the plants are some kind of dope?"

"Or maybe we don't know anything about her way of living. Maybe she moves in a fast circle of bright young people always eager for the newest way to get high. Maybe these plants could make her very popular in a certain social set. She and the Japanese guys obviously were willing to take lots of trouble and take lots of chances to get them. And there's obviously something illegal or secret about the whole thing, or else they'd just dig them up and take them away."

"What do you say we go find her?" Vi Coteau said. "I'm more than ready to start searching for her, even if she might be dead in that pile of rocks back there. At least let's do something about this poor little dead guy and get out of here. He gives me the heebie-jeebies lying there like that."

"Right," McIntyre said. "Let's get going. I need something to do, because I still can't get that stone cairn out of my mind. We said it looked like two people had built it. So if she's in it, who was the other person? And . . . wouldn't Tadashi have asked Kiyoshi the same thing? What a puzzle."

After packing up Tadashi's belongings, including the stone tip from the spear, McIntyre and Vi Coteau wrapped the small body in its woven poncho and lashed it face downward across the packsaddle. As McIntyre explained, their most logical course of action would be to go on up the valley until they struck the Flattop Mountain trail, then follow the trail down to the lodge. After arranging for someone there to take Tadashi to the coroner and after reporting to the S.O., he could come back and make a second trip over the mountain to retrieve the tent and any other camp gear they'd left behind.

"And let's keep alert," he told her. "Kiyoshi's still out here somewhere and he might be every bit as hungry and desperate as our friend Tadashi here. For all we know he's been sampling the seeds, too. Might be acting crazy."

The track was faint and narrow. In places it was nonexistent, which made it awkward for Vi Coteau and McIntyre to ride side by side. But she would rather dodge a few tree branches and detour around boulders and bushes than ride behind the packhorse. It made her shudder to look at the wrapped figure draped across the saddle.

"I wish I hadn't killed him," she said.

"I know," McIntyre replied. And he did know, and understand, because he, too, had been forced to shoot men in the name of duty. Killing for preservation of a life. It left an awful bitter taste in the mouth, a bitterness that stayed strong for weeks or months and felt like something that would linger forever.

"Funny, isn't it," she went on. "The Bureau lets us go to the firing range and shoot and shoot until we can hit a two-inch circle at a hundred yards. But you find yourself in a real-life situation and you don't know what to shoot at. I wish I had tried for his leg, at least."

"No use ragging yourself about it," McIntyre said. "It's over with. You stopped him from clobbering me with the rock. You had an unfamiliar weapon in your hands, you decided to shoot, it was the right thing to do, you did it. It's too bad, but it's over. Now, look: a few more miles and we'll strike the Flattop Mountain trail, ride down to the lodge, call the sheriff; he'll most likely send the coroner for the body. We'll find you a nice bed at the lodge, and a hot shower, and things will be brighter tomorrow. Okay?"

They didn't cut the Flattop trail after all. Instead, the track left by the Japanese stone-movers made two sweeping switchbacks at timberline and ended up on top of the mountain itself. Riding toward the alpine meadow, McIntyre called a halt and drew his revolver.

"There's somebody up there," he said. "At the medicine wheel. They're kneeling down, right there on the south side. See him?"

The kneeling figure heard the two riders coming. He stood up and waved.

"Why, it's Howard!" Vi Coteau exclaimed.

Howard? "Who, Professor Warren? What's he doing up here?" *She calls him Howard?*

Professor Warren kept waving excitedly, like a schoolboy who had just spotted his best friends at recess. McIntyre, scowling, assumed that Warren's agitation was caused by the pleasant surprise of seeing Vi Coteau again. Which was possible. However, the botany professor also had news of a discovery he had made.

"Couldn't wait to come up here again!" he told them when they had dismounted. "My God, I think we've got a whole new species here! Now, I may be wrong. I need to do more analysis. Method, you know, scientific method. I need to remain methodical and not get overly excited."

"I'd say it was too late," McIntyre said. "Or was it the altitude that left you short of breath?"

"Yes!" Warren exclaimed. "Exciting! Look here, look here! Many of these white rocks are sheltering a plant!"

"Plant? What kind of plant?" Vi asked.

"I went back to campus," Professor Warren explained. "The next day, I cabled my colleague in Japan with my description. Well, not a description of me. You know what I mean. Taxonomy, you know. He consulted his specimens and his sketches and cabled me back. It is *Eutrema*! No doubt of it. But what is exciting is that it does not appear to be *Eutrema japonica*! No! That plant, you see, appears in the north of Japan, the region known as the Snow Country, in conditions much like those where we are now standing! Barren of trees, extremes of cold and heat, high winds, subsurface water. Even the latitude there is practically the same as where we are standing."

"That's interesting," Vi said, "but in layman's terms, if it isn't *japonica* then what is it?"

"Possibly an undiscovered plant! I'll know for certain once I receive the sample from the Japanese university, but this may be a previously unrecorded variety. In layman's terms? This could well be an unknown variety of what you might mistake for the wild mustard."

"The Japanese guys have killed people over some mustard?" McIntyre said.

"You misunderstand. No, it's nothing like the yellow stuff you smear on your hamburger," Professor Warren said. "No, indeed. If anything it would more resemble the green gunk that the Japanese put on fish. Look here. Some of the plants have already gone to seed, see?"

He held out his hand to show a few very tiny seeds the size of a pinpoint.

"In Asia, seeds very much like these are more valuable than gold. They are terribly toxic, but hallucinogenic. Which means, before you ask, that any man brave enough to risk ingesting one or two of these will experience wild euphoria."

"So my guess was right!" McIntyre said. "What sort of 'euphoria' are we talking about?"

"His awareness of color, light, and sound will increase fifty-fold. He'll probably go through a temporary loss of consciousness and have fantastic dreams. With one seed, or half of a seed, he might become raving and violent. Depends on his metabolism. Anyway, that's what I believe these seeds to be. That's what they can do, if my supposition is correct. Mind you, I wouldn't eat one in order to be certain. I'll experiment with laboratory rats. But I think my hypothesis will withstand scrutiny. These are related to the *japonica* of Japan."

"Wow," said Ranger McIntyre. "You know, a couple of native Indian tribes have stories about plants that can make you have medicine visions. I thought maybe they smoked it in pipes, like kinnikinnick."

"Really?" Professor Warren replied. "I should look into it. At any rate, while traveling to get here I began deliberating the details of your investigation. I believe it's possible that when your man was assailing people like some sort of stone-age wild man, he could have been acting under the influence of one of these seeds. Very possible. I would go so far as to hypothesize a sort of imaginary drama for you. Let us imagine that he was working above timberline and somewhere along the ditch route he came across a flat, open, rocky space where this *Eutrema* grew. Perhaps he recognized it, or at least recognized that it looks like a Japanese euphoria plant. He chewed a seed or two, felt the strange effect, realized he was looking at a fortune if he could propagate it. If he could gather the seed and smuggle it to Asia. Or sell it in any large U.S. city with an Asian population. Better yet, if he could move the plants to a secure location and propagate them, the opium dens would pay enough to make him a rich man."

"I figured it was the seeds," McIntyre said. "I didn't make the Asia connection. I figured he was going to cut Fannie Painter in on the deal for a share of the seeds."

"The fellow—name is Tadashi, I remember—he knows his plants, probably lived in the region the Japanese call Snow Country. Where *japonica* grows. Sorry. I already told you that. Where is Tadashi, by the way? Did you locate him?"

"We did," McIntyre said. "That's him, on the packhorse."

"Oh, dear! What did he do, resist arrest?"

"You might call it that," McIntyre said. "But let's get back to these seeds for a minute. I'm having a hard time believing how one teeny-tiny seed can pack such a punch."

"You know something, Ranger?" Warren answered. "I have students who say the same thing about other plant seeds. Here, let me show you."

The professor smiled patiently, like a teacher preparing to explain calculus to a kindergarten. He squatted down to open his field case. On the outside it looked like an ordinary valise; inside, it was a laboratory in miniature. There were little drawers, snug-fitted compartments for magnifiers, tweezers and probes, a small rack of straps holding a little rock hammer, a chisel and pliers, a tiny trowel. He opened a little drawer and selected a small glass vial containing miniscule black seeds like one might buy in a packet to plant in one's flower garden. With the tweezers he removed one no larger than a caraway seed and placed it in McIntyre's palm.

"Perfectly safe," he explained. "It's merely *ratibida*, what many might call a wild coneflower. A type of prairie sunflower, if you will. Now, go ahead and bite down on it. According to folk legend, the plains Indians used it for toothache."

McIntyre bit down on the tiny seed. Within seconds he felt his tongue going numb, followed by a sensation that his gums and part of his cheek were dead and swollen.

"Wowsh," he said. "Thash reashy shom thin."

"I take it you see my point," the professor said. "Like mushrooms, or like your death camas, it doesn't take much to affect the human nervous system."

"You're drooling," Vi Coteau observed, looking at McIntyre.

"I'm . . . ?" McIntyre wiped the corner of his mouth with his sleeve. There was spit dribbling from his lips and he didn't even feel it.

"Tadashi had more plants in his backpack," Vi told the professor. "In fact, our deep woods detective here already suspected a connection between the white rocks and the transplanted plants."

"Grmmphh." McIntyre attempted to reply to Vi's "detective" remark, but his lips felt puffy and hard to move.

"Indeed," the professor said. "Indeed! And may I say it's 'damn clever'? If you'll excuse my language?"

"The ranger is damn clever?" Vi asked sweetly.

"No, no!" Professor Warren said.

McIntyre glowered.

"No," the professor continued. "I mean the whole rock situation. These *Eutrema*, you see? They almost certainly thrive in conditions identical to those you see around us. They do need a bit of shelter from wind, which the rocks provide. Moreover, when spring comes, the white rocks would store heat to help warm the soil but being white would not become hot as the dark granite does. Or should I say 'would'? No matter. Now, any plants and rocks arranged in a line or planted in clumps, etcetera, they would look artificial, man-made, like a garden. Too obvious to the passerby, you see. However, if they were added to an existing archaeological phenomenon such as this massive medicine wheel . . ."

"Nobody'd shee the li'l plansh or shink anyshing about 'em," McIntyre volunteered.

"Go to the head of the class," the professor said. "And one last thing. The white rocks are a type of limestone. You arrived as I was finishing up a field test of the soil acidity. The one chemical additive these *Eutrema* seedlings would require is a bit of lime. Rain falling on these white stones and snow melting on them would leach adequate amounts into the soil. As I said earlier, this Japanese chap knows . . . knew . . . his horticulture. I would not be surprised if Japanese growers use crushed limestone to nurture their Snow Country *japonica*. And now . . ."

"Now what?" McIntyre asked. His mouth felt as if it had said "meow gut" but then again, his mouth also felt as if the cat had taken a nap in it.

"Now," the professor said, "we know how clever Tadashi and his accomplice were to rescue these plants from the construction machinery and to salvage limestone to start a garden hidden in plain view. If you don't mind, I would like to return to what I was doing. I need to inventory the plants and make notes to record the growth stage of each one. I may attempt to retrieve recently planted seeds, but I doubt I'll find all of them."

"Will you be safe here by yourself?" Vi asked. "We still have Kiyoshi unaccounted for."

"And don't forget Fannie Painter," McIntyre said. "Who might be dangerous. She's damn—excuse me—darn unpredictable."

"Fannie Painter?" Vi exclaimed. "No! What are you talking about? She's dead, remember? We found her buried in a stone cairn down at the foot of the valley!"

"Well," McIntyre drawled, wiping his mouth, glad to discover the effect of the coneflower seed wearing off, "you like to kid me about being a spruce sleuth, but I've been doing some detective-type thinking about that. I said it looked like two people had built the cairn, remember?"

"Yes."

"What if Kiyoshi and Fannie built it, working together to fool Tadashi? What if Tadashi had gone out of control, demanding to take her horse and try to haul rocks on the saddle? What if he threatened her and she knew that she had to escape from him? But she couldn't bring herself to walk away from her share of the plants. So, maybe one day Tadashi was lugging a rock up the mountain and ordered Kiyoshi and Fannie to go back to the cache and bring another one. Sick and tired of being his slaves, they got the idea of a burial cairn. If Tadashi thought she was dead, Fannie could vanish into the woods and eventually make her way to the lodge. Kiyoshi could tell Tadishi they had quarreled and he had struck her and killed her. Tadashi might have been relieved to be rid of her. Maybe Kiyoshi planned to watch for a chance to sneak off and rejoin Fannie. The two of them would simply wait until Tadashi either wore himself out or finished the transplanting. They didn't need to be in a hurry.

They knew the value of the plants, knew where they were. All they had to do was hang around until the plants flowered and produced seeds. They'd collect enough seeds to make themselves rich. She could stay at the lodge. Or go back to Denver and return when the time was right. Heck, she could even say she had found Kiyoshi wandering in the forest and was taking him to a Japanese family in Denver until he could go back home again. She probably knows a Japanese buyer for the seeds."

"Sounds almost plausible," Vi Coteau agreed. "By the way, you need to wipe your chin again."

"And don't forget her history," McIntyre said, taking out his bandanna. "The first time she came here for a publicity stunt. All that guff about being a 'nature girl' living in the raw up in the mountains when she was really staying in a comfy lodge. Misleading people is a specialty of hers. She knows how to survive in the wild. But she knows how to swindle people, too."

"You think she and Kiyoshi are somewhere out here together? Hiding, waiting until maybe Tadashi returns to the construction gang or starves or something?"

"Not just somewhere," McIntyre said. "I think I know exactly where they are. If you still want to stick around, Professor, and study your plants, you stay on your toes. Finish up whatever you have to do, but be sure to stay alert. Fannie Painter and the kid could turn out to be darn dangerous."

"Not to worry," Professor Warren said cheerfully. He opened a pocket on the back of his field case and pulled out a heavy pistol, an Army-style 1911 Colt .45 automatic. "I may be a trifle nearsighted, but I assure you I can protect myself."

"Aren't you worried that he might shoot somebody?" Vi Coteau asked McIntyre as they rode away down the mountain.

"There's probably not much chance of him actually hitting anything. Those military .45 automatics are reasonably accurate, but accuracy takes lots of practice. He could accidentally shoot his own foot with it."

"It's sweet of you to worry that he might hurt himself," Vi said.

"I'm only worried that I might have to go rescue him. It could ruin my free weekend."

CHAPTER TWELVE
IN WHICH ALL IS RESOLVED. ALMOST.

"This way," Ranger McIntyre said, reining Brownie off the main trail and across the tundra toward a forest of stunted evergreens and krumholtz. The thicket looked all but impenetrable.

"Where are we going?" Vi Coteau asked. "The lodge is the other direction. Down the trail we just left. You remember. The lodge? Four walls? A real roof? Hot food and soft beds? My shiny new yellow convertible waiting to take me home?"

"We're heading for a hidden campsite," he replied over his shoulder.

"Camping? We left the tent in the other valley."

"We won't need it," McIntyre said.

"You know," she said to his back, "when I told you I'd like to have more camping experience I was thinking of going at it more gradually. Maybe begin in a tent with a stove and folding cots. I could slowly work my way up to having no stove, then perhaps sleeping on the ground. Lying down in the open with no shelter wasn't what I had in mind. Not to mention the fact that we have a corpse with us."

McIntyre kept on toward the twisted trees and tangled brush.

"Hush now," he said. "Sometimes sound carries a long ways up here near the tundra."

Without another word he undid the flap of his holster and brought out his revolver. Vi levered a cartridge into the Winchester, lowered the hammer for safety, and focused her attention on the thicket ahead.

Brownie's ears tipped forward.

McIntyre quietly slipped from the saddle, holding up his hand for Vi to stay where she was. She watched him creep into the thicket on the left, apparently planning to circle around whatever lay ahead. She could see the tension in his back, sense the intensity in the way he moved so stealthily. There was no mistaking it: the ranger was heading into a situation of deep danger and he knew it. Somehow. She wished she had her Thompson submachine gun instead of McIntyre's little carbine. His green tunic went out of sight among the crooked trees and undergrowth. The next few minutes seemed unending. She kept twisting in the saddle to look behind her, looked all around, bent down trying to peer into the trees.

McIntyre's explosive shout startled her.

"Hey! Stop there! Dammit, stop!"

Brownie began tossing her head and shaking her mane. The ranger needed her help. It was really dumb of him to leave his equine partner behind, but it wasn't the first time he had done it. The mare charged forward, heading toward the hidden camp. The livery horses stayed where they were and whinnied in alarm.

Vi Coteau hurriedly dismounted and hitched her horse and the packhorse to the nearest tree branch. She half-ran, half-stumbled in the direction Brownie and McIntyre had gone, her thumb poised to cock the carbine as she went. In a minute the krumholtz opened up and gave way to a long clearing where she saw a small figure in brown, a figure no bigger than a boy, carrying a brown packsack, running away from McIntyre. It looked as if he might make it to the shelter of the taller trees below the meadow. The ranger wasn't fast enough to catch him, but the ranger horse was. She thundered past McIntyre without slowing down.

"Brownie!" McIntyre shouted. "Break it up! Grab him!"

He and Jamie Ogg had spent many winter afternoons training the ranger horse. Now with loose stirrups flapping and reins flying, Brownie raced on, plunging headlong down the bare stretch of slope. She caught up with Kiyoshi and grabbed his shoulder in her teeth. The boy stopped running and instantly found himself sitting down. The mare's mouth felt like a carpenter's clamp squeezing his shoulder.

"Watch for Fannie!" McIntyre shouted at Vi as he hurried toward Brownie and Kiyoshi. "She can be anywhere!"

Vi held the carbine at the ready, scanning the wall of tangled brush, her eyes taking in the sleeping area beneath the krumholtz, the small campfire, and brown blankets. There was no sign of movement.

Vi walked down the hill to where Kiyoshi sat rubbing his sore shoulder. McIntyre was standing over him. The boy looked hungry, small, pitiful, and resigned to whatever fate the tall forest ranger might decide for him.

"Did the other man force you to work for him?" Vi asked.

"Yes," Kiyoshi replied. "The one man. All right man. Not Tadashi. Tadashi very bad. Very crazy."

"The one man? Who?"

"Man in San Francisco. Man told father, maybe boy come work. Come contract gang. Good money. Money for family. He said. There . . ," he pointed north to the distant mountain range, ". . . he told me go Tadashi, other men. Carry water, cut tree. Not where digging, we are . . ."

He couldn't find the words to explain the small crew that had been assigned to go ahead of the ditchdiggers and blaze the route.

"Did they pay you?" Vi asked. "Money? Did they give you money?"

Kiyoshi shook his head.

"No? Food only? If there was no money, no wages, the FBI wants to find these men. FBI arrests men who make slaves of other men, understand? Slaves?"

Kiyoshi nodded. He went on rubbing at his sore shoulder where Brownie had nabbed him. The mare was ignoring him now, cocking her head and looking off in the direction of the camp and the trail through the brush where the other two horses waited. *She wants to go tell the livery horses what a good ranger horse she is. She's a show-off.*

"The woman Fannie? You know? Fannie? Did she hurt you?" Vi asked. Kiyoshi nodded yes and shook his head no.

"Did she promise to help you go home, go to San Francisco? Or to your people in Denver? She said you would go to the city?"

"Promise," Kiyoshi repeated. "Yes."

"Listen to me, Kiyoshi," Vi said. "This tall man is a forest ranger. He is very nice. He is kind. You go with him, go with me, and we'll help you get home to your family. You stay with us. Okay? No running away, okay?"

"Okay," Kiyoshi said.

"Great," Vi said. "Where is the woman? Fannie? With you?"

Kiyoshi pointed back toward the camp where he and Fannie Painter had hidden from Tadashi. She had rice, Kiyoshi tried to explain. Kiyoshi used his hands to show them how he had made another fish trap to put in the creek. When the tall man with the horse found them, the woman ran away into the twisted trees. Kiyoshi ran, too, but the wrong way. The horse caught him.

"So she's hiding somewhere nearby," McIntyre observed. "Probably come out on her own, once she figures out we can't really arrest her for anything. Maybe I could give her a ticket for . . . what does the rule book call it? . . . when you collect wild food growing in the park, like mushrooms or berries or chokecherries . . . foraging, that's what they call it. Supposed to be illegal. Their campsite might be illegal, too. There's a new rule against camping outside of established sites. But I don't know if it's gotten into the books yet. She needs to pay the lodge for a horse and saddle, but that's nothing to do with park rules. She's guilty of scamming the newspapers with her 'nature girl' routine, but that's not my problem, either."

"I agree," Vi said. "There's really nothing serious you can charge her with. What do we do next?"

"Mount up and ride back to the lodge. Kiyoshi can ride behind me on Brownie. As for Fannie Painter, or Eve, or Agatha, or whatever her name is, we'll let her hoof it back on foot. She can make it before dark. Or she's welcome to go on hiding up here. The way I see it, I don't have to worry about her, not unless there's reason to believe she's in distress or is a criminal, and I'm getting tired of worrying about her."

The three of them walked back up the slope and into the krumholtz where the other two horses had been left. Brownie followed along behind. She held her head high and kept an eye on Kiyoshi in case he made another run for it. She had captured the fleeing boy and he was her prisoner. Some people, people who don't own horses, will say it's impossible for a horse to look smug. But they are wrong.

"By the time we make it to the lodge, it'll be too late in the afternoon to phone headquarters," McIntyre said. "I'll ask Ken if I can bunk down for the night. Tomorrow I'll need to ride back up over the mountain and collect the tent and the stuff we left in the other valley. The sheriff can come for Tadashi's body. Can you drive Kiyoshi to the city without frightening him to death? He hasn't broken any park rules that I know of. Rearranging the rocks, maybe. Nothing we could prove, at least. So I've got no reason to keep him. But you and that interpreter what's-his-name will want to question him about the labor contractor."

"Bob," she said. "Bob Daley."

Bob, she said. McIntyre was beginning to realize something:

it bothered him to hear her call another man by his first name.

"Right," he said. "You and . . . Bob . . . should be able to guide Kiyoshi through a legal deposition. Make sure it's done right, so a judge can't find fault with it. Afterward can you fix him up with some decent clothes and shoes and put him on a train for California? Agent Canilly can wire the FBI agent in San Francisco to meet the train and help the kid find his family. Case closed. End of story. All problems solved."

"Happy to do it," Vi said. "And now I see we have a new problem."

She pointed to where the packhorse stood tied to the stunted tree. All alone. Vi's saddle horse was gone. She had hitched it to the same tree, but now the animal was nowhere to be seen.

"Wandered off?" Vi suggested.

"I doubt it," McIntyre said. "He might have gotten loose, but probably wouldn't leave his stablemate. Could be around here somewhere. Grazing, looking for grass. Do you want me to show you how a girl should tie a proper rein hitch?"

"Do you want me to punch you in your Scotch nose?"

They searched the area and found nothing except hoofprints leading back toward the main trail. Carbine at the ready, Vi Coteau followed the tracks a short distance until they became blurred and confused with others, then gave up in disgust and rejoined the men. McIntyre and Kiyoshi left her to guard the remaining horses while they returned to the hidden camp to smother the campfire and collect the blankets and cooking pot. McIntyre took a chance by telling Kiyoshi to go smash the fish trap, thinking the kid might make another run for it. But in minutes he was back and the two of them carried the gear to where Vi and the horses waited

They wrapped everything in a blanket and lashed it onto the packhorse behind Tadashi's body. There was no sign of the missing horse; McIntyre expressed a sneaking suspicion that Fannie Painter had circled around back to the camp while he and Vi were chasing Kiyoshi. She had taken Vi's horse and was now on her way down the trail toward the lodge.

Once they were clear of the brush and out on the open ridge again, McIntyre held the stirrup while Vi Coteau swung up into Brownie's saddle. She rose in the stirrups and peered into the distance.

"You're right!" Vi said. "I just caught a glimpse of her! She's 'way down there where the trail comes out of the trees and crosses a hill. At least I saw somebody on a horse, moving fast."

McIntyre's impulse was to mount up and go galloping after Fannie. The very first rule of traveling in the mountains, however, is never, ever, leave your group. He had two people to look after, plus a corpse and two horses. Much as he would have loved take Brownie racing after the crazy dame, his duty was to stay with the group. He explained as much to Vi.

"Anyway," he said as he helped Kiyoshi into position behind her on Brownie, "it's not like we don't know where she's going. Look at the bright side: now the sheriff can charge her with horse stealing."

"If you won't ride," Vi said, looking down at him, "promise me if you feel tired, we'll stop and change places. I don't mind walking, really."

"A few minutes ago you were going to punch my nose," he said. "And now you're being nice to me? Criminy, make up your mind. But this arrangement makes the most sense. My legs are longer than yours . . ."

"You peeked!"

". . . and my boots are a heckuva lot better than those sandal things Kiyoshi's wearing. And I'm used to hiking. With me walking we'll make better time."

★ ★ ★ ★ ★

Unless weighed down with a sixty-pound backpack, your average mountain hiker has a "trail speed" of approximately three miles per hour. Given a path reasonably free of furrows, small rocks, and roots, Ranger McIntyre could do four miles per hour. Before long they were back down in the tall timber and it wasn't long before they caught the scent of woodsmoke from Bear Lake Lodge. In less than two hours they broke out of the forest and saw the buildings.

Four guests were playing croquet on the lawn. Two more were enjoying themselves at a game of horseshoes and half a dozen others were lounging in deck chairs or on blankets, simply enjoying the late afternoon. A young couple out for a stroll looked curiously at the small wrapped object lashed to the packsaddle and no doubt everyone who saw the new arrivals wondered why an RMNP ranger was walking beside a horse carrying a fashionable young woman and an oriental urchin. Were the woman and boy under arrest for something?

The three went on past the lodge and were almost at the stables when Ken, the lodge owner and manager, came up to them.

"Ah!" he said. "There you are! Miss Painter said you'd be here in about an hour. I helped her load the cases. She told me to tell you she'd be waiting at the car."

"Cases?" Vi said. "What car? What cases?"

"Her suitcase and yours. She said she's going to leave her trunk and we'll ship it to her later. Apparently the two of you need to hurry if you're going to catch the late train out of Denver."

McIntyre looked toward the parking area, which was across the road and half-hidden by the main lodge building.

"Which car is hers?" he asked.

"Which one?" Ken replied. "No. She said the ladies were going to use Miss Coteau's car. I put the suitcases in Miss Coteau's car."

Vi Coteau let out a very unprofessional oath—unless swearing was one's profession—and she dropped from the saddle to the ground, nearly knocking Kiyoshi off as well. She hit the gravel running, making a beeline toward the parking area. But she was not in time: the thrum of the Marmon's six cylinders accelerating to maximum rpm ripped through the quiet mountain afternoon and with a spray of gravel from the rear tires the coupe sped away.

McIntyre yelled for Vi to wait, but he had his hands full with the two horses. He helped Kiyoshi dismount by unceremoniously jerking the boy from the saddle. He handed him the reins.

"Here," he said. "Lead them on over to the stable. Ken will show you where it is. Ken? Can maybe you and Kiyoshi unload the dead guy and find a place to store the body until we can call the sheriff?"

"Dead guy?" Ken said.

"I'll explain later. Use your phone?"

"Sure," Ken said. "Go on in the back way, through the kitchen. Hey! Look there! She's got your truck!"

"What?" McIntyre said. "Who's got my truck . . . ?"

It was McIntyre's turn to utter an unprintable remark. Or two. More of an unprintable phrase, really: his Small Delights pickup was tearing out of the parking lot with Vi Coteau at the wheel. The engine whined like it was about to fly apart; the rear end fishtailed dangerously in the gravel as Coteau headed for the Bear Lake road at a speed the little Model A truck had probably never experienced.

Ken and McIntyre stood motionless, watching until the pickup flew out of sight and the road dust began to settle again.

"Ken?" McIntyre said, forcing himself to speak slowly and calmly.

"Yes?" Ken said.

"There's a lesson to be learned here. And I'm afraid Miss Fannie Painter's about to learn it. You can cheat on a woman and maybe get away with it. You can take her money and she might forgive you. But never, ever, mess with her automobile."

Ranger McIntyre sat down at Ken's desk and lifted the telephone receiver. He recognized the voice of the operator who said "Number, please?"

"Jane," he said. "How about connecting me with 060-R1?"

There was a rattling buzz as the connection clicked open.

"Moraine Park Entrance," the voice said, "Ranger Post speaking."

"Don? This is McIntyre. Are you the only one on duty?"

"No. Ranger Pedersen is here, too. She brought the mail and a box of brochures a while ago."

"Good," McIntyre said. "Look, there's a woman in a stolen car coming your way. I want you to block the park entrance and arrest her. It's a new Marmon convertible coupe. I don't think she has a gun, but don't take chances, okay? My pickup will probably show up right behind her. The FBI lady is driving it."

"What do you want me to do with her?"

"For one thing, if you value your life don't get between her and the woman who stole her Marmon. Oh, you mean the one who's driving the coupe. Let me see . . . okay, get Jane at the telephone exchange and ask her to locate Sam Bartlett. There's a good chance he's in the village somewhere. He can arrest Miss Painter and take her to the county seat."

"What charges?"

"Let's start with auto theft. And horse stealing. Vandalizing a protected area on federal land. Oh, and aiding a person engaged in slavery. FBI calls it peonage. When you've got her in handcuffs, call me. I'm up here at Bear Lake Lodge."

"Understood," Ranger Post said. "Anything else?"

"Maybe find somebody to shuttle my pickup back to me? Vi Coteau will no doubt leave it there and take her coupe back."

"Sure. Somebody'll run it over there for you. Okay to let Ranger Naturalist Eleanor Pedersen drive it? She's been sitting here counting tourist brochures and needs something less boring to do."

"Why not? If she doesn't mind driving a truck marked Small Delights. Some women find it kind of comical, I guess."

"No kidding?" Ranger Post replied. "I wonder why?"

With nothing to do but wait, Ranger McIntyre went into the dining room and accepted the cook's offer of a sandwich and cup of coffee. A couple of tourists broke into his boredom when they spotted his uniform and hurried over to ask questions about the national park. The questions proved to be the usual unanswerable ones, such as "where can we see elk and deer?" and "when will the aspen leaves begin to turn color?" and "are the bears dangerous?" and one of his favorites, "how difficult is the hike to Dream Lake?"

How difficult? He was tempted to reply. *Well, considering the pack of cigarettes I see in your shirt pocket and the hundred pounds of belly flab you're carrying, not to mention your shiny city shoes, I would say you'll find it quite a challenge.*

At least the visitor inquiries helped while away the time. When the tourists ran out of questions McIntyre asked what had brought them to Colorado and where they were from. One of the pair, a middle-aged housewife teetering on the edge of matronhood, had barely begun her lyrical paean to the scenic wonders of Ames, Iowa, when McIntyre was summoned to the telephone.

"Ranger McIntyre," he said into the mouthpiece.

"Sheriff Sam Bartlett here. Listen, I'm at the Moraine Park

entrance station. I was at your village police station when Ranger Post phoned to see where I was. Funny, huh. Anyway, have we got your affidavit to arrest this woman, Fannie Painter?"

"Affidavit? Yeah, I guess you can go ahead. I've got witnesses who saw her take the car. And Ken says he'll write out a complaint that she took a horse without leaving a deposit, and she never returned it. Or the saddle. Also, the FBI wants to talk to her about the way she aided and abetted a guy named Tadashi. He forced another guy to work for him, a kid named Kiyoshi."

"Okay, I'll lock her up. But you need to come down to the county courthouse in the next few days and tell everything to the judge. Otherwise we'll have to let her go."

They agreed on a day and time and McIntyre hung up. Forgetting the Iowa tourists, he walked out the open double doors of the lodge and onto the wide covered porch where he stood wistfully gazing at Flattop and the dark forested valleys around it. How simple it would be, he thought, to take Brownie and ride back up the mountain, over the ridge and down the far valley to where his tent waited for him next to a cold mountain creek, a creek where tasty little brook trout were waiting to be caught.

"What was that?" Ken said, coming up behind him.

"What was what?"

"I thought I heard you sigh a big ol' sigh. Maybe it was a sniffle. Got asthma troubles, do you?"

McIntyre didn't have time to answer: both men heard the six-cylinder growl of a heavy car. Through the trees they caught a glimpse of yellow approaching the parking area.

"I need to go see the cook about the breakfast menu," Ken said, heading for the doorway.

"Coward," McIntyre said.

★ ★ ★ ★ ★

For Ranger McIntyre, every tourist season in the park reinforced his conviction that Dante's levels of Hell included at least one level for people who ask questions. In this particular instance it was the judge at the county courthouse who was doing the asking. To McIntyre the session seemed to stretch into infinity.

What was the time of death? The judge wanted to know. How do you account for the chips of granite found in the wound in the victim's head? In your opinion, did Miss Coteau intend to kill the Japanese gentleman, or was it an accident? Do you have the address of the deceased's next of kin? How did Miss Coteau come to be in possession of your rifle? Would you say he was killed (a) while resisting lawful arrest, (b) while posing deadly threat to the public, (c) while fleeing from authority or (d) while engaged in sabotage or other activity with the potential to cause lethal harm? If Miss Coteau is only a secretary with the FBI, why would she need to be armed with a firearm?

Judge, if you were to be the one who annoyed Miss Coteau, you'd be the one who'd need a firearm.

Please describe again the circumstances, the judge said. Were you in uniform with your badge in plain sight? Had you given warning to the accused attacker before the shot was fired? Why didn't you survey the area into which you intended to ride, to be certain it was safe? Do you customarily loan your rifle to non-park personnel? Did you hand the lady the gun in order to impress her, or did you do it hoping she would use it to shoot the man you were pursuing? Why didn't you keep the rifle and give her your pistol instead?

The judge eventually dismissed McIntyre and had Supervisor Nicholson brought in to answer a few more questions.

The drive back up to the village took over an hour, but there was very little conversation between ranger and supervisor. A few muttered observations about the weather, the condition of the highway, the possibility of a dry autumn, and the two were through talking. Back at his office, however, the supervisor leaned back in his swivel chair, told McIntyre to stand in front of the desk, and unloaded on him.

"Goddammit," Supervisor Nicholson said, "all I wanted—all I ever wanted from you—was a simple explanation for a bunch of white rocks. What do I get? A dead climber, maybe murder? A poisoned geologist, probably murder? A ranger larking around in the woods with a gorgeous woman, probably hanky-panky? A dead foreigner, shot with a government rifle that the ranger "loaned" to that same dame? A parade of Japanese kids, horticulture experts, wranglers, innkeepers—rangers—sheriffs and coroners coming through my office drinking my coffee and eating my doughnuts? If you don't mind my asking—and since I'm the damn park supervisor I think I have every right to know—what the hell did you do about the rocks I sent you up there to take care of in the first place? And don't tell me you threw them out in the woods or I'll have you up there personally carrying each and every rock back to wherever it came from."

"Nick, I've got it all under control," McIntyre answered. "Miss Coteau took Kiyoshi with her back to Denver and after he tells the FBI about the slave ring—peonage, they call it— she'll fix it so he can return to his family. The coroner is finished with Tadashi, and since they can't find anybody to claim the body they'll bury him at the county cemetery. Those white rocks? I think they might as well stay there. The whole medicine wheel is man-made, for crying out loud. Besides, once the story gets around, maybe people will want to come look. Good for business, you might say."

"Great," Nick snorted. "That's all we need. People finding out we've got weird rocks up there. Not to mention your damn hallucinogenic plants growing wild."

"That part's taken care of, too," McIntyre said. "Professor Warren's dealing with the plant problem. He's happy as a pig on a parlor cushion. I told him he could have all the plants for his research back at the university. He's probably up on the mountain right now, grubbing out the last ones. Don't know where they came from . . . somewhere on the irrigation ditch project would be my guess . . . but there won't be any more left in the park by the time he's finished."

"I suppose it might turn out all right," Nick grumbled. "What about your lady friend? Is she all squared away about the auto theft thing?"

"Yeah, I assume she is. Haven't spoken with her recently. I've been kind of busy with judges and coroners and such. Besides, I think she's interested in Howard Warren. Calls him 'Howard' for cripe's sake. But there is one more thing."

Supervisor Nicholson eyed McIntyre suspiciously.

"Yes?"

"I'd like three days. Three or four days. I need to borrow a packhorse from Bear Lake Lodge and go retrieve the tent and cooking gear I left in the mountains."

"Is there a trout stream up there I don't know about?"

"No! Well . . . there's a little creek. Might have a few small brookies in it."

Supervisor Nicholson's sigh seemed incredulous. He shook his head and looked at McIntyre like a father listening to his small son explaining why he shaved the dog. He sighed again and called to the office secretary.

"Does this mean I wouldn't see anything of you for three days?"

"Yes, it does."

"Dottie?" Nicholson called. "Could you please bring me the duty roster for next week?"

Chapter Thirteen
The Lonely Ranger Rides Again

Ranger McIntyre did all he could to postpone the inevitable. Soon, or hopefully later, the moment would arrive when he would need to sit down at his desk and write the report. Worse yet, Dottie expected him to submit an expense sheet with it.

Rather than begin the paperwork, he shoveled horse droppings from Brownie's stable, split a goodly supply of firewood, swept the cabin porch, and rinsed out his dirty laundry. Indoors he found that he couldn't possibly begin until he had oiled the squeak in his swivel chair, made neat little stacks and arrangements of the stuff on his desk, and relocated the desk lamp. Four times.

Why did he dislike writing his reports? It didn't take long, nor did it require much thought or effort. But, as he told himself while deciding whether to polish his extra pair of boots, writing an account of his activities was like answering a bunch of questions. It was like having to explain things to people. He'd done enough explaining to last a long, long time.

The telephone jangled. Somebody else wanting to ask questions. As he picked up the phone, he felt an impulse to throw it through the window.

"Fall River Station. Ranger McIntyre," he said dutifully.

"Good morning!" chirped the voice on the other end of the line. "This is Polly! How are you?"

"Hi, Polly. Long time since I've heard from you."

"You bet it is! Say, Tim, listen: I don't like long-distance charges any more than you do so I'm getting right to the point, okay. It's going to be a beautiful weekend down here in Denver and we're going to crank up my Jenny and go flying. Wanna come? I know you do. Come fly with us!"

"Gee, Polly, nothing I'd like better. Except I really need to make a trip into the backcountry and retrieve some camping equipment. Darn it. My boss said if I finish my reports today I can take off the next three days. Four, counting my normal day off. I was looking forward to having the time alone."

"Ah, heck!" Polly said. "Johnny and I, we were thinking you and Miss Coteau could meet us at the aerodrome and we'd take turns going up in the Jenny! Make it a picnic kind of time? I'll bring the picnic!"

"Well," McIntyre said, "it sure sounds like fun. I'm not too certain Vi would be interested. I kinda think she's miffed at me because I spoiled her car chase with a roadblock. And then there's this botany professor she calls Howard. I'm not sure but I think there's something going on between them."

"Darn," Polly said. "Hey, I'll phone her! See if she'd like to go with us! I'd love to take her flying in my Jenny. Maybe go looking for those booze runners, huh?"

"Sure," McIntyre said. "Why don't you phone her. Sorry I can't make it."

"I'll ring her up right now! If she can't come at least we can have a girl chat on the phone. Maybe I can find out about this professor. Okay, talk to you again soon? Bye!"

" 'Bye, Polly."

The ranger rode alone, but a shadow woman rode beside him. Most of the time, when he rode alone, she was there.

In days past she had been the phantom of his first and most passionate love, the woman who had died in the automobile wreck; on this particular lonely ride, however, Vi Coteau had become the ghost. As the sounds of Bear Lake Lodge faded and vanished behind him, leaving the voice of the mountain wind in the pine boughs humming to the steady rhythm of Brownie's hooves, he found himself carrying on an imaginary conversation.

Wonder what Ken and the wrangler were smirking at back there, he said. *It's like they knew something I don't know. Something seemed funny to them. Seemed like it was awful funny that I would be riding over Flattop and into the north valley alone. Don't know what's so darn amusing about it. Maybe they think I look funny in my civvies instead of my uniform. Maybe my fly's unbuttoned? They were grinning like I had my hat on backward. Or like I had egg on my face and didn't know it.*

Whatever had amused Ken and the wrangler so much, it didn't matter now. The Flattop trail curved into the trees, shutting off the last sight of the lodge and the lake, and the familiar calming silence of the forest folded around him. In the rhythm of hooves and creaking saddle leather he felt his muscles relaxing, found his mind finally slipping free of the white stone mystery.

Wilderness again, he said to his imaginary Vi Coteau. *Nothing but a narrow dirt trail connecting us with the world of people. I wonder if any of the tourists who use this trail ever, ever realize how much wilderness there is on either side? They go up to the mountain on this trail, make their Kodak pictures of each other, eat their sandwiches, come back again, and brag to their city friends about being "outdoor" people. If they were ever to leave the trail and wander for an hour in practically any direction, they wouldn't be anything but tiny, weak animals surrounded by the wild.*

With things waiting to kill you, the imagined Vi replied.

Darn right. The cold air alone can kill you. The rain, gravity itself, starvation, lightning. Even a broken ankle can be fatal. And the predators, like the ones you're thinking of. But there's always a few of us who are drawn to the place. Blindfold us, take us anywhere in the world, spin us around, and we'd head straight for the nearest wilderness. If we can't hike into the wilderness we'll stand and stare into it. Or if we're too old or too crippled or too poor to travel to the edge we'll read about it and look at pictures of it. The worst thing would be if it wasn't there. If we knew it wasn't there anymore. If the day ever came when the entire wilderness was gone, something would be gone inside us, too. We'd soon be gone, too.

There you go, she replied, *talking all philosophical again.*

He could imagine the movements of her lips as she pronounced the word, "philosophical." Her eyes would be smiling.

Right you are. Why don't let's enjoy our fresh mountain air and think about something else. How about we reminisce about that certain evening after the formal dinner in Denver. Remember? When we went to your place after the dinner party . . .

You'd better stop thinking about that night and get me out of your head, Vi whispered to him. *You're coming up on a party of trail walkers. Can't have them see a man riding along mumbling to himself and smirking like a little boy after his first kiss.*

The four hikers heard McIntyre coming and stepped off the trail to let the horses pass. He stopped to exchange greetings: since he was out of uniform maybe they wouldn't pester him with tourist-type questions.

"Good morning," he began.

"Great morning!" one of them agreed. "Are you heading for the top, too?"

"No," McIntyre said. He pointed away into the deeply forested mountain valleys to the north. "I'm headed north. There's a place where . . . uh, where I'm going fishing."

"Hey, a good place? Lots of trout? Maybe we could go there!"

"Actually it's an ordinary little creek with little brook trout. I'm mostly after the peace and quiet."

"Oh, roger that. Boy, there's lots of peace and quiet up here, right? We're going to find the medicine wheel place. Take pictures for the folks back in Missouri. Ever been there?"

"Missouri, or the medicine wheel? A few times," McIntyre said.

"I guess nobody knows who built it. Stone-age Indians, some say."

"So I've heard," McIntyre replied. "I'd better be going now. You folks stay safe, okay?"

One of the hikers laughed.

"You sound like a ranger!" she said. "Or my mother. Or both!"

Another mile up the trail he paused at a trickle of an alpine creek and let the horses drink. Brownie and the packhorse tasted the water and snorted loudly to let him know it was freezing cold. But they drank anyway, and he rode on. He left the last of the tall trees behind and entered the regions of krumholtz and stunted willow and he rode on. Off to his right he caught sight of the faint path leading to the hidden campsite and he shook his head to clear away the memory of a wrapped corpse bent across a packsaddle and he rode on. He arrived at the trail junction where one track led up toward the summit of Flattop Mountain and the other pointed north across a treeless ridge of alpine tundra toward the deep shadowy valleys beyond.

Here he paused and looked back, resting his hand on the cantle, without knowing why he had turned nor what he had hoped to see behind him.

What am I looking for? Other people, coming up the trail?

The wandering breeze that stirred Brownie's mane also whispered in McIntyre's ear.

Vi Coteau won't be coming, the wisp of wind seemed to say. *She's sitting at her desk in the city where she belongs. And you, Mister Ranger, you're where you belong, too.*

He turned his face north, touched a heel to Brownie's flank, and went on.

Ranger McIntyre could have saved himself a couple of miles of riding had he chosen the lower trail, the one which branched off in the forest and followed a wooded valley down the other side of Flattop. Not many people used it. He would have found his solitude there. The trail that led up and over the tundra, however, held a particular attraction. He could feel it the instant he emerged from the timber and caught the first hint of alpine breeze on his cheek. Up here a man could see for miles, could see seemingly endless mountain ranges rising, could look back and see the flat plains stretched to the horizon. A man squinted from the sun's shining, which was unfiltered by any dust or smoke. He could see every contour of ground, every lichen-covered stone, every animal burrow. Yellow and purple alpine flowers seemed to pop out of the mossy soil like bright spots of paint.

Here he rode more slowly and here he breathed more deeply. Clock time lost meaning for him as if he had entered into a realm of God's finest infinity. No lavish breakfasts waited for him here, no jigsaw puzzles, no deep streams where German brown trout lurked. None of the things he loved could be found in the high, cold, treeless reaches at this altitude, yet every time he came up out of the forested slopes and onto the tundra he felt, if only for a few moments, it was where he would always belong.

With nothing in the air to hinder it, no city smoke, no haze, the morning sun warmed his back and shoulders, throwing a shadow of man and horses onto the tundra. Ranger McIntyre watched the shadow move along the ground, watched how it changed shape with each changing contour of the earth. He found himself remembering a winter's evening at the ranger barracks. There was a hot and heavy game of pinochle going on and Ranger Don Post brought out his Victrola record machine and played his newest records, including one called "Me and My Shadow." After hearing it four or five times the whole group could sing along.

McIntyre smiled a wry smile. *Me*, he thought. *Me and my shadow. And a horse. All alone and feelin' blue.*

"My dad always said everything had its price," McIntyre told Brownie. "I guess if a guy is hired to do a job where he can live in country like this, have all this to look at, well, I guess there's a price. The price might be that you almost always have to be alone to enjoy it."

They arrived at the crest of the ridge and rested while they gazed down into the maze of wooded valleys below.

"All downhill from here, girl," he said.

But he was thinking about what had happened down there. And up at Flattop. Three men were lying dead and stiff in the coroner's cooler. If he had only figured out the pieces of the puzzle earlier . . . granted, there was no way he would have known about those plants, but he felt like he had let the white rock thing distract him. He fooled around too long, going up in an airplane to survey the scene, putting big pieces together while one or two small ones might have been enough.

He uttered the word "dammit" aloud. Brownie turned her head toward him, hearing a word she had come to associate with herself—as in "Brownie dammit stop it."

"Not you, Brownie," he said. "Me. The minute I heard the climber say he'd been attacked I should've scoured the whole area for tracks. Maybe I could've found Tadashi before he hurt somebody else. Or himself. Or maybe I'm thinking too much. Nuts to it! A guy all alone up here, he never knows what notions are going to pop into his head. C'mon. Let's head on down to the valley and find our tent. Instead of taking another day off maybe we'll ride back home tomorrow."

He touched a heel to the mare's flank. Horses, man,

phantom, and shadows left the ridge of tundra and made their way down toward the dark green forest. The forest seemed to be waiting.

Brownie was the first to catch a whiff of woodsmoke. The ranger and his horses were carefully picking their way through heavy timber, following the faint traces of the path used by Tadashi and Kiyoshi. But less than a mile from the camping meadow Brownie began tossing her head up and down to get the ranger's attention. He had been busy watching out for low tree branches and hadn't noticed her nostrils flaring and twitching. She tossed her head again, jerking the reins. Brownie didn't know where McIntyre's brain was, but she knew it wasn't paying enough attention to his surroundings.

"Smell something?" he finally asked.

Another couple of minutes went by and the ranger smelled it, too. Smoke. Smoke from burning wood.

McIntyre scanned the sky, or what he could see of it between the tall spruce and fir trees. Clear blue. No plume of thick white rising to show there was a forest fire. No sign of forest fire anywhere, which was good: the last place you want to be when a forest fire breaks out is in heavy timber with dry branches and deep piles of needles and cones everywhere.

"It's a campfire," he told her. "Maybe."

More minutes passed before he drew rein. This time he didn't need the swiveling of Brownie's ears to warn him. He heard the gunshots himself. Four shots. Pop! Pop! Pop! Pop!, in close order.

McIntyre had consumed innumerable dime westerns and

countless detective stories during the long snowbound months of winter in his cabin. Gunshots in those books usually "rang out" or "echoed" or "shattered the silence" but in reality any distant gunshots you hear in the mountains are simply noises like a kid's balloon bursting. Shotguns closer to you give off a drawn-out whoomph. Rifles shots are quick and sharp like a wooden plank cracking in half. Small caliber pistols make more of a champagne cork noise, while a heavier pistol like a .45 has more of a booming sound.

These were pistol shots. Smaller, probably a .38 or .32 caliber.

Someone somewhere near the meadow ahead was shooting a pistol, presumably shooting at something. Most likely a pine cone or tin can, possibly an animal. People could be camped in the meadow and one of them decided to take a few pot shots at a stump. Or they might be killing animals illegally. Some guys couldn't resist shooting at squirrels or birds. Killing any animal in the park, except in self-defense, was illegal. Even carrying a loaded gun was illegal.

"Brownie," he said in a whisper as he dismounted, "I'm going to leave you here to take care of the packhorse. I need to sneak ahead with the carbine and see what's up. Stay here. Stay."

He slid the carbine from the scabbard and crept ahead down the track, moving with caution, alert to every sound and sign of movement. His mind was sifting and sorting all the possibilities, making and discarding theories and deductions. This time he was going to figure out what was going on before anyone got hurt. As he picked his way through the woods he called up his memories of the small meadow and arranged them into a picture. The tent sat on the west side, facing the morning sun; the creek was about fifty yards farther on and down the slope. There was a stand of aspen downstream, with a thick carpet of grass; the thing to do would be to circle through the spruce trees, slip into those aspen and come up on the back of the tent, then stay out of sight until he identified who the campers were.

Pop! Pop! Pop! Pop!

McIntyre dropped to his belly in the grass of the aspen grove. The shots had come from the direction of the creek. He could see his tent just as they had left it. He could also see most of the meadow. A solitary horse grazed there. Nothing else moved. Probably one person camping alone.

A person shooting four shots in quick succession. Whoever it was, they were doing target practice. When you shoot at an animal you only shoot once, or twice real fast if you didn't hit it with the first shot. You save your ammunition until you see if the animal is down. You might need to dispatch it with a third shot. Now, why only four shots, if they're doing target practice? Using a five-shot revolver with one chamber left empty for safety reasons? Better not assume anything about the gun. Treat it as loaded and deadly. Don't take chances. Might be a six-shot revolver and the shooter saves two live rounds "just in case." Same with an automatic. A guy might save two or three rounds in the clip so as not to be caught with an empty gun.

Cripes, McIntyre thought. *A little while ago I was enjoying being alone with the mountain and the forest and now all I can think about is whether some clown is shooting an automatic or a revolver.*

One shooter, one gun. Now, where was he? Somewhere near the creek, obviously. McIntyre was lying on his belly behind a fallen aspen, trying to see the creek, but there was only a teasing little glint of sunlight on water farther down the slope. He cradled the carbine in his arms and slithered from log to bush to tree. He crawled ten yards, twenty yards without seeing anyone. Now a stone's throw from the creek he could finally peek around the trees and see the shooter.

In fact, he could see quite a lot of the shooter. She wore no shoes, no socks. In fact the only thing Vi seemed to be wearing was a clingy garment, probably silk, held up by thin shoulder straps and reaching barely to mid-thigh. Her other clothing was in a pile next to her and her pistol was on top of the pile. McIntyre stood up and stepped out of the trees. Vi Coteau looked back at him over her bare shoulder.

"Hello, Mister Ranger," she said.

"Going swimming, are you?" he replied.

"Is there any law against a girl washing herself beside a stream?"

"Nope. But the park does have rules about shooting guns. Lucky for you I'm off duty," he said, clearing the live round from his carbine while walking toward her.

"My weekly target practice," she explained. "I'm afraid I've killed one of your pine cones. I'll reimburse you for it. So . . ." she asked innocently, "are you just out here doing some sightseeing?"

"I'll say I am. Wow."

"Thank you. And were you wondering what I'm doing here?"

"I figured you'd get around to telling me, sooner or later. No rush. I'll stand here and wait. You go on with what you were doing."

"You're a naughty ranger, aren't you. And you've got grass and leaves on your shirt and pants. What did you do, try to sneak up on your belly?"

McIntyre brushed himself off.

"Okay," he said, "so what are you doing here?"

"It was Polly," Vi replied. "She said you couldn't go flying because you were coming up to retrieve your tent and stuff. So I thought I'd surprise you. Agent Canilly thinks I'm over at the irrigation ditch project looking for more cases of peonage. I wasn't really expecting you until later in the afternoon, though."

"So I see," McIntyre said, picking the last pine needle from his trousers.

"Yes, you do," Vi Coteau said.

"I think I'll go find Brownie and the packhorse now."

"Fine."

"Give you a chance to, you know, put some clothes on."

"Fine," she repeated. " 'Bye, now."

" 'Bye."

"And Tim?"

"Yes?"

"Look where you're walking. If you keep your head turned around watching me you'll trip over something."

The afternoon passed slowly for them, as afternoons often do in the luxurious privacy of the wilderness where all schedules are cancelled and where worldly pressures vanish like a blue smoke. Ranger McIntyre investigated the fishing situation, deciding to wait until morning to catch a mess of brookies for breakfast.

"You can have your fancy fish dinners," he told her, "but nothing, absolutely nothing, can beat the taste of trout right from an icy mountain stream into the hot frying pan. I even brought bacon to lay over them."

"Speaking of which," she said, picking up another piece of firewood to add to the bundle in her arms, "maybe it's time we began thinking about supper. Before the sun drops behind the mountain."

"Right you are," the ranger agreed. "The air turns chilly early up here. Let's carry the rest of our firewood into camp, make sure we have enough water in the pot, then get to cookin'."

"Gettin' to cookin'," however, turned out to be the cause of their very first disagreement.

"I brought you a surprise," Vi said, opening her pack.

"I've already seen it," he said. "Down at the creek?"

"If you're going to be a silly ranger I'm not going to share with you. Look!"

She held up a bottle of French red wine.

"Remember Mr. Leup? The formal dinner party?"

"Where you made me wear a tuxedo? Who could forget?"

"Well, he was grateful for our help and insisted on giving me four bottles from his private stash. Very legal. He bought it before prohibition and keeps it for private use only. And look here!"

The second surprise was an oilskin packet that turned out to contain a nicely matched pair of thick T-bone steaks. Vi laughed to see the wolfish gleam in McIntyre's eyes. She reached into the pack once more.

"And potatoes," she said proudly, setting them beside the fire. "If you'll put a pot of water to boil and pass me the large frying pan, we'll be dining in style!"

"What's the water for? Washing dishes?"

"No, silly. To boil the potatoes."

"We'd better slice 'em and fry 'em."

"Fry them?"

"Sure. I've got a jar of lard here in my food bag somewhere."

"Did you say lard?"

"Sure."

"Tim?"

"What?"

"Have you ever noticed my figure? At all?"

"Once or twice. Maybe more. A gentleman doesn't like to say."

"This is not the shape of a girl who eats lard. Now boil the water."

"No."

Had she been standing rather than sitting beside the fire, she would have stamped her foot at him. If she could not have her potatoes baked, with a nice garnish, she would have them boiled.

And since it was she who had bought them and brought them all the way up the mountain, it was she who would decide. She reached for the pot.

"No," he said, taking it from her hand and setting it out of reach. "We'll fry the potatoes alongside the steaks."

He saw the color come to her cheeks. As his father used to say, she was getting her Irish up.

"You are so stubborn!" she exclaimed.

"True. But I'm also hungry. Boiling those potatoes would take six or eight hours before they'd be soft enough to eat."

"What *are* you talking about?" Vi emphasized the word "are."

"Boiling water. Any idea how high we are? Ten thousand feet above sea level. Up this high, water boils away before it's hot enough to cook eggs, beans, potatoes, anything. Your spuds would sit there soaking in warm water for hours. Not to mention the amount of fuel it would take. You slice the spuds. I'll open the lard and grease the pan."

McIntyre didn't particularly like the way she was glaring at him as she drew her hunting knife from its sheath.

"Tadashi and Kiyoshi, they had rice," she said.

"Probably precooked. Either that, or they soaked it for a couple of days and fried it in grease."

"Okay, Mister Clever Camper, so what's the pot of water for?"

"Might want to wash our hands. Might want to douse the campfire. Or I might decide to rinse out my socks."

Watching her guillotine the potatoes with her hunting knife, McIntyre decided he had better say no more, for the time being.

It was a very contented ranger who lay back on the packsaddle to sip his early evening coffee. The endless blue mountain sky had begun to turn steely gray, the individual spruce trees were showing up as sharp-edged silhouettes on the ridge, the fire was burning without dark smoke to irritate the eyes, and he was full to the brim with good meat and wine. Best of all, he could look across the campfire at Vi Coteau reclining on her own saddle.

"What do you want to do tomorrow?" she asked. "Ride back to the lodge?"

"Oh, heck no. No hurry. No, if you don't really intend to ride on over to the irrigation project, I'd like to do one more thing to clean up the case of the white rocks. I'd like to open the cairn we found and make sure there's no body in it."

"I thought you said there was, the way Brownie reacted?"

"I think she was smelling the dead horse," McIntyre said.

"Might be someone else in the cairn."

"No. I'm sure it's a fake. Darn, we should've asked Kiyoshi about it. I forgot."

"I bet we'll find a body if we tear it down," she said.

"Oh? What do you want to bet, Miss Smart Aleck?"

Vi poked a stick into the fire and stirred the coals. She took a sip of wine from her tin cup. Finally she looked across the fire at the ranger.

"Okay," she said. "From close observation, I have deduced that you enjoy eating."

"You're a regular detective, you are."

"There are places to eat in Denver. We call them 'restaurants.' The best of them are very posh, very hoity-toity. Formal clothes only. Orchestras for dancing. There's one called the Archives. It's on Capitol Hill. Senators and congressmen go there."

"So what?" he said.

"So here's my bet: if there's a body in the cairn you'll buy me dinner at the Archives. If there isn't a body, I'll buy you dinner. Same place, anything on the menu. If you win you won't even have to dance with me unless you want to."

"Let me guess. You'd be wearing a dress that would make me want to?"

"Bingo!" she said.

The sun vanished behind the peaks, darkness crept slyly up into the mountain valleys, allowing the million stars to pop out one by one. Having covered the fire and cached the food, having set the water canteens within reach, along with the flashlight, the pair snuggled down into their sleeping bags. Vi was nearly asleep when she heard McIntyre swear in the inky blackness.

"Damn," he said.

"Forget something?"

"No! I realized something! You're a conniving little devil. It took me this long to figure it out. Whichever way our bet goes, I'll still have to put on that darn tuxedo and take you to dinner. And it'll turn out to be one of those restaurants where they give you six spoons and five forks and your own tiny saltshaker that you're never supposed to use."

"You got it," she said. "You figured it out. And you're the one who's supposed to know all about traps and snares."

"Oh, that was nice!" Vi Coteau said. She was standing and stretching her arms into the blue morning sky.

"Brook trout, eggs, and bacon," McIntyre said. "And boiled coffee. Up here it's pretty much lukewarm when it boils. Still, there's nothing like it anywhere. It always tastes extra good when you're outdoors."

"I mean the whole thing," Vi replied. "Sitting by the fire and chatting far into the night, watching all those jillions of stars, the nice cuddle before going to sleep. Waking up with sun pouring into the tent. I see what you meant about having a three-sided tent."

"I never did like waking up inside a pup tent, particularly,"

McIntyre said. "Or even in a pyramid tent, anything where you're all closed in. The air in the morning inside one of those things, it seems . . . I don't know. Secondhand? Stale."

"Shall I help you clean up?"

"Not much to do," he said. "The bones, eggshells, and fish guts we'll bury in the woods so as not to attract four-legged visitors. I'll take the plates and pan to the creek and scrub them with sand and we'll be ready to go. Tomorrow it'll be your turn to wash up."

Vi Coteau stretched again.

"Time really does seem to slow down here, doesn't it? Here we are, up and dressed and fed and I haven't looked at my watch even once." She laughed. "Come to think of it, I don't even know where it is! In my coat pocket, I guess. Who cares? What a perfectly perfect summer day this is! Look how blue the sky is. And the patches of white snow on the mountaintops . . . what did you call them? Not glaciers?"

"Snowfields. Glaciers move. They slide down the mountain. What we call permanent snowfields stay in place all summer."

"I bet you'll be sad to see winter coming," she said. "No more camping or long rides in the mountains. What do you do up here all winter, anyway?"

"That's exactly what the tourists keep asking. Say! You're not an undercover tourist are you? Sent by the motor club, disguised as an FBI secretary, trying to find out ranger secrets? Waiting for a chance to feed chocolate bars to my chipmunks?"

"Darn!" Vi said. "You got me, Officer. Put the cuffs on and take me away."

She held out her hands. And he took them.

"So . . ." she said. Because he was holding her hands she spoke more softly. "What is a ranger going to be doing this coming winter, for instance?"

"Weekends usually bring people up from the city with their

sleds and skis, which means I do a lot of patrols. Mostly pulling cars out of the ditch, doing first aid on skiers who have run into a tree. Or doing first aid on the tree. Let's see: I catch poachers, I cut cord after cord of firewood, I haul hay for Brownie, teach her new tricks, play gin rummy at the ranger barracks. I keep tabs on the closed-up lodges and cabins. Empty the rat traps, check to see the doors and windows are secure and so forth."

"Like when we inspected Fall River Lodge together. Wow, was it cold and dark in that building! Gave me the shivers."

McIntyre picked up the tin plates and the frying pan and started toward the creek. Vi followed him.

"There was another motor club spy at the lodge the other night, I think," she said brightly, making conversation as he knelt down to scrub the plates.

"At least that's what Ken thought he was. Motor clubs hire writers to stay at places and write critiques for their guidebooks."

"So you did stay at the lodge," McIntyre said.

"Sure. Wanted to surprise you. I came up the night before and arranged for horses and food and packs, got everything ready for an early start. Ken was very helpful. He even hid the Marmon for me so you wouldn't see it. It's under a tarp out back of the lodge."

"You know," McIntyre said, "when I saddled up and told them where I was headed for, Ken and that wrangler of his were both grinning like the girl in the toothpaste ad. Now I know why. Nothing funnier to a man than watching another man about to get ambushed by a woman."

"Anyway," Vi went on, "there was this guy at dinner. Very curious about what the area looks like in winter."

"How so? I mean, how's that unusual?"

"He started out the usual way, asking Ken and the waitress, and me, how many people live up here in winter. He wondered what kind of security there was, whether somebody goes around to all the cabins and lodges when they're closed. He asked if the sheriff ever comes to the village on patrol or anything like that. Oh, and how difficult it is to drive to some of the places like Bear Lake Lodge when there's deep snow on the roads. Did they keep the roads plowed, and so forth."

"You're right. Sounds suspicious. I bet he's secretly a skier or snowshoe guy looking for winter recreation. Very sneaky."

"He was curious about lodge and cabin décor, too. Kind of odd for a man, unless he's a decorator."

"Décor?" McIntyre said.

"He asked about photos. He wondered if the village library or a local photographer might have photos of the interiors of various lodges and summer homes. Or if anyone remembered whether any of the places had paintings on the walls. Framed oil paintings. Said he was an amateur collector and always on the lookout for old paintings. But later on, Ken said the art collector story sounded thin. It was more like he was collecting information."

"Might be," McIntyre agreed. "Maybe he's another one of those college professors. A historian, probably. Either way, it's none of my business."

He handed her the clean plates and pan and stood up to brush sand from his knees. He was relieved to hear Vi Coteau chatting about other people again: maybe she had put Tadashi's death out of her mind. He knew her well enough to know that she always preferred things to be orderly, logical. Manageable. Although she had said little about the shooting incident, McIntyre sensed that she was deeply disturbed by it. Instead of killing Tadashi she might have yelled a warning, or she might have aimed for his leg or even fired a shot over his head to distract him. Aiming for the rock had been a tragic mistake. She had taken a human life. What made her feel even worse about it, McIntyre guessed, was having the corpse lashed across a horse that would be with them all the way back to the lodge.

Poor gal, he thought. *It'll be a long time before she'll be able to point a gun at anybody. I know how she's feeling. No more gunplay for her, not for quite a while.*

She spoke of it several times during the day. There seemed to be no getting away from reminders of the incident. After putting the campsite in order and watering the horses and picketing them in fresh grass, McIntyre saw Vi stroking Brownie's flank and looking absently at the mountaintop as if remembering that dead horse in the woods. They went for a hike, following the faint trail across the creek and up the next ridge where McIntyre could point into the distance at a faint line of dirt cutting across a mountain. He told her that they were looking at the irrigation ditch project and she fell silent again. She remained silent most of the walk back to camp.

She was cheerful again by lunchtime, kidding him because he hadn't brought the makings for egg salad sandwiches.

"Didn't know you were coming," he said.

"What now?" she said, when they had finished the bread and cheese and cold steak leftovers. "Shall we have another lesson in wilderness camping?"

McIntyre didn't reply, but got up and went to the tent. Their sleeping bags were draped over the ridge pole to air. He took them down and spread them out beneath the awning where they would be shaded from the sun.

"Always keep the sun in mind while you're up here," he told her. "The air is so clear, you see. And thin. It can feel nice and cool, but that ol' sun will be frying your skin."

She watched with interest while the ranger stretched himself out on his sleeping bag and closed his eyes. He was actually going to take a nap.

"At the risk of repeating myself," she said, "what now?"

James C. Work

"Siesta," McIntyre replied without opening his eyes. "Sit down, relax. Or lie down. We're not on the clock, you know. I'm going to have a little nap. Afterward we'll go take that cairn apart and find out if there's anyone in it."

She came under the awning and lay down beside him. *It is very relaxing,* she thought.

Almost an hour later, Vi's relaxation was ended by the sound of a horse snorting nearby. She blinked, yawned, stretched, felt a twinge in her back as she propped herself up on one elbow, and found Tim standing there with both horses saddled and ready.

"Have a good nap?" he asked. "Let's go have a look inside that cairn, whenever you're ready."

CHAPTER FIFTEEN
A PARTING SHOT. OR TWO.

Ranger McIntyre was all business the next morning as they broke camp. To his way of thinking, the worst part of a camping trip was packing up and saying goodbye to a place. It was like burying a comrade, or a pet animal, a process you wanted to do quickly and carefully and be done with. Everything should be picked up and packed up and the place should be left looking so natural that you couldn't even imagine, or remember, exactly how it had looked with tent and fire. Better to pack away the good memories. Wipe away the place where something had happened but would not, in that place, ever happen again.

Neither he nor Vi Coteau had very much to say while they rolled the sleeping bags and fastened them with straps, nor while they folded the tent. He carried the tent poles into the trees and tossed them here and there; he used a tree branch to sweep away the remains of the ash from their campfire and used a stick to knock down and spread the clumps of horse manure. When they were mounted and riding away they both looked back and, except for a small black charred circle that would soon recover and some flattened grass where the tent had stood, there was nothing left to see.

They rode quietly, as if everything had been said around the campfire the evening before, each topic had been explored; it was as if both of them were mentally basking in the morning afterglow of those wonderful hours of talking and laughing. Twice he spoke to thank her for coming to the mountains to surprise him, and for bringing steak and wine, and twice before they reached the cairn site she said what a beautiful day it was and how much she regretted having to go back to Denver.

"You're repeating yourself," he said.

"I know. Should we stop and rebuild the cairn, do you think?" she asked as they drew near the spot. "Or scatter the rocks so it's all natural again?"

"I don't think so," the ranger replied. "It was good to bury the broken saddle because it's nothing but trash, but we can leave the rocks. Maybe someday, somebody will discover a man-made pile of rocks covering an old log and maybe they'll wonder who made it, and why. I thought it was pretty cute of Kiyoshi and Fannie Painter to build their cairn over a log like that . . . it saved them having to find twice as many stones."

As for the dead horse there was nothing to do except salvage the bridle and bit and leave the carcass to slowly return to nature. When McIntyre came back out of the trees carrying the bridle, he found Vi Coteau sitting on her horse, her face like a mask without expression.

"Still thinking about it, huh?" McIntyre said.

"Yes," she said. "I was thinking about his family, too. Tadashi must have family, somewhere. I wonder if they would under-stand. Why he died, I mean. There might be a wife waiting for him."

"Could be," McIntyre said. "The coroner and the others, they'll do everything possible. They'll notify the contract company and the company will know who to inform. Nothing you can do about it."

He tucked the bridle under the packsaddle lashing and re-mounted.

"If there's a family," Vi Coteau continued, "maybe our government has some kind of compensation. You know, a fund of some sort for innocent victims."

"Well," McIntyre said, "you can find out when you get back to your office. Right now and right here it's a beautiful sky-blue day, we're on our way to timberline and we'll make it to the lodge by late afternoon."

"You really love your world above timberline, don't you?" she asked.

"You bet," he replied. "A friend of mine calls it 'real country.' Whenever he and I get up onto the tundra he looks all around and says 'Tim, now we're in real country.' I love it when everything is taken care of, too, when a problem is settled and we don't have anything to do except ride along and enjoy the sights. Everyone and everything is accounted for. Once you and I get back to work there won't be anything to show what happened, except for some official reports stuck in some dusty ol' filing cabinet."

"My filing cabinets are not dusty," she said, trying to smile.

Their path took them up and up into the valley and neither of them spoke when they went by the cliff where Tadashi had tried to ambush McIntyre. But the ranger did look at Vi and saw the faraway expression again. Poor kid.

"You know," she said after they had left the last of the timber behind and were working their way through the maze of krumholtz, "I doubt that I'll ever be able to point a gun at anyone again. I'm officially an executive secretary, you know? I think I'll stick the .38 in a drawer and concentrate on being a good little secretary. I'm just not sure, Tim. I'm not sure. The only thing I'm convinced of is that I'm not cut out to be a field agent. I thought I was. I wanted to be. But now . . ."

McIntyre raised his eyes to the summit of Flattop Mountain as it came into view.

"Got an idea," he said. "It'll mean getting back to the lodge late, but I think we'll stop at the medicine circle."

They tied their horses at the foot of the final pitch and

dismounted to climb up to the flat alpine expanse that gives the peak its name.

"Want to tell me what we're doing?" Vi asked.

McIntyre stopped to rest on a boulder.

"I'm not certain it'll work," he said, "especially since we don't have time to put you through the whole ritual of fasting and resting and letting your mind go blank, but it might help a little. I know it helped me a couple of years ago when I was going through an awful dark time. In fact, that was the first time I saw the medicine circle. Yankee Horse, he showed it to me."

"Yankee who?"

"Yankee Horse. Part Cheyenne, part Arapaho, part something else and a quarter part lunatic. But he's kind, and he's awful wise sometimes. The thing is, there's a relatively quick way—when your mind's preoccupied with a problem you can't shake off—to find the best perspective, the best way to look at things. Your medicine direction, that's what Yankee Horse would call it."

He got up off the boulder and led the way up over the edge and out onto the flat, treeless tundra.

"I'm not taking off my clothes and lying in the moss," Vi said.

McIntyre laughed.

"Darn," he said. "And here I was, planning to steal your duds and run away leaving you in your bare-skin birthday suit. But no, it's nothing like that. We don't even need the medicine circle, particularly, but it helps to get the mind into the right mood."

The air was dead calm and the sun was hot as they walked together toward the circle of rocks.

"Got your gun on you?" he asked.

"Sure. Why?"

"We can use it for this quick way I mentioned. When we get there, I want you to stand in the center with your pistol in your hand. I'm going to blindfold you with my bandanna. Then you're going to take your shooter's stance and very, very slowly turn while pointing the gun at the horizon."

"And what's it supposed to prove?"

"You'll see. If it works. Yankee Horse had me do it, only with my fly rod. I kept turning and making false casts. Pretty soon I realized that there was one particular direction that felt the best. Can't explain it, but when I made a blind cast in that one direction it felt, well, it felt more right. More natural."

"More right?" she said, smiling a little at his grammar.

"You'll see. It'll be your medicine direction, your guide to how to look at the Tadashi thing. Somewhere in the four directions, if we're lucky, we'll discover your best way to see things. The thing is, in the four directions we've got north for wisdom, south for innocence, east for perspective, and west for insight. Like I said, it's quick and it may not work. But might help a little. Shall I tell you about medicine animals?"

Vi stopped and sighed and pretended to look at her wristwatch.

"Go ahead," she said.

"Okay. Sometimes you've got a natural way of dealing with a problem, only you don't know it. Now, north, that's the buffalo direction. The old buffalo, he stays out on the open prairie where he sees everything. He's calm and thoughtful. He knows that the grass and the flowers need to die so he can live, just as he knows that he will die so that a wolf or a man can live. So maybe you need to look at it that way. Or there's the eagle. He's the east. Yellow direction where the sun is brightest. Eagle sees everything from high, gets the whole picture all at once. Sees how it all fits together, how everything belongs somehow. Not like your mouse. Little mouse—she's the south direction of in-nocence—she doesn't need to be concerned with big pictures or wise perspectives; she just needs to follow her whiskers to a bit of food. She runs from shadows, like a hawk makes, but that's good for a mouse to do."

Vi was smiling at him again.

"Sorry," he said. "Got carried away there."

"No," she said. "Go on."

"All right. One more animal. Maybe your medicine is bear medicine. She's the west, where the sun goes away and things get dark. She gathers food, sure. She knows where things belong in her world, too. But mainly she goes into her dark den and curls up and thinks about being bearish. She's the introspection animal, see?"

"You think we'll find out that I'm a bear?"

"Dunno. I wouldn't doubt it. I'm guessing you'd be somewhere between bear and mouse. I think your best way of being Vi Coteau is to scurry here and there, exploring everything close up, but also to pull into yourself and think about you."

"Geez, I'm with a ranger philosopher! What are you, a buffalo?"

"What are you, a wisenheimer? C'mon. Let's get you started. Get your gun out."

"Look away," she ordered.

Vi Coteau was still reaching for her .38 when the first pistol shot boomed across the tundra. The bullet skidded across a flat rock with a screaming whang and went whistling off into space.

"Down!" she yelled. "Over here! Quick!"

McIntyre didn't need to be asked twice. Crouching low, zigzagging across the few yards separating him from Vi, he dove into the shallow depression in the tundra alongside her. He pulled out his own revolver.

"You okay?" he asked.

"I'm fine," she said. "I think it came from that direction."

As if to prove she was correct, a second shot boomed and echoed and they heard the ricocheting bullet whine away.

"Who the hell . . ." McIntyre swore.

"You're the super tracker," she said. "Did you see any sign of a third person? An accomplice? Somebody who'd be up here looking for those doggone plants?"

"Never even thought about it," McIntyre said. "It seemed logical to assume that Tadashi didn't know anybody who would help him, especially somebody with a gun. Where would he find help? Although it could be a friend of Fannie Painter, I suppose."

"But she's in the lockup. Would she have had time to contact someone and send them up here for plants? Or seeds? I can't really envision her doing it. Send a killer, I mean. She's not the type."

"Dunno," the ranger admitted. "No idea who it is or why they're trying to shoot us. But instead of lying here and speculating about it, we'd better figure out what to do. Don't you think?"

Vi snapped open the cylinder of her revolver, checked to be sure all chambers were loaded, then flipped it shut again.

"Are there any bullets in that .45 of yours?" she asked.

"Of course," he said. "Why do you ask?"

"Because I'm getting to know you. Let's take stock of our situation real quick. We're out here in the open with no cover anywhere around. He's probably over the crest of the hill."

"Where the medicine circle is," McIntyre suggested.

"That does seem logical," she said. "Okay. I'm smaller and I'm faster than you, so I'm going to make a dash to the right, see if I can keep the rise of ground between me and him. Why don't you go left, stay as low as you can, circle around, and maybe you can pop up behind him. You concentrate on getting behind him, I'll focus on watching for him. Try not to get in my line of fire, either, because the first movement I see, I'm going to shoot. Got it?"

"You sound like my old squadron commander," he said with

a grin. "One of these days I need to sign up for an FBI tactics class. How about if I fire a shot over him before we make our move. Just to let him know we're armed? Maybe he'll surrender."

"You fire a shot over him if you want to," Vi said, "but I'm going to save my ammo. Whoever that bastard is, he scared the heck out of me. If he pops off another shot at me I'm going put five .38 slugs in him."

"Miss Coteau!" McIntyre said. "I'm shocked! Such language!"

"Oh, be quiet. You'll hear worse if that misbegotten *pistolero* catches us lying here in this hole. I'll count to three and we'll run for it."

The *pistolero* turned out to be a lucky man on three counts. First, there had been only two bullets left in his .45 automatic; when McIntyre came rushing up with his own gun drawn, the shooter was sitting on the ground trying to reload. Second, it was lucky he was sitting on the ground. Had he stood up to see what was going on, he might have provoked Vi Coteau into unloading her weapon into him. Third, McIntyre recognized the open laboratory case, the tweed jacket, and the figure of none other than Professor Howard Warren, horticulturalist.

The professor heard heavy breathing behind him, twisted around, recognized Ranger McIntyre, and uttered a single word.

"Bear!"

"What?"

"A bear! Attacked me! I shot at him, but I don't think I hit him! He went that way, over the rise!"

McIntyre grabbed the empty .45 automatic out of Warren's hand and yelled to Vi.

"Coteau! Coteau! All clear!"

"Who's that?" she called back.

"A ranger!"

He hurried toward the rise, meeting Vi halfway.

"All yours," he said, handing her the automatic. "Be careful, though. He's still armed with a magnifying glass and tweezers."

A bear, McIntyre thought as he went striding over the tundra. A ten-foot silvertip grizzly, probably. Probably the same one that nearly mauled the nature girl. The short grass and dry ground showed no tracks, but at least the treeless, flat tundra allowed him to see hundreds of yards in every direction. He kept going.

And then he saw it. An unmistakable black shape, more of a cinnamon color, hunched over with its fat round backside toward him. With the breeze in his favor McIntyre was able to approach within a few yards before he spoke.

"So it was you," he said calmly.

She looked up from the kinnikinnick bush she'd been combing for berries, then rose up and twisted around to face him. A small black bear, a sow, and from the looks of things she had birthed a cub or two earlier in the spring. They were probably hanging around somewhere. Waiting for mom to find them some food.

"Did you frighten the professor back there?" McIntyre asked. "Bad bear. Did he look like another bear to you? Because he was wearing brown clothes and was probably down on all fours looking at his plants? I bet you surprised him, huh?"

The sow cocked her head slightly. To McIntyre it looked as if she wished he would go away so she could get back to hunting for berries.

"Did he yell at you? That was a bad human. Well . . . I'll go have a talk with him about shooting his gun. He damn near hit me, you know? Bad professor. Okay, bear. See you later. Enjoy your hibernation."

★ ★ ★ ★ ★

"Did you find the bear?" Professor Warren asked. "Did you shoot it? I didn't hear any shots?"

"I found her," Ranger McIntyre replied. He was very glad to notice that Vi Coteau was noticeably calmer. "She didn't mean any harm. She saw you down on all fours, wearing those brown clothes, and took you for another bear. Couldn't smell you because the breeze was in the wrong direction, so she came up to you to investigate. Bears have good eyesight, but it doesn't make them any the less curious."

"How do you know she did all that?" Vi asked.

"I interviewed her. It's standard operating procedure to interview animals when humans have frightened them. It kind of lets them know we care, see? Speaking of eyesight and seeing, though, Professor, how are your eyes?"

"My eyes? Not that good. I wear these glasses. For driving and for seeing distances. When your bear came up, however, I was wearing my reading glasses. And you're right; I was down on all fours with my magnifying glass. Suddenly I saw a shadow and then a big brownish shape next to me."

"So you screamed, she ran away, you went for your firearm, and fired two shots. Miss Coteau and I only happened to be in the way. Since no harm was done and I don't want to do all the paperwork, I'm going to say this case is closed. I should give you a citation for carrying a loaded gun in the park, but the bear says she won't press any charges. All I can do is give you a verbal warning. I'll need to confiscate the weapon. When you leave the park you can pick it up at the supervisor's office in the village."

"Fine," said the professor. "I'm very sorry to have frightened you like that."

" 'Sorry'?" Vi answered. " 'Sorry'? You could have killed a ranger. I could have killed you. Or Tim might have. What kind of a dumb stunt was it to go shooting off a gun when you don't know who's out there, especially when you can't see enough to tell what you're shooting at? Well? And tell me this. What were you going to do if you actually hit the bear but only wounded her? Well? Let her crawl away and spend hours, maybe days dying? Boy, people like you really get my goat. You have to own a big gun so you'll feel safe, but you've got no idea about when to use it. Or how. You're a lucky, lucky little man, you are. Instead of poking around looking at seeds and dirt you might be pushing up the daisies right now. Or headed for federal prison for shooting a ranger."

"I was merely trying to wrap up the last of the details for my report. I was going to drop it by your office later in the week. And I am sorry."

"Forget the report," she snapped. "I don't need more paperwork to clutter up my files. I suggest, Professor, that you get packed up, get your horse, and get back to your ivy tower."

Vi and Tim started back toward their own horses, deliberately taking their time. Vi wanted the extra time so she could calm down. McIntyre wanted the extra time in order to let Howard Warren get packed up and headed down the trail ahead of them. The last thing either of them wanted, that afternoon, was to have the professor join them on the trail back to the lodge.

"You certainly gave him an earful," McIntyre said as they walked along over the tundra.

"Well, he made me mad."

"I hope you never get mad at me," he said. "Frankly, I'd rather face an angry bear."

"To tell the truth, I feel a lot better now," she admitted. "I don't think I was looking forward to seeing my office again. Sitting behind my desk copying letters, opening the mail, wishing the phone would ring. Or wishing that the building would catch fire. But popping off at the professor like that, getting my blood going, it pushed the Tadashi accident farther away, if you know what I mean. I feel better."

"You're more talkative, too," McIntyre said. He couldn't help smiling at her. "But see? I told you the medicine circle would help you find your right direction. I knew it. I remember one time when I was struggling with a decision as to whether to let a local poacher go, since he had a family and no money . . ."

"Speaking of talking," Vi Coteau said.

"What about it?"

"Shut up and ride."

High above the Continental Divide, soaring on the afternoon thermals, the prairie falcon tipped her head and with lazy, almost careless movement dipped one wing and lifted the other to perform a wide descending spiral. She saw the cinnamon bear go ambling down into the trees. The two humans also went away, riding their animals and making their harsh, almost unceasing mouth sounds. The falcon's spiral carried her over the medicine circle, a fine open ground where there was little cover to hide any rodents or small birds from the sudden talons of death.

GLOSSARY
THE LANGUAGE OF THE LOCALS

Alpine: no spruce, no fir. ("all pine," get it?) Locals think that "alpine" means no trees at all. No trees and thin air, since much of Colorado's alpine region is two miles above sea level. Winter blizzards are horizontal. Summer's unmitigated sunshine makes exposed human flesh look like overcooked bacon. (Europeans use the term "alpine" to mean any picturesque high mountains where men wearing leather Bermuda shorts stand around yodeling while little girls do the goat herding.)

Altitude: far enough up a mountain to brag, as in "we were hiking at altitude," or as in "we were camped at altitude." Usually above the tree line (see "timberline"). "Relative Altitude" is a local real estate term. As in "Sure, the front yard is covered with rocks and the slope is steeper than a barn roof, but there's a million-dollar view!" Which will be added to the price, so enjoy it.

Belay: (1) A safety rope used in climbing. (2) The act of holding one end of a rope while your partner climbs the cliff, as in "don't be afraid to let go, I will belay you." Safety tip: if you rely on your partner to belay you while you climb, it's better if you are below him or her. If you climb above your belay and you slip, remember to wave as you plummet past them.

Bowline: a rope knot used to make a loop that doesn't slip. Very handy for hauling people up out of perilous places and also for securing a boat to a dock. Like a "line" on the "bow" of the boat? With a big loop to drop over the bollard on the dock? Get it? Learning to tie a bowline knot usually involves a story about a rabbit, a tree, and a hole in the ground. Come to think of it, so does a story about Alice.

Cabin camp: a collection of tiny cabins, a step up from a tent camp. A slight step. A typical cabin camp consisted of five or ten one-room uninsulated 10 × 12 cabins, each furnished with one or two beds, a woodburning cookstove, a single light bulb hanging from the rafters, and a small table with two chairs. If advertised as "rustic," it meant the cabins had an outhouse up the hill and a water tap in the middle of the parking area. "Semi-modern" meant there was a community bathhouse with hot and cold showers and maybe a flush toilet. Having a cold water tap inside the actual cabin itself was considered a luxury. "Modern" got you a cabin with a bathroom inside, unless that particular cabin had already been rented, in which case you got "semi."

Chimneying: some climbers enjoy finding a cliff with a long vertical crack that looks like a chimney with one side missing. The challenge is to put one's spine against one side of the chimney and one's feet on the opposite side and squirm one's way upward until the top is reached OR until one's muscles become fatigued. In which case, see "gravity" in the glossary.

Chinook: a warm wind, often called "the snow eater." The phrase "chinook wind" is regarded as redundant and makes you sound like a tourist. It is permissible to say "it's chinook-ing" even if it makes you sound like a non-English speaker. A chinook becomes most noticeable in winter when warm air sliding down from the Divide turns the snow sloppy. In a matter of hours a ski slope can go from three feet of packed powder to twelve inches of slush. Some skiers do not like chinooks.

Chipmunk: countless scientific man-hours have been spent cataloging the characteristics of this point-nose little rodent. Thanks to all those generations of intrepid biologists and illustrators, we can now say with confidence that a chipmunk is not a ground squirrel, gopher, prairie dog, or marmot. Some tourists, however, have yet to appreciate the difference and gleefully send Junior to give peanuts to the "chipmunks," which actually turn out to be black bears.

Creek: In the Rocky Mountains, any dribble of water that appears to be moving can be labeled as a creek. But it is required to have an unimaginative name. Thus we have Willow Creek, Beaver Creek, Rock Creek, and Pine Creek. If those seem too daringly descriptive, you resort to calling them North Fork, Middle Fork, or Miller's Fork. "Fork" of what is hardly ever specified. When a dribble grows too deep, wide, or turbulent to wade across it is termed a "river," much to the amusement of out-of-state visitors who live near real ones.

Crevice, crevasse: being primarily granite and suffering extremes of heat and freezing, the Rockies are prone to cracking. Any crack may be called a "crevice," mostly for dramatic effect as in "wow, would you look at that crevice." The exception is any crack in an ice field (which locals erroneously refer to as "glaciers"). In an ice field the term becomes Frenchified into "crevasses." If you fall into a crevasse, crevice, you don't care what they are called. You only want somebody to come haul you out.

Clearing: for reasons no one has adequately explained, forests sometimes have expanses of open grass, usually flat and fertile, where no trees, or only a few trees, grow. Some clearings are created with chainsaws and bulldozers but will revert to forest if left alone long enough, for reasons I can't adequately explain, either.

Divide: the Continental Divide, an imaginary line running along the top of the Rocky Mountains but not always at the highest points. It is called the Divide because creeks and streams on the west side (known as the Western Slope) flow toward the Pacific Ocean, while those on the Eastern Slope of the Rockies drain toward the Atlantic.

Dry fly: an emblem of fruitless hopes. It consists of feathers, thread, and chenille wrapped around a hook in a pattern that the fisherperson is convinced resembles an actual insect. The dry version is intended to float on the surface of the water and attract trout. The wet version is intended to sink beneath the water and fool the fish into thinking it is an emerging insect. Samples of both versions may be seen festooning willows, aspen, pine, dead logs, rough logs, and articles of clothing, not to mention protruding appendages such as noses, ears, and fingers.

Elk: local jokers have a story about a tourist who asked "what time of year do the deer turn to elk" hah hah hah. Elk are taller and heavier than deer and have longer antlers and can run faster, which is good to remember if you are ever tempted to send Junior out onto the meadow to pose with one of them. Local lore also believes that "the Indians" (whoever they were) called the elk "wapiti," a word no one could pronounce until a ranger with nothing else to do came up with the rhyme "hippity hoppity it's a wapiti."

Front Range: I don't know about other states the Rockies run through, but in Colorado the long line of high mountains dividing the state into two halves is itself divided up into "ranges." To the north we have the Mummy Range, so named because the collection of peaks resembles either a reclining mummy or a severely constipated boa constrictor; the Never Summer Range, in which there actually is summer every year; then the Front Range (for which there is no correlative Side

234

Range or Back Range); then the Arapaho Range named for the Indian tribe we stole it from (sometimes referred to as the Indian Peaks, but God help any Indian who would try to claim any of it).

Gate, The: as in "who is manning the gate" or "I'm only going up to the gate and back" or "they will give you a map at the gate." The term refers to one of the automobile entrances to the park, where there are no actual gates unless that's what you call orange traffic cones.

Kinnikinnick: In the Rockies, kinnikinnick is an ankle-high plant whose glossy leaves resemble mistletoe. Non-natives sometimes call it "bearberry," but I've never actually spoken to a bear who has eaten the little red berries. According to legend, Native Americans smoked kinnikinnick or added it to tobacco to smoke. However, it was never made clear to us whether they smoked the dried leaves, the dried bark, the roots, or the crushed and dried berries. Trying to answer this question, local high school boys have inhaled most of the local kinnikinnick patches.

Lichen, Krummholz, and Skree: crusty moss on rocks; stunted and twisted trees at altitude; and loose sliding stones where you want to walk. (My sister, who is an RMNP Volunteer, has other words for krummholz and skree, but we can't print them.) I've also been told, by unreliable sources, that "Lichen, Krummholz, and Skree" is the name of a pop music group. Either that or it's the title of a story about three squirrels.

Lodge: (1) a large private home made of logs chinked with ten-dollar bills and credit card receipts; (2) a tiny summer shack with grandiose names like Nest of the Eagle Lodge or a silly name such as Wee Neva Inn, Dew Drop Inn, or Lily's Li'l Lodge; (3) a big establishment with a few rental rooms inside and a dozen or more cabins outside, plus a livery stable upwind of the dining room and a volleyball court no one has ever used.

Moonshine: illegal alcohol. According to folk legend, it was distilled by the light of the moon in order to avoid the authorities. Also known as "shine," "hooch," "popskull," "varnish remover," "who-hit-John," and even "beer."

Moraine: few terms confuse visitors as much as does the term "moraine." Locals use the term sparingly, because they don't understand it, either. Some say it means a big ridge of rocks that looks as if it was dredged up and stacked by huge machines—it was actually done by a prehistoric glacial flow—while others say it refers to a big treeless clearing. Locals sometimes take visitors to Moraine Park and point at the distant ridge, the flat meadow, and the campground and say "that's the moraine." Residents along Fall River Road have actually built homes on no fewer than three moraines and none of them knows it.

Mountain sickness: also known as "altitude sickness." Do you feel clammy, yet feverish? Dizzy and diuretic? Have a hangover-size headache? Nausea, aching joints, death wish? Have you been bitten by a wood tick lately? Have you sipped water from one of our trout streams? If not, then it's not tick fever or giardia. You probably have mountain sickness. Go home.

National Forest: a usually vast area set aside and under the protection of the U.S. Department of Agriculture and managed "for the greatest good of the greatest number in the long run." Land within National Forests is used for logging, mining, grazing, and recreation.

National Park: a usually vast area set aside and under the protection of the U.S. Department of Interior and managed so as to preserve and protect it in its natural state for the benefit and enjoyment of future generations. The principal ideal is expressed in the slogan "take nothing except pictures, leave nothing except footprints." (Which, by the way, will get you arrested in the Louvre.)

Park: a flat open space in the mountains, often named for a pioneer and ranging in size from a few acres (Allenspark, Hermit Park) to hundreds of square miles (South Park, North Park). Locals joke about tourists who arrive in Estes Park Village and ask where to find the roller coaster and Ferris wheel, or the caged animals. No one in human memory has ever laughed at that joke.

The park: Rocky Mountain National Park, the only important industry of Estes Park and the only reason for the village's existence. Villagers speak lovingly of trails and peaks and lakes in "the park" but roughly seventy percent of residents have never ventured off the pavement.

Pass: (1) a slip of paper allowing you to bring your car into the park. But you already knew that. (2) In local parlance, a "pass" is a route over the mountains. There are more of these than you might assume, most of which are inaccessible. Foreigners to Estes Park might be confused by the fact that El Paso del Norte in New Mexico lies south of the village, while South Pass crosses the Wyoming Rockies to the north.

Pika: a chubby little alpine rodent. If you wander into their territory you'll think you're surrounded by puppies playing with squeaky toys. Can you tell a hamster from a gerbil? No? Then you probably can't tell a pika from a hamster, either.

Piton: a device formerly used in rock climbing. A strip of metal about as thick as a ruler and as long as your hand, pointed on one end and having a large hole in the other end. Early rock climbers would secure themselves to a cliff face by "whanging" or hammering pitons into little cracks in the rock where (they hoped) the soft metal would become permanently stuck. With their climbing rope threaded through a metal ring attached to the pitons, climbers were safe. From everything except gravity.

Ranger: there are two kinds, and woe to him who confuses them. In the USFS (which see below) a ranger is an important chieftain in charge of a very large district of the National Forest. In the NPS a ranger might or might not be a temporary summer employee, i.e., a schoolteacher wearing a uniform and badge. A National Forest symbol shows Smokey the Bear wearing a flat ranger hat, which National Forest rangers don't wear but national park rangers do. Park rangers are known locally as "flat hats" and sometimes "tree cops." National Forest rangers can cancel your permit for grazing, mining, logging, or commercial recreation and thus are known locally as "sir" or "mister."

Rappel: in French, the word means "coming back to oneself." In rock climbing, it means taking a rope that is between 120 and 260 feet long, doubling it through a piton ring or some other secure place, wrapping it around your body, and leaping off the cliff. The rope, by the way, is approximately the same diameter as your middle finger. Oh, and nowadays it is made of nylon; if you descend too rapidly on it, you'll find that it can get hot enough to melt and fuse itself to your other equipment, a phenomenon that gave rise to the American phrase "don't leave me hanging."

Sam Brown: in addition to the iconic flat hat, park rangers used to wear iconic Sam Brown belts (presumably invented by the iconic Sam Brown), a wide leather belt that had a narrower leather belt that went over the shoulder. Some say the function of the shoulder strap was to support a heavy pistol and holster. Some say it was left over from WWI, when the shoulder strap was used to drag wounded soldiers out of harm's way. Some say the function of the shoulder strap was just to make the uniform look cool.

Skree: a steep slope of unstable small rocks. See "talus."

The S.O.: supervisor's office, or the central administration building from whence flows a relentless stream of orders, regulations, recriminations, requests, and regrets. For some reason, employees seem to like pronouncing "S.O." with a suggestive pause after it as if a letter were missing.

The S.O.P.: a manual of standard operating procedures, kept in the S.O for reference. Updated on a weekly basis until no office shelf is sturdy enough to hold it, the S.O. S.O.P. dictates How To Do Everything, from what to tell people in the event of nuclear holocaust (pray) to how to install restroom toilet paper (roll from the top, not the bottom). Temps in search of answers to questions (I just saw a bear climb into a visitor's car, what do I do?) have been found years afterward as desiccated corpses hunched over the S.O.P. Equally useful is the Compendium, revised almost annually, which tells everyone how to do everything and what not to do. It has been said that the flat hat rangers won't even visit the restroom without taking the Compendium along.

Sub-alpine: When the first Rocky Mountain explorers saw the stunted high altitude trees, it reminded them of a pod of submarines with only their periscopes visible, hence "sub" alpine. That isn't true. Actually, the existence of the term "sub-alpine" shows what happens when scientists are allowed to wander unsupervised. They seem driven by a need to name everything. First they decide that "alpine" will mean a place with no trees. Then they notice that there's a zone slightly lower in elevation where there ARE trees, but the trees are wind-twisted and stunted and so are the bushes, although the flowers are still pretty like the "alpine" ones. So they call it "sub" alpine. Kind of like calling a Chihuahua a sub-dog.

Summer hire: with more than a million visitors traipsing through the national park each year, the park depends heavily on summer employees to keep everything (particularly restrooms) clean and functioning. They maintain hiking trails, clean toilets, paint signs, clean toilets, direct traffic, clean toilets, answer questions, clean toilets, and pick up trash. Sometimes the rangers help them clean toilets.

The Canyon: there are two major highways between Estes Park and "the Valley." One of them follows the Thompson River and is always called "the Canyon" as in "I'm going down the Canyon to the Valley to load my car with stuff at Sam's Club if you need anything." The other route, Highway 36, doesn't have a name. It also doesn't have much of a canyon.

Talus: a steep slope of unstable large rocks. See "skree."

Tarn: (1) a mild swear word uttered by a person who has problems with preaspirated glottal stops and therefore cannot pronounce "darn" correctly; (2) a hydraulic anomaly usually associated with tundra and occurring due to accumulation of atmospheric moisture in depressions caused by glacial excavation or terminal moraine occurrence. In other words, an itty-bitty pond 'way up in the big mountains. It gets water from melted snow and rain. Tarns are shallow and inviting, but don't jump into one. The water is cold enough to freeze the patellae off a brass tourist.

Telephone exchange: Not where you young whippersnappers (see def.) go to swap smartphones. There are persons still living who remember how telephones had wires. The wire from the phone was attached to the wall wire, which went out of the building and was attached to a wire strung on tall poles (known as "telephone poles" because calling them "wire poles" sounded silly), which led to a building known as the telephone exchange. An "operator" there, usually female, sitting at a switchboard, would see or hear a signal that you had picked up your end of the wire and she would ask "Number, please?" Then she'd connect your wire to that number's wire.

If you wanted a number other than a local number, she would write it down and would also write down how long you talked. The long-distance charge would then appear on your monthly statement for you to explain to your parents. My own father went to his grave still wondering who I had talked to in Parsons, Kansas, for forty-five minutes.

Timberline: 10,500 feet above sea level. Or thereabouts. Early settlers discovered that at that altitude the trees would not grow large enough to be cut down for lumber. And "timber-line" sounded more euphonic than "lumberline." Some modern fussy little know-it-all decided that it should be called "tree line" instead, which confuses things because stunted, runty little trees can be found higher than 11,000 feet in some locations. But that fact, like having a word like "timberline," has little or no significance.

Tundra: in Russian, the term "tundra" means "if you plan to sleep on the ground bring plenty of sheepskins." It is an area above timberline, usually flat except for the place you chose to pitch your tent, devoid of trees, bushes, tall grass, and any kind of public restroom. Mosses, lichens, and flowers grow there although (by definition) the subsoil is permanently frozen. As you will also be if you try to sleep there on the ground without a sheepskin. In fact the only creatures who sleep there are mountain goats and bighorn sheep, who bring their own sheepskins.

Up top / Up on top: locals who say they drove "up top" or took guests "up on top" are referring to the highest section of Trail Ridge where they can see snowbanks in August at two miles above sea level. They can also enjoy driving a two-lane highway that (a) has almost no guardrails and (b) drops off more than a thousand feet from the edge of the pavement to the bottom of Forest Canyon. Restrooms are available Up Top. Sometimes for a reasonable gratuity a local high school student will agree to pry your fingers from your steering wheel and drive you back down to your lodgings.

The Valley: one Estes Parkian might say "I'm going down to the Valley" and another will ask "which one?" and the reply will be "Longmont." This may confuse those who don't know that "the Valley" may refer to any town or city between Loveland and Denver. However, one goes "up" to Fort Collins and "over" to Greeley, both of which are approximately two thousand feet lower in elevation than Estes. You also go "over" to Grand Lake, which is on "the other side," and you go "down" to Allenspark, which is higher than Estes Park (unless you're looking at a road map you've tacked to the wall, in which case, being south, it appears to be below Estes). I hope this clarifies the matter.

Whippersnapper: Just kidding. I haven't a clue why the young and stupid are called whippersnappers. But I made you look.

ABOUT THE AUTHOR

When **James Work** was about to enter third grade, his parents moved the family to a rustic cabin camp a mile from the entrance to Rocky Mountain National Park. He grew up roaming the mountains. He came to know the plants, trees, and rocks, learned to recognize animal tracks.

As soon as he could ride a bicycle and carry a backpack, he began venturing farther into the park, exploring valleys and rivers, creeks and meadows, and eventually the open tundra above timberline. He followed the stone cairns, which, according to ranger naturalists, marked the route of early-day Arapaho Indians across the Continental Divide. He found hidden tepee rings and prehistoric stone walls.

In college James discovered that physics required calculus, and agriculture and forestry majors required him to pass chemistry, which he was unable to do. So he gravitated into a literature and creative writing program. He eventually earned an M.A. and Ph.D. in Victorian poetry. Currently he is a professor emeritus at Colorado State University and has published twenty books including mysteries, Arthurian westerns, personal essays, and literary anthologies.

The employees of Five Star Publishing hope you have enjoyed this book.

Our Five Star novels explore little-known chapters from America's history, stories told from unique perspectives that will entertain a broad range of readers.

Other Five Star books are available at your local library, bookstore, all major book distributors, and directly from Five Star/Gale.

Connect with Five Star Publishing

Visit us on Facebook:
   https://www.facebook.com/FiveStarCengage

Email:
   FiveStar@cengage.com

For information about titles and placing orders:
   (800) 223-1244
   gale.orders@cengage.com

To share your comments, write to us:
   Five Star Publishing
   Attn: Publisher
   10 Water St., Suite 310
   Waterville, ME 04901